THE NEW HUSBAND

BRIAN R. O'ROURKE

INKUBATOR
BOOKS

Published by Inkubator Books
www.inkubatorbooks.com

ISBN (eBook): 978-1-83756-220-6
ISBN (Paperback): 978-1-83756-221-3
ISBN (Hardback): 978-1-83756-222-0

PROLOGUE

I hit my brakes just in time. The two children continue to pedal their bikes through the crosswalk, oblivious to the fact that I almost drove into them. I can't believe I didn't even see them coming.

I tighten my grip on the steering wheel to still my hands. They're shaking.

But they're not shaking from my having almost run into those kids.

My hands were already trembling before that.

Normally when I'm having a bad moment like this, I'd call Brent. But I can't call my husband now. I literally just ran out of the house to get away from him. Brent's not the same person ... he's changed.

A car horn blasts me from behind, snapping me out of my panic. The driver motions angrily in my rearview mirror. I wish that was all I had to worry about right now, another driver blocking the street for a few seconds. But, instead, my whole world is falling apart.

I wave apologetically, my heart racing as I pull through the intersection.

How did it come to this?

Brent went away for a month. He was supposed to come back better ...

But he's gotten worse.

As I pull into the parking lot of the diner, I check my mirrors. It's a new habit I've picked up in the last few weeks. I don't see anybody following me. But that doesn't mean they're not there.

I sit in the car and try to keep from having a full-on panic attack.

I can't believe this has happened. Who Brent has become. Who we've become. I know wellness retreats are supposed to be transformative but ... I don't recognize my husband at all.

And now I don't trust him anymore.

1

WEDNESDAY – MAY 10

"Are you excited, or are you nervous?" Paige asks.

I offer her a nervous smile, which I hope looks excited. "Both, I guess."

"Remind me," Paige goes on while I fill out a balance transfer form. "How long has Brent been away?"

I fill in the amount, double-check the form, and slide it across the counter. The bank is usually empty on Wednesday mornings, which is exactly why I'm here. I'm not agoraphobic. At least, I've never been *diagnosed*. But I don't like crowds.

"It's been a month," I remind her.

Paige has been my friend since high school and is, honestly, one of the reasons I do my banking at this branch. We were really close all the way back in senior year, but then lost touch when she went away to college and I stayed home. I don't do social media and am a proud homebody, so it was completely by accident that I ran into her at the grocery store a few years back. Nowadays she's my closest friend. We see each other once or twice a week, usually over coffee and sometimes getting dinner.

"Wow." Paige takes the balance form and goes to work on her computer. "That is *quite* a long time to be without a man. I think I'd go crazy."

She gives me a wink, and I feel my face turn red. Paige's sex drive has always been a lot higher than mine. If she knew how infrequently Brent and I had been intimate before he went away, she'd probably be shocked. Paige has been married twice already and can't seem to go more than five minutes being single.

"I miss him," I say. "That's for sure."

Paige finishes with the form and hands me a receipt. Then she leans in and lowers her voice. "Joanne went to one of those places," she says in almost a whisper. "And she was a totally different woman when she came back. Like, *totally.*"

Joanne is one of our mutual friends from high school, though I probably haven't spoken to her since ... gosh, has it been that long?

"Really?" I say, trying not to get even more worked up than I already am. Brent and I were both very nervous about his trip, but ultimately we thought it was for the best. That being said, the idea of him coming back a totally different man is scary.

"Oh yeah," Paige says. "Joanne walked into her job the next day and quit on the spot. A week later, she'd opened her own online business. Once that got off the ground, she finally divorced that good-for-nothing. Now she's single and doing *great.*"

All this talk of a person completely changing, of leaving their job and then their spouse, is not helping matters. Paige finally realizes how uncomfortable she's made me.

"Oh, I'm sure things will be great with Brent. He's such a good guy."

He is. He really is. He's just been struggling for a long time. Nobody knows this, but Brent suffers from depression. He's really good at hiding it. He learned at an early age to put on a brave face. He had to act like nothing was wrong, or he'd get it from his parents. Paige knows where Brent has been, but nobody else does. We told our friends and people from the neighborhood he was traveling for work. Some nosy neighbors tried to pry and ask me lots of questions, but I shut those conversations down immediately. It's none of their business.

"Yeah," I say. "I hope so."

Paige smiles at me. "It's going to be great. I'm really excited for you, Mary. Give me a call later, and let me know how everything is, okay?"

"Okay." I really am grateful to have Paige. I don't have a lot of friends, and she genuinely cares about me. Paige is also good at getting me, occasionally, to come out of my shell. "How about coffee on Friday?"

"Sounds good. See you then."

I leave the bank. Outside, the spring air is warm, and the sky is clear. It really is going to be okay. It really is. I need to keep telling myself that. Brent is supposed to be home in a few hours, which gives me plenty of time to get the rest of the house together. Brent has never cared about how neat— or messy—the house is, but I really wanted to make it look nice for his return. I wanted this day to be special, to be as perfect as it could be. I really want everything to be better, for him, for me, for both of us.

But as I cross the parking lot, I get the eerie feeling that I'm being watched. I spot a gray SUV parked on the far side of the lot, far away from all the other cars, just sitting there by itself. The engine is running. There's a man behind the wheel, but I can't see him that well.

Relax, Mary, I tell myself.

I get into my Prius and take deep breaths. I'm on edge. I get this way a lot, but it's even worse today. I haven't seen my husband in a month, and now I'm worried he'll come back a totally different man. That he'll quit his job and ask for a divorce.

My knuckles are white on the steering wheel. I ease up and take more deep breaths. Everything is going to be fine.

2

I have some time and a lot of nervous energy to kill before Brent is due. Even though I've kept on top of the house since he's been away, I keep myself busy with household chores that don't really need doing. I pass the vacuum, tidy the coat closet, mop the spotless kitchen floor. I scrub the toilets again and am standing around, wondering what else I can do, when I remember I forgot to defrost the meat for tonight's meal. It's going to be cutting it close, but I take the beef out and put it in the sink.

It's almost noon, and Brent is due home any minute. I check my phone for the umpteenth time this morning, but there's still nothing from him. Brent's not a big texter, but it's strange he hasn't sent me a note just to confirm he was on track and would be home soon. Brent wasn't allowed to have his phone where he was, but he should have gotten it back this morning.

I look out the window by the front door for, like, the thousandth time of the day. All I see is the same old street I grew up on. Ms. Ryers's house is opposite ours. She's on her porch, as usual, doing her crossword puzzles. I've known her for literally all my life. She lived in that house before I was born. She was older than Mom, but the two of them were friends for quite a while before they fell out of touch when my parents retired and moved to Florida. Mom passed not long after the move, and Dad died suddenly almost a year to the day after she did. I miss them terribly.

A woman wearing a tank top and stretch shorts jogs by, her ponytail swooping back and forth in time with her strides. I peer out a moment longer, but there's still no sign of Brent.

I try to keep myself busy. Noon comes and goes. One o'clock, two o'clock, three o'clock. I wonder if I got the date wrong, even though I know that's impossible. Brent and I talked about this trip *so much*. He was in the kitchen when I wrote the date of his return on the calendar, along with the time. But all the same, I go into my email and pull up the confirmation note Brent forwarded, which included all the information. Yep, it says it right there: he was supposed to be home three hours ago.

I'm beginning to worry that something's happened. Was Brent in a car accident on the way home? It's possible. Oh God, I can't think like that.

Or ... did something happen while Brent was away? They were in a very secluded area and were supposed to spend a lot of time outdoors. This part of the trip did not appeal to Brent, whom I jokingly call Mr. Suburbs. The group was supposed to go on some hikes ... maybe he disappeared?

I shake my head. That's stupid. They would have called me if my husband had gone missing, surely. I'm being ridiculous.

But then, where the heck is he? If he was going to be late, why didn't he let me know? He should have been able to call, or at least text, by now. Brent can be absent-minded sometimes, but he's never *thoughtless*. He would have let me know if he was going to be *several hours* late.

Now I can't stop thinking about what Paige said. People who go on trips like this, sometimes they come back very different. Has Brent changed? I find it hard to believe that in thirty days, he would turn into a complete asshole, forgetting to text me to say he wouldn't be home on time. I'm sure he's nervous about coming home, but he'd also have to know how nervous I'd be. Our marriage wasn't in the best place when he left—I mean, that's *one* of the reasons why he went in the first place. So why wouldn't he call to tell me he'd be late?

I text him:

> Hey, honey. I'm looking forward to seeing you. I thought you were going to be home at twelve. Is everything okay? Love you.

It's the first text I've sent since he went away. There were nights when I wanted to write him, when I missed him so terribly that it literally hurt. But I didn't. I knew he wouldn't get any of the messages, and I also didn't want him to be bombarded with texts from me the moment he got his phone back.

I read the text over before hitting send. The note sounds a little awkward, like I'm trying to sound like his wife. I want everything to be perfect. I really do. But I can't think of a better way to phrase the text, so I hit send.

There's no immediate response. I distract myself by trying to find more things to clean in the house. I dust everything. Again. I pass the vacuum. Again. Even though there's literally only one can to go out, I take that one can out to the recycling bin. Back inside, I check myself in the mirror. I don't usually put on makeup. My lips are naturally pretty red. But today I made an effort. Lipstick, eyeliner, a little rouge. I even made sure to wear the gray pants and pink blouse that I know Brent really likes. I haven't fit into either in a while, but while he was gone, I decided to lose a few pounds. I think I look pretty good. I hope he thinks so too.

Now it's four o'clock. My phone buzzes. I rush over to the end table by the front door where I left the phone, expecting there to be a text from Brent.

But it's not.

It's a note from Paige:

> Thinking about you, girl. How's everything going?

I start to write her back that Brent isn't even home yet, but I stop short. Paige is a good friend, but I don't want her to know that he's late and hasn't contacted me. It's ... embarrassing. But I can't *not* respond. Paige can tell I've read her text. I fret for a moment before deciding to put the phone down. I'll tell her later that I saw her text while I was in the middle of something and couldn't respond right away. I'll write her back once Brent is here.

Hopefully, he will be soon.

I get started on dinner, making Brent his favorite. The steak is thawed. I get to work, preheating the oven and getting the vegetables out. I can't wait for dinner to have a glass of wine—I'm too on edge. So I uncork a red and pour a glass. Just as I'm about to bring it up to my lips, I hear a car pull into the driveway, and my heart stops.

I put the glass down and hurry to the front door. It's Brent's car! I'm really nervous. My hands are shaking. It's nervous excitement. But I'm also angry. Why the heck didn't he let me know he was going to be this late? I hear his car door close. I close my eyes and take a deep breath, not at all sure how I'm going to greet him, or how he's going to greet me. Now that he's here, I almost don't want him to be. I can't stand the uncertainty of everything.

I open the door and step onto our porch. Brent is coming up the stairs, and he looks ...

Hot.

I mean, really. Like, really hot. Brent has always been attractive. He's more handsome than cute. But right now, he looks—

"You look *amazing!*" he blurts out.

Brent drops the suitcase where he's standing and rushes up the stairs with a big smile on his face. He's lost some weight, he's got a tan, and he looks like he just got a haircut. But really, it's his shoulders. Brent has always had good shoulders, but now these things look like they've come off a statue. Standing there in his gray T-shirt and tan slacks, he looks like a personal trainer.

"Brent ..."

Before I can say anything, before I can even figure out what I'm going to say, he scoops me up. Brent hasn't picked me up in years. I can't help it. I wrap my legs around him like I'm a schoolgirl hugging her first crush, and then his lips are on mine. And ...

Oh.

My.

God.

We haven't kissed like this in a long time. And neither of

us are normally affectionate in public. I know Mrs. Ryers is watching right now. But I don't even care. She can stare all she wants. My husband is home. Everything is okay. I'm sure there's a perfectly good explanation for why he didn't text to say he'd be this late. I feel his body against mine, every *part* of him pushing into me.

When Brent pulls away, we're both out of breath. I look into those dazzling blue eyes of his and want to shout with joy. I just know everything is going to be fine. This trip was totally worth it.

But his eyes look different. The blue isn't as dazzling as it usually is.

"Hi there," he says, still smiling.

"Hi."

He frowns. "What's wrong?"

I want to tell him his eyes are different. But I can't put into words how they've changed. And besides, it would spoil the moment entirely.

"Nothing." I smile and give him another kiss. "Nothing at all. I'm glad you're home."

He kisses me back. "I'm so sorry I didn't text. They lost my phone."

"They lost your phone?" I ask.

He shrugs it away. "Whatever. They're paying for a new one."

"Okay, well, that's good."

"And sorry I'm late," he says, still smiling. "We got held up this morning. Everybody wanted to do one more hike. I really wanted to get back here to you, but, well, I made a few friends, and they really wanted me to stay. I kind of became ... God, I have so much to tell you."

He really does look amazing.

Almost like a totally different person.

"But first," he says, putting me gently down on the porch. "I think we should go upstairs."

"What about your suitcase?" I ask.

"I'll get it later."

3

It's only been a month, but you'd think neither of us had sex for years. We've torn each other's clothes off before we even reach the stairs, and we barely make it into the bedroom before we're intimate.

We do things we haven't done since we were dating. And Brent is different in surprisingly good ways. Normally our lovemaking is sweet, almost shy, but today Brent takes charge and turns it almost into a workout. We're a complete sweaty mess when we're done and then decide to shower together, which leads to more things ...

When I'm finally putting my clothes back on, I remember I haven't put the steak in the oven. He's standing there, still naked, watching me get dressed with hungry eyes. Even though we just made love, his intense gaze makes me blush.

"Don't be shy," he says. "You are *hot.* You should walk around naked more often."

I'm all for body positivity, but sorry, Brent, that's not going to happen in this lifetime.

"Someone made me forget all about dinner," I say. "I've got to get the steak in the oven."

"Why don't we go out?" he says. "I wanted to take you some place nice."

"Oh, we don't have to—"

"We're going out," he says. "To Rindella's. I know how much you love that place."

I really do. And we haven't been in a long time. It's really expensive and usually fully booked. And it's not the type of restaurant you can just walk into without reservations.

"Brent," I say, "why don't we keep it low-key toni—"

"Come on, baby." Brent walks up to me. He's still naked. I swear, he must have put on fifteen pounds of solid muscle while he was away. Brent has always kept himself in decent shape. It comes naturally to him, without much effort. But now he's got well-defined abs. His chest is bigger. And those shoulders ... oh boy.

Brent presses his lips gently to mine, and I want to melt. "You probably haven't been out to dinner all month. Let's make it a special night. What do you say?"

It already is a special night. I'm just glad he's home, and it seems like the trip has worked wonders. He really does seem different. In a good way.

"Sounds great," I say.

"I'M SORRY, SIR," the host at Rindella's says. He's an older gentleman with a gray mustache, dressed all in black. "But we're fully booked this evening."

I knew this would happen. Like I said, Rindella's isn't the type of restaurant you can just walk into and grab a table.

And my stomach is grumbling. You can't wear whatever you want to a place like this, so I had to put on this black dress and ·do my hair. Rindella's isn't around the corner either. I was planning on having dinner at five, and now it's almost seven thirty. At this point, if we pass a fast-food spot, I'd be happy.

"I have seating for tomorrow night," the host says, consulting his computer at the stand. "Would you like to reserve a table?"

"That would be nice," I say, rubbing Brent's shoulder. "Want to come back tomorrow?"

Brent does not look at me. Instead, he keeps his eyes on the host. The other man fidgets under Brent's gaze.

"We're hungry now," he says. "And you know, we've been coming here for ten years. We drove almost forty-five minutes tonight. Couldn't you set aside a table, maybe in that corner right there? It's only the two of us. We won't order any specials, and we'll be in and out quickly."

I frown, not expecting the unusual tone in my husband's voice. Brent isn't what I'd call a pushover, but he is normally reserved and polite. It's not like him to speak this way to someone who's only doing their job.

"I'm sorry, sir," the host says, "but we are—"

"Could I speak to the manager?"

The host pauses. The two men regard each other. Brent's eyes never waver. The host is first to look away.

"Of course, sir. I'll go get him. Please give me a minute."

Once the host is gone, I grab Brent's forearm and lower my voice. "What are you doing?"

"What?" He smiles like this is all perfectly normal. "We're hungry."

"Brent, you know they only seat you with reservations," I say. "Let's just go somewhere else. I'm starved as is."

"Relax," he says. "I'll handle this."

A party of five has queued up behind us. I move out of the way to let them get by, because I assume they have reservations. But Brent doesn't budge. He towers over the host stand. The host returns with the manager, a man who looks about ten years older than us. He's dressed all in black as well. The party of five waits patiently for Brent to move out of the way, but my husband doesn't. In fact, I don't think he even sees them.

"Good evening, sir," the manager says. "How can I help you?"

"You can help us by giving us a table. You know, we've been coming here for ten years."

I want to die. My face feels like a million degrees. I catch two of the women in the party eyeing us up. I turn away so I don't have to exchange glances. I can't believe how Brent is acting. The manager goes on to explain how sorry he is, but they're fully booked. It's just the same thing the host already told us, so I don't know why Brent thought this exercise would prove fruitful. Meanwhile the host is craning his neck to look around Brent and address the party of five. Brent pretends like he doesn't notice this, but he must have realized he was standing right in the way.

"I understand," Brent says, reaching into his pocket. "But listen, tonight is a really special night for my wife and me. We just found out ..." He lowers his voice. "We just found out we're pregnant and wanted to celebrate."

Brent's hand comes out of his pocket. There's money in it. I can't tell how much. It's folded up in his palm. He presses it into the manager's hand.

"So if there's any way you can help us out," Brent says. "That'd be great. Like I said, we've been coming here for years."

The manager takes the money, pocketing it discreetly. While the host is seating the party of five, the manager gestures at one of the idle busboys. In a hushed voice, he tells the young man to set a table in the corner Brent mentioned a moment ago.

"If you'd give us a moment, sir," the manager says, "we'll be happy to accommodate you."

"Thanks," Brent says. "We appreciate it."

The manager hurries off to help the busboy. They move a small table out of a side room and throw a white tablecloth on top. Inside a minute, there is silverware and place settings and we're being shown to our seats. A few people in the restaurant stare at us pointedly. It's not that loud in here, so Brent's exchange with management did not go unnoticed. I feel like everybody's watching us as Brent stands behind me and pushes in my seat for me. My face must be really red.

Brent sits on the other side of the table from me. "See? No problem."

"How much did you give him?"

"What does it matter?" he asks. "Tonight's special. I'm home, I feel great, and we're together."

I'm trying not to laugh at how crazy this has been. I whisper, "But you told him I was pregnant."

He shrugs. "Maybe you are. It's too early to tell yet."

His comment only makes me blush even worse as I recall our rather wild exploits from only a couple of hours ago. I know it's impossible, but I feel like everybody looking at me knows exactly what's on my mind right now. When our server appears, a young woman who looks like she just graduated from high school, Brent has to order for me. I'm still too embarrassed to even speak.

"We'll start with the chardonnay," Brent says. "And bring me a lager as well."

The server says she'll be right back with our drinks and some bread for the table.

I just stare at Brent dumbly.

"I know," he says, giving me a knowing look. "I've changed. I'm sorry. It must be jarring. But—"

"You *have* changed," I say carefully, "but it's not about that. I mean, it's not totally about that. I was only confused."

"Confused about what, honey?"

He smiles at me sweetly. He really does look great. He's wearing that pinstripe navy blue suit he hasn't fit into since one of his college friends got married. I've always found my husband attractive, and all of my girlfriends have said as much over the years. But right now, there's only one word to describe him:

Hot.

I can't believe the change that's come over him. He looks great, he's much more self-assured, and there's this air about him now. My husband has a *presence*.

He's also never seemed so alive.

I consider changing the subject. I'm afraid if I ask the wrong question, it'll ruin the evening.

But it's important.

"One of the reasons you went away," I begin, "was because, you know—"

"Oh, alcohol?" He waves a hand like it's nothing. "Not a big deal anymore."

I gape at him. "Not a big deal?"

"Nah." He shakes his head. "I decided I can drink alcohol and be fine. I don't have a problem."

I don't know a lot about alcoholism, but I'm pretty sure you can't simply decide you're not an addict and continue to indulge.

"I know," he says, smiling at me. "We really do have a lot to talk about."

"I'll say."

"And I can't wait to share every step of my amazing journey with you," he says. "But I want to hear about you."

I'm not the one who spent the last month on an incredibly expensive self-help retreat. "About me?"

"Yeah." He reaches for my hand. His fingers are icy cold. "You're my wife, Mary. Tell me what you've been up to this whole time."

The problem is, not much. I'm kind of a boring person. I like it that way.

"How's work been?" he asks.

"Oh, the same." I work from home as a data analyst. Aside from the occasional phone call, all my exchanges with other human beings are completely electronic in nature. Brent has always shown a polite interest in my work before, but I know it's not exactly scintillating.

"Are you happy?"

"Happy?"

"Yeah," he says. "With work."

I'm not passionate about what I do, but I don't hate it either. The job pays the bills and came in handy a few years ago when Brent lost his prior job and then more recently when we agreed he should take a leave of absence.

"Sure."

"Are you sure?" he presses. "Really?"

"I like my job, Brent," I say defensively.

He holds out a palm. "Okay. If you say so. I'm just thinking, honey, we only get one race around the track. If there's something else you'd be interested in exploring, you should go for it."

Brent has always been very pragmatic. His attitude tonight is surprising.

"I haven't given it much thought," I say. "I mean, it's always helped with the bills, we've got a nice 401k, and we live comfortably."

"Well, give it some thought," he says. "You deserve to be happy, you know."

The server returns with the bread and drinks. Brent pours me a generous glass of chardonnay and waits for me to taste it before he has any beer.

"They think I'm pregnant, Brent," I say.

He waves my concern away. "Pregnant women drink. It's a thing again. One doesn't hurt."

That's true. But all the same, I steal a quick glance at the host stand to make sure nobody's watching before I taste the wine.

"Good?" he asks.

It's delicious. And the bread here is to die for. Seriously. I could come here and just eat the bread, it's that good. I order the eggplant parmigiana, while Brent orders—you guessed it —steak. I could have just made that at home for him, but he was insistent on making an evening out of everything.

"I am happy," I say. "I like my life."

"That's good." He tears his piece of bread in half. "I'm glad to hear that. But you don't sound *excited* to me. That's one of the things this place taught me. It was really eye-opening, Mary. Routine normalizes mediocrity. It's true."

Routine normalizes mediocrity. That sounds like one of those expressions that Brent and I used to hear and roll our eyes at. But he appears to have bought into it, big time.

"How about sex?" he says casually, like there aren't two groups of people sitting only a few feet away from us. "Are you happy with our sex life?"

"Brent." I look down. I'm blushing for, like, the hundredth time since we got here. "Can we not talk about that right now?"

"Why not?" He looks around. The woman sitting nearest to him has clearly overheard this piece of our conversation. When I catch her stealing a glance at Brent, she quickly looks away. "It's as good a place as any. And besides, sex is perfectly natural. Everybody in this restaurant is having it, or wishing they had it."

Okay ... so Brent has a healthy sexual appetite. (I do too.) But he's never liked *discussing* the topic with me. Usually he gives me *the look*, and that's enough to initiate things if I'm in the mood, or I'll rub his thigh, and he'll know what I'm after. But talking about it? No. Uh-uh. When we were younger, we tried discussing it, and it was really awkward. We told each other about the things we liked, and ever since then, that's what we've basically stuck to. We've never had a conversation since.

This is too much. "Brent, you're making me uncomfortable."

He reaches for my hand again. "Sorry, honey. You're right. We can talk about that later. *In the bedroom.*"

As embarrassed as I am, I can't help but be taken in by his sexy smile and those blue eyes of his. Earlier I thought there was something different about his eyes, but I don't see it now. I burst into laughter as I take his hand. We stare into each other's eyes for a moment, and I'm so grateful that he seems to have found something that's turned his life around. So far, this retreat seems to be just what he needed.

"Did you see any of your friends?" he asks. "Paige or maybe Gwen?"

"Just Paige," I say, frowning.

A couple of months ago, I had a falling-out with Gwen. It was kind of a big deal at the time, and I told him all about it. Now, our relationship wasn't in the best place at the time, and Brent was struggling at work, so maybe my spat with Gwen went in one ear and out the other. But still, it's hard to imagine that Brent would have completely forgotten about it. I don't have a lot of friends, so losing one of them is kind of a big deal.

"Not Gwen?" he asks.

"No." I study his eyes. He genuinely does not recall. "Gwen and I had a fight, remember?"

"Oh." He perks up, embarrassed. "That's right. Before I went away, I was all in my head. It completely just—God, I'm sorry."

"It's okay."

I smile. I don't want to make him feel bad right now. I don't want anything to ruin this night. My husband is back home, and he seems so much better.

"Love you, Mary," he says, giving me a wink.

"Love you too, Brent."

4

THURSDAY – MAY 11

Brent cannot keep his hands off me.

After dinner last night, we shared a bottle of wine at home on the couch. I barely got through one glass before Brent was pawing me. Then, this morning, before he announced he was going to the gym, he woke me up for some more fun.

"Wanna come with?" he asks as he laces his sneakers.

In the past, it was usually me asking Brent if he wanted to go to the gym together. He usually went when I asked, but a lot of times it was very begrudgingly. He's one of those annoying people who can eat basically whatever they want, never work out, and still look presentable.

But this morning, Brent's the one pushing for the gym. We didn't sleep much last night, and we were up early again. I don't know where he's getting all this energy. If I weren't such a homebody, and if it weren't so expensive, I'd seriously consider attending this wellness retreat Brent just went on. I could use some more energy, and I wouldn't mind losing a few pounds and looking more like I used to.

I roll over in bed, still coming off the high from this morning's escapades. "I can't, honey. I have to get started with work soon."

He reaches under the sheets to give me a good squeeze. "Suit yourself. I'll be back in a couple of hours."

I stick my head up. "A couple of *hours*?"

Usually, Brent is good for forty-five minutes at the gym, tops. Most of the time I find him waiting for me in the lobby, scrolling through his phone when I come out of my Zumba or yoga class.

"Yeah." He smiles. "While I was away, I got back into the swing of things. Now I can't get enough exercise."

Brent stands up. He's shirtless. Raising his arms in a classic bodybuilder pose, he flexes his biceps. I can't help it —I giggle. It's so silly. But Brent isn't laughing. He stands there proudly, showing off his new physique. I still can't believe that it only took him thirty days to look *that good.*

"Very hot," I say.

He pulls on a T-shirt and leans over to give me a kiss. "See you in a little bit."

* * *

AFTER A GOOD, long, steamy shower and a big cup of coffee, I feel much more awake. I settle down to work. When I was a little girl, I wanted to be a pop singer (ha) and then a marine biologist (double ha) and finally an accountant (triple ha). I went to college and studied accounting, but found myself more interested in studying the underlying financial data and looking for meaningful trends. After I graduated, I made a go of being an accountant, but it wasn't a good fit for me. I took a pay cut to switch careers and was lucky to get a job as a data analyst at the company I currently work for.

I have a lot of work to do this morning. I pour myself into it and finalize a report I couldn't close the loop on last week. By the time I come up for air, it's almost noon, and Brent still isn't back from the gym.

I head into the kitchen to make myself lunch. And by make lunch, I mean I open a box of spring mix salad and dump what's left into a bowl. I pour some balsamic vinaigrette onto my food, and voilà, I just made lunch.

It's a nice day, so I sit on the porch while I'm having my meal. Mrs. Ryers is out on her own porch, one knee crossed over the other. She's wearing her half-eyeglasses and has a pen in her hand. The woman probably does about ten crossword puzzles a day.

"Hey, Mary!" she calls out.

"Good morning," I say, then edit: "I mean afternoon!"

She rises slowly and a bit painfully from her chair. Mrs. Ryers is in her eighties and only just recently began showing signs of her age. She steps forward and rests her hands on the railing in front of her.

"I see Brent's come home," she says.

"Yes," I say. "Long business trip."

I've already told Mrs. Ryers this little white lie. But it never hurts to repeat information like this so the neighbors don't get any ideas. I don't want the whole world knowing Brent was severely depressed, potentially alcoholic, and was basically forced into taking a leave of absence from his job because the quality of his work had declined. As sort of a last resort, we dipped into our savings to pay for this thirty-day wellness retreat. He was in a bad way, and our marriage was too. But that's nobody's business.

"That's good," she says, nodding slowly. "He looks ... different."

"He's been working out a lot too." I smile. "And watching what he eats. He's lost some weight."

I can't help but call to mind the image of my husband standing shirtless next to the bed, pumping his muscles like those bodybuilders do onstage. Brent isn't as big as any of those guys, but the more I think about it, he's now got the chiseled physique to be a fitness model.

I'm giddy at the thought of how hot my husband has become.

"Oh, well, that's nice, dear," Mrs. Ryers says. "But that wasn't what I meant."

I frown, not understanding. Mrs. Ryers saw Brent from a distance, and I'm not trying to be mean when I say this, but her eyesight at her age isn't the best. What else could she mean?

"He looked, I don't know, taller," Mrs. Ryers says.

I pretend to think it over, even though the idea is silly. Brent could not have gotten taller while he was away. I mean, I've heard of people doing yoga for years and years and, over time, lengthening their spine by an inch or so. But those are all anecdotes, most of them passed down by discredited gurus. I'm not sure that's real.

"I've seen you two together a lot," Mrs. Ryers goes on. Apparently, she's determined to prove her point. "You normally come up to his shoulder. But yesterday, when he came home, you didn't quite reach."

I like Mrs. Ryers a lot. She was always very sweet to me. I don't want to tell her she's clearly mistaken, that she observed us briefly from across the street yesterday, and hurt her feelings. But I also can't come up with a polite response.

"And there was something else," she goes on vaguely. "I couldn't put my finger on it. He just seemed—"

Brent's car comes roaring around the corner. Normally Brent is very good at actually stopping at the stop sign there because there are a lot of young children on our street. But today he only slows a fraction and slides around the corner like he's a race car driver. He waves to me as he flies into the driveway and brakes hard to a stop.

"Hey, babe," he says after jumping out of the car. "What are you up to?"

He must have gotten a shower at the gym, because he's dressed in a nice shirt and khakis now. After popping the trunk of his car, he pulls out his gym bag.

"Eating," I say, holding up my salad bowl. "You were gone a while."

"I know." He grins from ear to ear. "I got a lot of work done."

I can't help but feel Mrs. Ryers watching us from across the street. Brent is usually very good with her. We used to joke that it took him two hours to rake the leaves: thirty minutes to push the leaves onto the street and ninety minutes to speak with Mrs. Ryers while she sat on her porch. She's kind of that old lady on the street who watches everybody. Not exactly nosy, but not exactly minding her own business either.

"Work?" I say, trying to ignore Mrs. Ryers, who is very openly staring at us. "What do you mean?"

Brent knew he was coming home on a Wednesday, but decided to take Thursday and Friday off as well and return to work on Monday. He wanted some time to readjust after his trip and didn't want to go running back into the office.

"Yes." He looks me up and down. I'm wearing old, baggy

sweatpants and a T-shirt, an outfit that's not exactly sexy. But he's checking me out like I'm wearing a thong bikini. "I wanted to tell you last night, but there was just too much to discuss."

He must feel Mrs. Ryers's gaze on him. Brent turns and sees her. They always got along so well, I'm expecting him to give her a big greeting, but all he can muster is a half-hearted wave.

"Hello, Brent," Mrs. Ryers responds, with about as much enthusiasm.

"Come on," he says, coming up the steps quickly. "Let's talk inside. I don't like that old bag listening to everything we say."

I could die. Mrs. Ryers might not see so well anymore, but her hearing is fine, and I'm pretty sure she just over-heard what Brent muttered a bit too loudly. He takes me by the hand and pulls me inside. I offer Mrs. Ryers the best smile I can manage at an embarrassing moment like this, while I pretend like Brent wasn't just as rude as all heck.

When we're inside, Brent closes the door quickly behind me. I put my salad bowl down on the end table by the door because I feel like we're about to have an important conversation.

"Brent, what was *that* all about?" I ask, unable to help myself. Everything between us since he came home has been really good, but I can't act like he wasn't very rude to our neighbor just now. "You and Mrs. Ryers have always gotten along so well."

For a moment he has that deer-in-headlights look, but then he recovers. "*Mrs.* Ryers? *Mrs.*? What am I, four years old and living in the nineteen fifties? I'm a grown-ass man. If

I want to talk to her, I'll call her by her first name from now on."

I'm shocked by how angry he is. Of the two of us, I'm the one with the shorter fuse. It usually takes a lot to get Brent angry, though when he's mad, he can stay that way for days. But I've never seen him snap like this over ... I still don't even understand what set him off.

"She's in our business too much," Brent says. "I've never liked her. I don't want us talking to that woman anymore. I want her returning that spare key to our house too. I don't want—"

"Brent." Where is this coming from? Mrs. Ryers can pry at times, but she's never been outright nosy. "Slow down. Why are you so angry? You used to talk to her all the time."

"I was just being polite," he says. "And I'm done with *just being polite*. Just because someone's nice doesn't mean they're good or worth your time."

His anger is frightening me. I've never seen him this worked up before over nothing.

"Okay, Brent," I say, trying to think of a way to calm him down. "You don't have to engage with her if you don't want. I'm sorry you felt like you had to before. I had no idea. It really seemed like you *enjoyed* speaking with her. You used to rake her leaves al—"

"I don't want *you* talking to her either."

I take a step back. Brent has never, and I mean *never*, told me to stop doing anything.

"I've known Mrs. Ryers my whole life, Brent." I fold my arms. "There was a time when Mom had to work, and the woman helped our family out by babysitting me a couple of times a week. I can't just *stop* talking to her. I won't. That's not fair of you to ask me."

He looks at me. There is a lot of anger in his eyes. For a moment, I'm scared of him. I'm literally scared of my own husband. But then that moment passes as his eyes soften, and he looks apologetic.

He reaches for me, and I put my head against his chest, grateful the argument is over.

"I'm sorry," he says. "You're right. I shouldn't, uh, tell you what to do."

I rub his back. My heart is still racing. "You got so angry."

He squeezes me gently. "I know. It's part of the whole process."

I look up at him. "Process?"

He smiles sheepishly. "Yeah, you see, I used to suppress all my feelings. You know my parents, I mean, you know how my parents *were*. We weren't allowed to express our feelings at home, so I learned to suppress everything and keep it all down. But that's really bad, you know? Our emotions are part of evolution, they are our mind's way of telling us something is not right, and we have to deal with it. Ignoring them doesn't make them go away, it only makes things worse."

I've heard that before, and it makes a kind of sense. Though there are plenty of times where emotions do not help a situation.

"Okay, Brent." I rub his chest. "I understand."

"I knew you would." He kisses my forehead. "It's funny, but you grow up thinking what your parents told you was best, and then you reach this age where you realize not all of it was very good. Then you spend the rest of your life basically unlearning all the bad things they beat into your head."

I wince at the word *beat*. Brent might have meant that literally. My husband had a horrible childhood. His parents took turns being completely disinterested in him or wickedly cruel. They physically and mentally abused him. His mother and father always preferred his brother, Christopher, who never got punished for anything. It got so bad that Brent worked up the nerve as a fourteen-year-old to contact child services. He got himself into foster care, graduated high school, managed to get into college, and at least tried his best to live a normal life. But all that psychological trauma has left him scarred. I'm convinced that his depression, low self-esteem, and alcoholism—even though he's saying he doesn't have a problem now—are all related to his childhood trauma. His parents really did a number on him.

I cling to him. "I'm sorry, honey."

He knows what I mean: I'm sorry for how lousy his life was as a kid.

"Thanks, babe, that means a lot." He begins to lead me into the kitchen, but I backtrack to retrieve my salad bowl. Brent drops his bag on the island counter and opens the fridge. "I'm *starved*. What do we have to eat around here?"

The way he says it, it's like he's expecting me to figure out lunch for him. Brent has never acted that way before. Thinking back to what he just told me, I wonder if he's always felt like I should have prepared meals for him, but never expressed this feeling, like it was one of those things he *suppressed*.

But that seems *so* unlike my husband. We both work full-time and evenly divide the chores and the cooking. It's only fair. And Brent never seemed like the type who expected to be waited on.

He turns around, leaving the fridge open behind him. "Kidding."

"Oh."

I laugh, but it's a bit forced. I feel like everything is

happening so quickly. I feel like I have to get to know this man all over again.

Brent starts making himself a sandwich, slicing a fresh roll, then adding some cheese and a couple of slices of bologna on top. He doesn't bother to get a plate out, which is weird. I wouldn't call Brent a neat freak by any stretch of the imagination, but he'd never eat anything without a plate.

But I don't want to ruffle his feathers right now. His surprising anger only just subsided. And everything has been going so well.

"So tell me about this work you were doing," I say, pecking at my salad. "I want to hear all about it."

"Oh, yeah," he says with a mouthful of sandwich. He drops his food onto the counter—again, not bothering to get a plate out or even tearing off a paper towel. "I think you're going to like it. Remember how I always said I wanted to start my own business?"

He says it like it's something he mentioned once, maybe twice, many years ago. But it's something we've discussed often and recently.

"Yes, honey, of course."

Brent begins pacing excitedly. "Well, I had the opportunity to really think about it over the last month. All that time away from the job was just what I needed to get my head straight and see things clearly. You know, when you're stuck in a routine, it's hard to imagine all the other possibilities that life has to offer?"

I think it's a rhetorical question, but Brent is waiting for my response.

"Yes," I say.

"I knew you'd understand," he says. "Anyway, I had a lot of time to think and actually, you know, come up with a business plan. After the gym, I went to that coffee shop right across the street."

It takes me a moment to figure out which one he's talking about. We don't go to a lot of coffee shops, and the one by the gym isn't close, so I've never been.

"I just spent the last two hours brainstorming," he says. "And it's like, you know, the ideas are just coming now."

He snaps his fingers multiple times while he paces back and forth. I've never seen Brent this excited about anything.

Well, okay. There are a few things that get him this excited. What I mean is I've never seen him this passionate about work.

"I'm a good coder," he says. "Why should I do all the work and the company keeps all the profits? I could do the same coding, all by myself, and reap all the reward, right?"

We have discussed Brent starting his own side business before. In the past, he's always wanted to do it on the cheap, maybe as a way at first of making a few extra bucks. But he never expressed interest in pursuing freelance coding before. As a matter of fact, just the opposite: Brent doesn't really enjoy what he does, so I can't imagine him now starting his own business doing the same type of work. To me, that seems like a recipe for burnout and disaster.

"*Coding?*" I say.

"Sure," he says. "Why not? I've put a lot of time and energy into it. I might as well leverage all this experience."

Over the last few years, Brent has spent a lot of time looking into new careers. Coding isn't the end-all, be-all that everybody makes it out to be, apparently. With all the second thoughts he's had about this career, I'm really surprised by this change of mind. I know he's been through what seems like a life-changing experience, and he's full of optimism right now, but I really don't think this is a good idea. I don't want to spoil his good mood and be the naysayer, but I don't have a good feeling about this. Before he went away, he was telling me he'd pretty much made up his mind: he was going to get out of this line of work.

"You know," he says, "all it's going to take is a little sweat equity and startup capital."

Brent can build his own website. Outside of registering a domain name, obtaining a PO box, and paying for an email service, his side business wasn't going to cost us anything. And all of those expenses are pretty cheap. If his side business were to take off, then he could quit his job and be his own boss. The way he always presented this idea before, it was low risk and high reward. At worst, we'd be down a few hundred dollars and Brent would have lost out on the opportunity cost of doing something else. Those were risks we were both willing to take.

But now, Brent is talking about *startup capital.* At some point, this idea went from a side hustle to big business. I don't know what he's got in mind now, but it's a heck of a lot riskier than before.

"So what were you thinking?" I ask.

"I've already contacted a few people I know in the business," he says. "To gauge interest. I'm fishing for silent partners."

Silent partners? As far as I know, Brent rarely interacts with his firm's clients. He does the coding work and hands off the project deliverables to the people who actually interact with the customer. In other words, he wouldn't get the opportunity to speak to people who have that kind of money for them to know who he is.

"You know," he goes on, like I don't understand what he

means, "silent partners. They're, like, angel investors. They're people who have a lot of money and want to get a nice, reliable return on their investment. But they don't want to spend any time managing a business. It's the best of both worlds: they bankroll us, and they leave me to run the operation. I just know they'd love my idea. I'm sure of it."

I'm not used to being the voice of reason in our relationship. As a matter of fact, I'm usually the glass-is-half-full one. But all this is too much for me. Brent could really use a reality check, but I don't know how to offer him one tactfully. Don't get me wrong: I love his newfound passion and energy. But there's something almost ... *manic* about it. I'm not a psychologist, so I'm not qualified to diagnose my husband at all. But that's how it seems to me. It'd be really weird for a grown man in his thirties to suddenly exhibit signs of mania, as far as I know, but that's the vibe I'm getting here.

What happened at this retreat? Did they give my husband a narcotic? I don't know anything about drugs. I've never even smoked pot. But could he be on something? It would explain some of his erratic behavior.

"What's the matter?" he asks.

"Oh, nothing," I say. "Tell me more about your business plan."

I can't bring myself to voice my concerns. Brent is so *happy* right now. So alive. I've never seen him like this before.

He's been home less than a day. I should let Brent ride this high. And who knows? Maybe he'll find some angel investors. But I really hope he doesn't ...

I don't even want to think about that right now. Hopefully he won't ask me.

5

BRENT – DAY ZERO – APRIL 11

As I let the soothing warm water of the shower run down my back, I can't believe I'm doing this.

Never in a million years did I think I'd pay all that money to attend a thirty-day wellness retreat. But something needed to change. Okay, *a lot* of somethings needed to change. I'm unhappy at work, I'm drinking way too much, my meds aren't helping with my depression anymore, and Mary and I aren't getting along.

It feels like I've reached several major crossroads all at once, professionally, personally, and psychologically. I can't keep going on the way I have. I can't keep pretending like everything is okay and I'll just "come out of it" somehow. I needed to really shake things up. I don't know if I'll stay at my job, but I do know for sure I want to make things work with Mary. She's been there for me in some very dark times.

That's why, tomorrow morning I will wake early, when it's still dark out, and drive out to the countryside. The retreat is being held at an old converted farmhouse that sits upon acres and acres of farmland. The rules are straightforward. No cell phones. No computers. No electronics of any sort. Follow the schedule. Do the work.

A detailed schedule was not provided in advance, but the people running the retreat clued me and the seven other participants in. Our days will involve several hours of mindfulness, exercise, and manual labor. We will rise with the sun and go on a nature hike first thing. Lights go out at nine o'clock. We are expected to be asleep by ten.

As for the work, it's both physical and, I hate to use this word, spiritual. I'm not a spiritual guy. I think most of this New Age stuff is a lot of hand-waving, woo-woo nonsense. But I've got to try something different. I can't keep doing all the same old things and expect better results. And from what I've read, there's been a lot of support in the scientific literature for mindfulness practice, so maybe—hopefully—there's something to it.

Still, I'm pretty nervous. I get anxious a lot, especially around new people. Seven other perfect strangers are going to watch me try to perform manual labor on a farm and be all outdoorsy. Neither of those things are exactly in my wheelhouse. Mary likes to joke that I'm Mr. Suburbia, and I can't really argue. As a kid, I never went camping. Nor have I ever had a physically demanding job before either. My brother, Christopher, seemed to inherit all the athletic genes. There wasn't a sport he didn't excel at, whereas I was always a step slower than everybody and a little clumsy. I also was never *aggressive* in the same way he was ...

Christopher.

He's been dead for a few years now, but it still doesn't feel real. I hadn't seen him in a long time. When my parents, whom I hadn't spoken to in years, contacted me to share the news, I didn't know what to say. My mother was crying over the phone, and my father was uncharacteristically quiet. I almost asked them why they had bothered to tell me, but that would have been heartless. My parents and I have our issues, but they were still people who had lost one of their children. So I told them I was sorry, but I didn't feel sorry at all.

Christopher was my only sibling. I didn't feel sad when he passed, and I don't miss him now. I know I should have, because Christopher was my brother, and you're supposed to love your brother, but we never loved each other.

I tried to like him when we were kids. I tried to be his friend. But he didn't want that. In fact, he made it impossible to like him. Any chance he got, he would hit me. Sometimes he'd do it right in front of our parents. Mom and Dad mostly turned a blind eye to the abuse, with Dad sometimes putting the blame on me.

"If you weren't so soft, he wouldn't walk all over you."

The older we got, the more sophisticated Christopher's torments became. He still hit me—that never stopped—but he also got me in trouble at school or in the neighborhood. He'd do something and make it look like I was the culprit. He'd get one of his friends to make up a story about how I threatened them, or how I hid their backpack, or how I cheated on a test or whatever. I was constantly in trouble, even though I was, for the most part, a reasonably well-behaved child.

The worst part?

Christopher *always* got away with it.

Not once did he get in trouble, not once did my parents

ever punish or even reprimand him. I didn't have a word for it then, but I became depressed. My parents didn't seem to love me, my brother abused me, and there was nothing I could do about it. I felt like there was no point to anything. I didn't think I could make it to the age of eighteen, didn't think I could graduate high school even, with all this going on. Christopher even managed to turn everyone against me at school, so I lost what few friends I had.

I began to feel hopeless.

I thought Christopher was pure evil, like he had been put on Earth by the devil or whatever to torment me. Now that I'm older, that idea seems silly to me. The reality is, Christopher was a sadist. My brother was the product of bad genetics and an even worse upbringing. I won't go so far as to say I'm glad he's gone, but I'm not sad he isn't around anymore.

I turn off the shower and towel off in the stall. Am I really going through with this? Part of me thinks I should just wake up at my regular time tomorrow and head into the office. Asking for a leave of absence from work was one of the hardest things I'd had to do in my life, honestly, because it required providing my boss with a doctor's note and admitting to someone I don't even like that I was struggling mentally. It was embarrassing as hell, and I'm sure the rumors will start up this morning, with my coworkers wondering where I am. I don't even want to think about my first day back and how mortified I'll be.

When I'm reasonably dry, I step out of the shower and wipe the mirror so I can look at myself.

I'm not a kid anymore. When you're mid-thirties, you can't claim to be young. You've entered that weird gray area where you're not old and not exactly middle-aged, but you're definitely not young.

There's a knock on the bathroom door.

"Hey, hon," Mary says. "Can I come in?"

I open the door. My wife is standing there in the doorway, wearing a T-shirt and pajama bottoms. She looks adorable. I tell her she's beautiful all the time, but Mary doesn't think so. She hates her nose and her ears, and she thinks she's too heavy.

"Hey," I say, unable to hide how nervous I am. "What's up?"

"You okay?" she asks.

"Yeah." I force a smile and put my palms on the sink. "Yeah, I'm fine."

She gives me a look. "You've been in here for a while. I just wanted to make sure."

"It's not too late," I say, looking at her. "I could still cancel."

She leans against the doorway. "What do you think?"

What do I think? I'm thinking a million things. This trip could be just what I need. I could go away and come back a new man, full of confidence and passion and maybe even some little peace of mind. I've never experienced any of those things.

Or it won't help at all, we'll have wasted thousands of dollars, and I'll have put my job in jeopardy by taking a leave of absence for no good reason. I know that, under the law, my employer can't hold my taking this time off against me, but let's be real, I know it's going to be in the back of my boss's mind forever now. Behind closed doors, they'll talk. They'll say things like:

"Can we really trust Brent with this major project? What

if he asks for a leave halfway through and we can't deliver on our promises to the client?"

"How long till Brent loses his mind again?"

"We have two candidates. One of them has never had any problems here. The other had to take a leave of absence for a month because he was depressed and couldn't perform his job duties. Which one should we promote?"

Mary steps into the bathroom and puts her arms around me. "I think you should try it. You can leave whenever you want, right?"

I hug her back. "Right."

"Just try it, then, for a few days. Okay?"

"Okay."

Her body shudders, and I realize she's crying. "I'm going to miss you."

"I'll miss you too."

She looks up at me with those beautiful green eyes of hers. Since we've been married, we've never been apart for this long. We won't be able to call, email, or text each other, and Mary is not allowed to drive out to see me either.

"Will you be here when I get back?" I ask.

"Of course." She smiles. "Promise you *will* come back?"

"Yes."

We kiss and hold on to each other for a moment. I miss this. We used to lie down in bed, put our arms around one another and talk for hours about everything and nothing. We haven't done that in a long time.

"I'm sure it'll be great," she says. "I'm really excited for you."

I'm not excited. I'm terrified. And I'm worried this is going to be a complete waste of time and money.

"What is it?" Mary asks, looking up at me again. "You seem like you want to tell me something."

My wife knows me too well.

"No," I lie. "I'm just nervous. I'll be okay."

She gives me a look like she doesn't believe me, but then lets it go. I breathe a sigh of relief.

There is something I haven't told her about this trip. And it's important.

6

FRIDAY – MAY 12

"**H**ey, babe."

Brent comes flying downstairs, full of energy. He's dressed for the gym and carrying the same bag as yesterday. He's also holding the backpack he uses to transport his laptop around.

"Hey there."

He zooms into the kitchen, gives my rear end a pat, which turns more into a grope; then he kisses the side of my neck, which he knows drives me *wild*. I have to put my cup of coffee down and turn to him. Next thing I know, our lips are locked, and my hands are all over him.

When Brent pulls away, he's smiling. "Wake up in a good mood this morning?"

We made love again last night. I don't know what it is, but we haven't been able to keep our hands off each other since he got home. I'm not going to lie, it doesn't hurt that he's lost a little weight and is in the best shape of his life. With those broad shoulders and tapered waist, his body has that delicious V-shape that I find irresistible.

"You're trouble, you know that?" I say.

He gives me another squeeze, then sets his things down on the island counter so he can root around in the fridge. I'm absolutely shocked when Brent emerges with an apple. This is another new development in his life. I don't think I've ever witnessed my husband willingly eating a piece of fruit before. He wraps the apple in a paper towel and puts it in his backpack.

"Alright, babe," he says. "I'm headed to the gym and then to the coffee shop to do more work."

"You could come home and work," I say. "I won't bother you."

He laughs. "Are you kidding? How can I get anything done knowing you're in the next room, looking that good?"

I'm wearing my trademark baggy sweatpants and T-shirt again. My hair is tied up in a messy bun. And I haven't showered. I don't know how in the world he can think I look good, but I'm not going to look a gift horse in the mouth.

Still, I've really missed him.

"It's just, you've been away for a month." I get close to him again, before he can pick up his bags, and put a hand on his side. "I really missed you, and you know, next week you'll be back at the office. I guess I was hoping we could spend a few days together before you had to start work again."

"I've missed you too, but if I'm going to get this business off the ground, I really need to get cracking. Once I'm back at the office next week, it's only going to get more difficult to work on this side business."

He gives me a good, long kiss; then he's off and running again. Throwing his backpack on, grabbing his gym bag, he gives me a wink.

"I might be a while today," he says. "I had some more

ideas last night. I want to take some time and think them through."

I can't hide my disappointment. "Alright. What do you feel like for dinner tonight?"

"Why don't we go out?" he says, his smile brightening. "There's this new Asian fusion place nearby."

I know. We've talked about it before. But it seems to be one more of those random things Brent forgot. It opened a few weeks before he went on his retreat, so maybe like the other thing, it went in one ear and out the other.

"Brent," I say, "we just spent a fortune at Rindella's the other night."

"Come on," he says. "We can afford it."

I make a face. "I don't know, Brent. We didn't have your pay coming in this month, and the retreat—"

"What?" he snaps. "The retreat what?"

I take a step back, puzzled by his reaction. It's no secret that his wellness retreat cost us some money. We had to dip into savings. Brent knows how reluctant I am to do that, but I was more than willing to do so to get him the help he needed.

"Brent," I say, trying to remain calm, "the retreat was something we didn't budget for."

"Are you saying it was a waste of money?"

He's getting very defensive. "No, honey, that's not what I'm saying. I'm glad you went. It seems to have helped—"

"You're damned right it helped," he says, losing the temper I never knew he had. "I feel great. I feel like my whole life has changed for the better. I can see the potential now. I can see all the *possibilities*. We don't have to be miserable. We don't have to work jobs we don't like. We don't have to worry about money. All we need to do is believe in ourselves a little bit and we'll succeed. That's it. The universe will provide."

Oh boy.

The man I married would never have been caught dead saying something like *the universe will provide*. Brent is the most reasonable—to a fault—man I've ever known. He's very skeptical when it comes to things like that and careful about what he accepts as true. In the past, if anyone had said those words to him, he would have rolled his eyes and walked away, unable to take anything else that person said seriously. Later, he would scoff at how silly some people can be. I can hear him now, the *old* him anyway, pointing out that the universe didn't provide when he was younger and enduring a terrible childhood, when he was abused physically and emotionally by his brother and his awful parents.

He shakes his head. "Do you doubt me?"

"Brent." I can't help it. Now I'm getting defensive. "I don't doubt you at all. I'm just worried about money."

"You're the last person who should worry about money," he says. "With everything your parents left you."

I stiffen. I don't know where this attitude is coming from. My parents left me some money, which is nice, don't get me wrong, but it's hardly enough to retire on. I mean, even if we were in our sixties, it wouldn't be enough right now. Brent and I are in our thirties and hopefully have a lot more living to do. Between now and later, we need to save significantly more than that if we want to retire. And, given my recent diagnosis, there's a good possibility I'm going to need a lot of money for expensive medical treatment in the future, especially when I get older. Lupus isn't a cheap condition.

Meanwhile, Brent is acting like I'm hoarding cash and being incredibly stingy. It's really not fair.

He finally reads my reaction, and his face softens. "I'm sorry. You're right to be thinking about the future, especially with your condition. Rheumatoid arthritis is no joke."

I do a double take. "I have *lupus*, Brent. *Lupus*. Those are two very different things."

Brent makes a pained face. His cheeks turn bright red.

"Jesus, uh, I, did I say rheumatoid arthritis? I'm sorry, God, I don't know where my head ... I meant lupus. I'm sorry, honey."

I fold my arms. I don't know how we went from having a great morning to having a bitter argument about money. His forgetfulness is hurtful as well. Lupus is a serious, lifelong medical condition with no cure. It's an autoimmune disease that, at best, can only be managed.

"I'm glad you went on this retreat," I say. "But I think we need to slow everything down here, Brent, and have a real conversation."

He frowns. "What do you mean?"

"I mean, you've been back for two days, and I still haven't heard anything about your trip. What you did, who you met. You seem like you've had a lot of epiphanies, and I don't know what they are or how you came to them," I explain. "I feel like we've been talking around each other since you got home."

Brent stares at me for a long moment. I've always been able to read him really well. But for the first time in our marriage, as I study his face, I literally have *no idea* what my husband is thinking. He could open his mouth and say anything. I really have no idea.

But then the spell is broken. Brent smiles and nods, moving in once more to wrap his arms around me.

"You're right," he says. "You're so right. Tell you what,

why don't you let me cook dinner tonight? We'll sit down to a nice meal together and talk. How does that sound?"

It sounds wonderful.

Or at least, it *should* sound wonderful.

But I can't shake the terrible feeling in my stomach.

I CAN'T KEEP my mind on work today. All I can think about is Brent and the argument we had this morning. He has never accused me of being cheap before, and I have to admit, it really hurt my feelings. When he first mentioned the idea of attending this wellness retreat, I *immediately* offered to pay for it, without hesitation or question. It's incredibly unfair of him to suggest I'm stingy right after my contribution.

My parents passed away before Brent and I got married. I remember one of the last conversations I ever had with my father, who'd spoken to me as if he knew he'd have a heart attack a week or so later.

"Your mother and I always liked Brent," he said. "I think he's a good man."

I had flown down to Florida to spend a long weekend with Dad in his retirement community. He seemed so lonely to me without Mom there, almost like a shell of his former self. We were sitting out on his balcony among the condominiums. I remember it was incredibly hot that evening. I was sweating profusely, but Dad kept complaining about how cold it was.

"I hear a but coming," I said.

My father looked over at me. "Brent has a lot of demons. That childhood of his, I wouldn't wish that on my worst enemy." Dad shook his head. "I know you two are thinking about getting married."

I hadn't told him that, but of course Dad was right. He knew me like the back of his hand.

"When I'm gone, there will be some money left for you," he said. "It's not enough to quit your job, but it'll give you a little security. You never know when you're going to need it."

"I don't want your money," I said. "I want you to live forever."

He laughed then, like I was being silly. "Not happening, I'm afraid."

"I'm still waiting for that but."

He nodded gravely. "If you two decide to get married, I want you to get a prenup."

"A prenup?" I laugh, thinking he's joking. Prenups are what very rich people get. Prenups are what famous actors make their future, non-famous, spouses sign. But Dad isn't smiling. "Wait, are you serious?"

"It's important. I want to leave what little money I have left to *you*, honey. I wish it was more." He looked away, as if embarrassed. "I worked hard all my life, but it never amounted to much."

"Dad, don't say that—"

He held out a palm. "It's true. We never wanted for anything, but it pains me how little I have to give you. But that's just the thing, Mary. I want to leave it to you, and to you alone. I like Brent. I think he's a good person, but like I said, he's got a lot of demons."

"Brent would never steal an inheritance from me. He's too good a person."

Dad pursed his lips. "When you get to be my age, you see so-called good people do all kinds of awful things. I'm no doctor, but I can tell Brent's got depression. I've seen him go quiet and get that hollow look behind his eyes."

I never shared that with Mom or Dad, but it was true. Brent had only recently begun to speak to a therapist and gotten himself on medication. I wanted to protect Brent's privacy, but I also couldn't lie to my father, who was only looking out for me. So I said nothing, and by saying nothing, Dad knew he'd struck home.

Dad said, "That's a terrible condition, don't get me wrong, but it makes people behave in unexpected, irrational ways. I saw it happen to one of my good friends. He had everything going for him, and then one night he up and killed his girlfriend, then shot himself."

Mom had shared this story with me before, but Dad had never opened up about it. I could tell reliving it took a lot out of him. He and this person had been very close when they were young men, working at the machine shop together.

"Mary, it's my job to make sure you're safe. If you don't get a prenup, then I'll put this money into a trust or something so that only you can get to it. Those finance guys know a million dirty tricks. But I'd really rather not do that, make you jump through a bunch of hoops. I want you to have access to it whenever you want."

I really didn't want to get a prenup. I felt like that was a horrible way to start a marriage. It's like saying, *I love you. Let's get married. Oh, by the way, this might not work out, so could you sign this document?*

"What difference does it make if I get a prenup?" I asked, playing devil's advocate. "If I have the money, then I could just give it all to Brent, right?"

I have never enjoyed talking about money, and that time was no exception. It was the last thing I wanted to discuss with my father, because it forced me to think about a time when he'd no longer be around.

"Once you have control of the money, it's up to you what you want to do with it, of course. If you decide to give it to Brent, then that's your choice. But at least it'll be your choice and no one else's."

When I returned from that trip to Florida, I discussed the future with Brent. I wanted to get that conversation over with so we could either move on together or decide to part ways. When I raised the possibility of a prenup, Brent didn't bat an eye.

"I don't want your parents' money," he said. "I only want you, Mary."

Dad passed not long after that.

I FINISH what I absolutely must get done for the week, then jump in my Prius and head out to meet Paige at the coffee shop in the same shopping center as her bank.

Paige is dressed in her usual slightly provocative fashion, her blouse open one too many buttons, and her black skirt terminating a few inches above the knee. We find a table in the corner. I go to sit, but she bumps into me.

"Mind if I take this seat?" she asks. "That way, I don't have to stare at the bank while I'm on break."

I take the other seat, which affords a view of Paige's bank. It sits on the other side of a busy parking lot, opposite the coffee shop we're sitting in. I guess Paige spends enough time in that building, and thinking about it, that she doesn't want to sit here and look at it while on break. Makes sense.

"So," Paige says, putting both hands around her cup of coffee. "How *are* things?"

"Good," I say. "I mean, really good."

Paige watches me for a moment. "Uh-huh?"

"Yes, really good," I say. "I think this is what Brent needed. He seems a lot better. He's happy, he's full of energy, and he's got all these new ideas. I think he's going to do it this time. I think he's going to start a side business."

Paige nods. She has seen right through my enthusiasm.

"You're red in the face again," she says. "Are you sure you're feeling okay?"

I immediately take out my compact. I didn't bother to give my appearance much thought today. Looking in the tiny mirror, I find Paige is right. One of the symptoms of lupus is a reddening around the face that takes the shape of a butterfly. Not good. When this happens to me, it usually presages a flareup.

I can't deal with *that* right now.

"Oh, this isn't bad," I lie, putting my compact away and pretending it's nothing. "I was rearranging the spare bedroom earlier—"

"You're not telling me something." Paige leans in, lowers her voice. "Have you two had sex yet?"

My God, have we. "About six times since he's been back."

"Mary." Paige pretends to be shocked. "I never."

I laugh giddily. "It's been incredible, Paige. I mean, the things this man can do to me ..."

Paige grins conspiratorially.

"That's great, Mary," she says. "I'm happy to hear that. But if sex isn't the problem, then what is?"

"Who said there was a problem?"

She tilts her head to the side. "Come on, Mary. Something's bothering you, I can tell."

"Uh, well ..."

The truth is, I don't know what *exactly* is bothering me. Or where to begin. I don't like the fact that Brent got angry with me, or that he implied I was cheap, or, come to think of it, that he was kind of nasty about Mrs. Ryers the other day. But I can't remember word-for-word what he said, how I responded, how he came back. I do my best to recall our conversations, but I don't do a great job of painting a vivid picture for Paige.

She sits back and thinks over what I've shared.

"You know, when people go away on these things, they're taken out of their usual environment so they can get a better perspective on things," she says.

"Yeah, Paige. That's kind of the point."

"Oh, look at Mary with the snark," she says. "I didn't know you were capable."

I laugh to make light of it, but she's right: I'm usually not snarky. With everything going on in the last two days, I'm clearly not myself.

"Sorry," I say.

She holds out a palm. "Don't be. I kind of like it. Anyway, when they come back, they're still in *retreat* mode, or whatever you want to call it. It takes a few days for them to get readjusted to regular, everyday life."

"Yeah, I guess you're right."

Paige shrugs. "Or I'm wrong, and he's completely different. I don't know, Mary."

We both have a laugh at that. It's really good to see her. Like I said, I don't have many friends, so I cherish every moment I get with Paige.

"I'm a little worried about him returning to work," I admit. "Just like me, I'm sure Brent's coworkers are used to him being a certain way. I don't know how they'll take his new demeanor, especially his outspokenness. I mean, his boss is *definitely* not going to like that. That man is a real jerk, and he's probably looking for any reason to zip Brent."

Paige's face darkens. "Yeah, about that ... I wasn't sure if I should tell you or not."

Oh no. "Tell me what?"

Paige takes a deep breath. "I'm sorry, but, you know, some of Brent's coworkers were in the bank the other day."

"Okay."

"While I waited on one of them, I overheard a few of the others talking and ... look, I really don't know whether I should say anything."

"You might as well tell me now, Paige."

She grimaces. Paige is a bit of a gossip. Normally I don't mind because I'm never the object of any local gossip. But right now I've got my back up. I don't like the thought of Brent's colleagues talking about him.

"I don't know how, but word got around the office that he was *away*, you know, for a *condition*."

I ball my fists. Where Brent was, what he was doing for the last thirty days, is nobody's business. Especially these people at his office, none of whom know anything about him really or what he's been through. If they knew about his brother, if they knew about his parents and how awful they were to him, how he found the strength to call child services when he was a teenager ... God, I really hate people sometimes. They can be awful. No wonder I'm such a homebody.

"Do you know who they were?" I ask.

"I waited on a man called Rich," she says.

Rich.

I know who he is.

He and Brent have worked together on a lot of projects. Recently, a new role opened up, which would be a promotion for both of them. Before Brent took his leave of absence, Rich apparently took to throwing his weight around, trying to dominate meetings and overstep bounds in the hopes it would lend him an air of authority. Brent thought it was Rich's immature way of establishing himself in the new role before it was even offered to him.

Now, I don't know with certainty if Rich started the rumors about Brent. But I wouldn't put it past the guy. They've never really gotten along well.

"But like I said," Paige continues, "Rich wasn't the one talking about Brent. It was the others, there were four or five of them. They were waiting by the door for Rich."

"What did they look like?" I ask. "Was there an overweight man there, one with a mustache?"

That's what Brent's boss, Aaron, looks like.

Paige thinks about it. "I don't really remember what they all looked like. I was waiting on Rich and had to pay him mind. I didn't get a good look at the rest."

"Wait, how did you know they were from Brent's office?" I ask.

"I've seen them in the bank before," she explains. "I've overheard them talking about Designed Solutions before."

That's the name of the company Brent works for, alright.

"What did they say?"

"I heard somebody say, *Do you really think he'll come back to the office?* And since I knew where they worked and I knew about Brent ..."

"What else?" I ask.

"Somebody else said they wouldn't if they were him. They'd be too embarrassed."

I hate people. "Assholes."

Paige nods sympathetically. "I'm sorry, I shouldn't have told you."

"No, I'm glad you did," I say quickly.

But as I sit and think about it, I'm actually not glad she did. I don't know what to do with the information. Brent seems like he's in a really good place right now, but if I share this gossip with him, I fear it will crush him. Honestly, I wouldn't blame him for feeling that way. I mean, who would want to go back to work when the whole office has been talking about their having to take a leave for a mental condition?

Or, maybe even worse, this information will spark Brent's newfound anger, and he'll stalk into that office Monday morning and start yelling at everybody, demanding to know who's been gossiping about his mental health. I wouldn't blame him for that, either, but I don't think it would help matters around the office much. This is not good. Not good at all.

Brent and I talked about how his taking leave might impact his job. We both knew there was a good possibility it would. He even admitted he should be prepared to look for another job when he returned, since his coworkers and boss might not be so welcoming. Right now, that is looking like a very real possibility.

"People just suck," I say.

"They really do," Paige says. She checks her watch. "I'm sorry, girl, but I have to get back. They're being real sticklers over at the bank these days. Apparently when they say twenty minutes for a break, they literally mean twenty minutes."

I laugh, and we hug goodbye. Paige hurries out of the coffee shop. I gather my things and stop at the trash can to dispose of my coffee. Looking out the window, I see Paige practically jogging across the parking lot. She runs right past a gray SUV that looks familiar.

I do a double take, trying to place where I've seen it before. It doesn't belong to anybody I know, but I remember seeing this vehicle recently ... and then it hits me.

That SUV was parked in the empty part of this parking lot the other day when I left the bank. A man was sitting behind the steering wheel, but from where I was, I couldn't get a good look at him.

The SUV is backed into a spot and facing toward the coffee shop. It's right next to my Prius today.

Whoever it is, they must do their banking here, or maybe they like this coffee shop. Or maybe they're here for an early dinner at the gourmet pizza shop next door. I step out into the afternoon sunlight and weave my way through parked cars.

The SUV's engine is running, just like it was the other day. And again, there's a man sitting behind the steering wheel. I don't know why, but the way he's parked, backed into the spot, the driver-side door right next to my own, gives me such a horrible feeling in the pit of my stomach. It's obviously just somebody who comes to this shopping center regularly, just like I do. But I can't shake the feeling.

The man is wearing a hat and sunglasses that obscure his heavily bearded face. And even though he's got those sunglasses on, I sense he's *watching* me from behind them. His head isn't tilted down like he's on his cell phone. His lips aren't moving like he's singing along to the radio. He's just sitting there, very still, looking out his windshield. I pick up my pace, growing ever more uncomfortable as I draw nearer to this man.

He didn't leave me much room to open my door, either. He's parked right up along the line separating our two parking spaces. And now I am freaking out, because it's going to be difficult to get into my car without asking him to move.

I squeeze between the cars. The man's head turns. He's definitely watching me. My skin crawls. I don't want to talk to him. I don't want to engage with him. Now that I'm up close to his vehicle, I notice that his SUV has seen better days. It's pretty dinged up. There are scratches all down the driver's side, and the rear bumper is hanging a bit low.

After unlocking my car, I open the door as wide as I can without bumping the SUV. That gives me about ten inches or so to squeeze my body in. I toss my bag inside, landing it on the passenger seat.

I'm being silly, I know. He's just a guy who comes to this shopping center often. I've probably seen half the other vehicles in this parking lot before but never paid them any mind. Why am I freaking out? I'm on edge because of Brent being away for so long and then coming back very different, that's all. I need to calm down.

I peek over my shoulder.

The man is turned in his seat, watching me.

My heart drops.

He's facing my way and not trying to hide it. With his hat, sunglasses, and beard, I can't really make out his face, but I can tell right away: I do not know this man. I have to get in my car. I have to get away from him.

He powers his window down. I pretend not to notice,

turning quickly and desperately trying to wedge myself into my car. In the process, I accidentally bump my door against his car. Now I'm really panicked.

"Hey, sweetheart," he says in a profoundly deep voice.

I don't like when men call me sweetheart. I know it's old-school and meant to be endearing, but I find it sexist and minimizing. Only Brent gets to call me that.

I freeze. I've got one leg and almost one hip in my car, but the rest of my body is out. Discreetly, I pull my door away from his SUV. I'm utterly relieved to discover I didn't scratch or dent his vehicle. The last thing I want to do is engage this man and exchange insurance information with him. Though, honestly, judging by the way he looks and the state of his SUV, I wouldn't be surprised if he was driving without insurance.

"Yes?" I say, like I just didn't tap his car with my door.

He sticks his head out the window and smiles at me. He's missing a couple of teeth, and the rest are yellow. There's also a bad odor emanating from his car. It could be pot. I don't really know, I've never tried it before.

"You alright?" he asks.

"I'm fine." I force a smile. It's really uncomfortable with half my body in my car and my head turned his way to look at him. I pull my leg back out of the Prius, making sure not to bump his SUV again with my door. "Can I help you with something?"

He doesn't answer. He just holds his gaze on me for a long, excruciating moment. I don't like this guy. At all. I should be ready to call the police, though I don't know what for. He hasn't technically done anything ...

I reach in my pocket, but then remember: I put my cell in my bag. My phone is in the car right now.

He pulls his sunglasses down the bridge of his nose. There's a nasty scar running along the side of his eye. The man looks me up and down like I'm wearing a string bikini. Gross. I can't take this. He's a total creep. Men don't understand what it's like to be ogled by a perfect stranger. They just don't get how scary that can be. This guy clearly doesn't, or maybe he *does* know and doesn't care.

He's not answering me, so I'm not engaging him any further. Just before I can swing my leg back into my car, though, he speaks.

"Hey, you want me to move my car?" He motions. "So you can get in?"

I want this interaction to be over. "No, I'll be fine. Thank you."

"Wait," he says, "it's no big deal. I'll—"

"It's fine," I say, squeezing myself in. But the problem is, it's not fine. I really cannot fit myself into the car with this little space. I *do* need him to move his SUV.

"Come on," he says, smiling toothily. "It's no big deal. Only take a sec. Sorry I parked so close, but you know, these spots are really small."

I can't help but look around the parking lot. There are plenty of other open spots on this side of the lot, places he could have parked where he wouldn't be next to anybody. He didn't need to be this close to my car. I feel like he did this intentionally so he could talk to me. He's a creep.

"Yeah," I say. "Okay. Thank you."

"You're really fit," he says. "But there's not enough room even for you. I parked way too close."

I feel like there are insects crawling all over my skin. I don't respond to what I guess was his compliment of my physique. I move so I'm standing in front of my car. He puts his SUV into gear, the brake lights go off, and he inches his way forward. The man doesn't get far when his vehicle stops suddenly. He's not far enough up for me to get into my car yet. The driver hits his horn at a pedestrian who was cutting through parked cars in the next row. The two men get into a shouting match, telling each other to watch where they're going, until the driver throws open his door and jumps out.

He's *big.*

I mean tall. And broad. He's well over six feet and moves like an athlete. There are tattoos up and down his arms and running down one calf. But that's not what scares me the most about him.

There is a handgun tucked behind his shorts at the small of his back.

"You wanna do something about it?" the driver yells at the pedestrian.

Seeing the driver's size, the other man turtles up and hurries away to get into his own car. Then the driver turns around. Before he gets back into his SUV, he gives me a smile.

"People can be so rude, am I right?"

It takes me a moment to find my voice. All I can picture right now is the gun. Not that this man even needs a gun— he could pretty easily throw me into the back of his car. Probably with one hand. That's how big and strong he looks.

"I'm sorry," I say. "I, uh, I really have somewhere to be. Could you move up a little more?"

The driver doesn't budge. He stands there, staring at me, saying nothing. Even if he didn't have a gun on him, he'd look *dangerous.*

"Sure, sweetheart, no problem."

My shoulders relax as he gets back into his SUV. He

edges forward, taking his time, giving me *just enough* space to open my door. Once I have room, I throw the door open and quickly jump inside, pulling the door closed behind me and locking it. I fumble with my keys, drop them onto the floor of the car, then panic as I scramble to pick them up and get the Prius started. Meanwhile, the driver is backing into the same space again. He pulls in as far as he can, so that the driver's window is almost next to mine. I can feel him looking over at me while I finally manage to get the keys in the ignition and start the car.

As I back out, the man gives me a creepy little wave.

While I wait for traffic to pass, I keep one eye on my rearview mirror. The SUV is still in the same spot. At least the creep isn't following me. When there's a break in traffic, I pull out onto the street. My phone buzzes with a text from Brent. I wait to read it at a red light.

> Hey, babe. Sorry, but got held up over here. Lot of great ideas, just trying to work through them. I'm going to be later than I thought. I know I offered to make dinner, but is there any way you could whip something together tonight?

The car behind me hits the horn. The light literally just turned green. I wave that I'm sorry and get into the flow of traffic. I turn off the main road onto a side street and pull over to respond to Brent's text.

> No problem. I'll make pasta. I have some sauce and can add bell peppers.

Before I get going, Brent has already written me back.

> I just had pasta with my steak the other night at Rindella's. Could you make something else?

I put the car in park.

Brent loves pasta. I'm pretty sure that, if left to his own devices, he'd eat it every night. He's never cared about eating pasta too often before.

More importantly, we have a dinner policy. So long as it's something we both like, whoever's cooking calls the shots. If you're not the one doing the job, you can't complain. That always seemed fair to us. I have to admit, I'm kind of annoyed with Brent right now. First, he got a little nasty with me this morning because he wanted to go out to dinner tonight and spend more money unnecessarily. His gesture of making dinner was really sweet and appreciated, because I was the only one of us working today while he was, technically, off from work. Don't get me wrong, I want him to spend time thinking about his side business, but clearly out of the two of us, Brent was the one with more flexibility in his schedule today. I wasn't even mad about him asking me to cook when he said he would. Things come up all the time, and plans change. It wasn't a problem until pasta became an issue for him.

Another text from Brent comes through.

> Sorry, honey, but I'm really trying to watch my weight. I don't want to eat a ton of carbs and turn into a lard ass.

Lard ass?

I don't think I've ever heard Brent use that expression before. It's not something I ever imagined him saying. He's never once made fun of people being overweight before. In fact, it's usually the opposite. He's often complained of coworkers making fun of a colleague's weight or talking pettily about how somebody's put on a few pounds. He finds that kind of talk and judgment infantile.

What has gotten into my husband?

I take a calming breath. Setting aside the unusual judgmental comment, Brent could have explained in the first place that he didn't want to eat too many carbs, and I would have totally understood. Over the years, we've both had times where we put on weight and then had to work hard to lose it. I appreciate the fact he wants to maintain this newfound physique. More power to him.

(Not going to lie, it's also nice for me.)

I also understand he's really excited about his new business idea. But, honestly, he had all day to think about dinner. Texting me at five o'clock to ask if I could prepare our meal, then asking me to come up with another idea is not cool.

I'm about to write him back when another text comes through.

> How about chicken and asparagus?

Brent has never liked asparagus. But it must be part of his new health kick. I like his idea, but there are two problems: I don't have chicken, and I don't have asparagus. I don't really feel like it, but I could stop at the grocery store around the corner on the way home. I hem and haw, then decide to stop. It is a healthy meal, and to be honest, now that Brent is in such fantastic shape, I feel like I should try a little harder myself.

Sounds good. See you at home.

I swing by the grocery store and pick up the chicken and asparagus and a few other things we could use around the house, including apples and bananas, now that Brent is actually ingesting fruit. I snake my way through the neighborhood. While I'm driving, I check my rearview mirror and gasp.

There is a gray SUV behind me.

It's not *directly* behind me. It's two cars back. I wait for my turn at a stop sign before proceeding through the next intersection. The car behind me turns right. The SUV doesn't come to a complete stop at the sign, however. Instead, it slides through the intersection and follows me.

From this distance, I don't know if it's the same vehicle from earlier. They're not following me that closely, so it's hard to tell. My hand goes to my phone. Little does this guy know, I can dial 9-1-1 faster than anybody else. I actually practiced it once.

The SUV continues behind me, but begins to slow. It's half a block away when I make the left onto my street. Relaxing, I let go of my phone and pull into our driveway. I peer up and down the street. There is no sign of the SUV.

I grab my purse and the grocery bag and hop out of the car. Juggling the two bags and my keys, I walk up the steps to the porch. Before I open the screen door, however, I hear a car coming down the street. My blood runs cold.

I turn to look, and sure enough, it's the gray SUV. It's moving along slowly, like the driver is unfamiliar with the street and checking house numbers. I turn away, not wanting the man to recognize me if it's the same person. I get my keys in the door and open it.

The SUV's brakes let out a little squeal as the vehicle comes to a stop in the street behind me. I freeze in the doorway. Should I turn around to see if it's the same guy? I want to know if it is, but my turning around might invite another uncomfortable conversation. And I don't want this guy, assuming it's him, to recognize me and know where I live.

I duck into the house, close the door, flip the deadbolt. My heart is racing. I put my bags down right where I'm standing in the foyer and, very carefully, turn to peek out the sidelite window next to the door.

The SUV is stopped right outside my house. The driver's window powers down, and I get a good look at the man behind the wheel.

It's the same guy from earlier. Hat, sunglasses, big and unkempt beard.

Though he probably can't tell I'm watching him, I still feel like he's looking directly at me. He lowers his sunglasses on the bridge of his nose, just like he did earlier, as if to get a better look at my house. God, I really wish Brent had stayed home today. Not that anybody could have foreseen I would have picked up a stalker this afternoon, but still.

I take my phone out. I am ready, willing, and able to call the police. I don't care if this guy hasn't technically done anything wrong yet. I am not going to wait for him to do so, especially since he's walking around town with a handgun tucked into his waistband. There's a good chance it is an unregistered firearm, judging by the look of him.

The driver grins ear to ear, like he's caught me watching him. As I bring the phone up to dial the police, the man sticks his hand out the window and gives me a little wave before driving off.

7

I'm finishing up with dinner when Brent finally comes home. It's almost seven o'clock. After the strange man drove off, it took me a while to calm down. I watched out the front window for a bit to see if he'd come back, then went room to room to make sure all our windows were locked. I even changed the bulb for the floodlight in our backyard. I've been meaning to do that for months.

"Hey, hon," Brent says, flying into the kitchen. He's just as energetic tonight as he was this morning. "How you doing?"

He comes in for a kiss, but I push him away. Brent frowns, pulling back.

"What's wrong?"

"Did you not get my text?" I ask.

"Text?"

"I also tried calling you," I say.

"You did?" Brent takes his phone out. "Oh, jeez, sorry. I missed both."

"Yeah, you did," I say.

I give him my back, turning to finish with the chicken. I stir-fried it. Brent's hand is on my shoulder a second later. I want to shrug out of his grip, but I'm too busy and just want to get done in the kitchen so we can sit down and eat, and this day can be over.

"I'm sorry I missed your text and call," Brent says. "What did you want?"

I drop the long wooden spoon on the counter, allowing it to spatter sauce everywhere.

"I think there's a man following me."

Brent's eyes narrow. "What man?"

"I don't know, I don't know who he is. I saw him in the shopping center on Wednesday when I stopped at the bank. Then he was there again this afternoon when I got coffee with Paige." I tell Brent about what happened in the parking lot. "Then, when I was coming home from the grocery store, he was behind me. He followed me onto the street and stopped right outside our house. I was going to call the cops."

"The cops?" Brent asks.

Why does he sound nervous right now? I *should have* called the police.

"Yeah, the cops. This guy was watching the house for a minute. Then he rolled his window down and *waved at me.*"

Brent purses his lips. "What did he look like?"

"I don't know, he was like, really big. Tall and he seemed muscular. He was built like an athlete. He had tattoos up and down his arms and also down one leg. He was wearing big sunglasses and pulled them down to peer at me. And he was carrying that gun."

"Right." Brent goes quiet. "That's really weird."

I glare at him. "Where were you? I texted and called right after all this happened."

"I'm sorry." He smiles apologetically. "There's not great reception at that coffee shop. In the future, I'll have to work somewhere else."

"You could work *here*, Brent."

He holds out his palms. "Whoa, honey. Take it easy, okay? I'm sorry I didn't realize you were trying to contact me."

"It's fine. Let's forget about it."

I turn away from him, swiping the spoon off the counter. I just want to finish with dinner and eat. I'm starved, I'm still a little freaked out, and I'm angry with Brent. He doesn't even sound like he's sorry or even worried that I had this terrifying encounter with an armed man today.

"Hey." He gets right behind me. His hands are on my sides. "I'm sorry, baby."

He kisses the back of my head, then gently loops his arms around me.

"That must have been scary," he adds.

"It was awful."

I can't help it. I start crying. I hate that I'm such a baby sometimes. Brent hugs me more tightly, and I let it all out. It's been a while since I've had a good cry. It turns out I really needed it.

"Can I take over in here?" Brent asks after I get myself together.

"Oh, sure."

The truth is, dinner is ninety-nine percent done already. But I appreciate the gesture. I take my wine with me and sit at the dining room table. A few minutes later, Brent brings our plates out. The meal turns out better than

I expected, especially since I scraped it together at the last minute.

"So," Brent begins, dropping his fork on the plate to signal he's done eating. "I know this afternoon was traumatic for you. But can we talk about it some more?"

I dab the corners of my mouth with a napkin. I don't really want to discuss it any further. "Why?"

"What did this guy look like?" Brent asks.

"I told you, I couldn't make out his face." Why is he going over this again? "He had dark hair and this big beard, and all those tattoos."

"Hmmm." He thinks it over. I don't know what he expects to do with this information. It's not like he's a cop. We don't know anybody in the police department. Brent can't just pick up the phone and call somebody. "How about his eyes? Did you get a look at those?"

"No, I told you, he was wearing sunglasses."

"But didn't you say he lowered them a few times to get a better look at you?"

"Brent." I can feel myself getting nervous again just talking about this. "What is the point?"

"Honey," he says, keeping his calm, "I want to get a picture of this guy."

"But why?"

He gives me a look like I'm really dumb. "Because there are things we can do about it. For one, we can—"

"What are the police going to do?" I ask. "I didn't get his license plate, and I don't really know what he looks like."

"I was thinking more a private detective," Brent says.

"A PI?" He's thrown me for a loop here. "Why wouldn't we call the police?"

"Well, like you say, I'm not sure the police will do a whole lot about this. They'll run it through their computer for five minutes, and if they don't come up with anything, they'll probably forget about it. But a PI would be working for us. We'd pay him, you know?"

More money. Brent wasn't always the best with money, but ever since he came home from this retreat, it's like he can't wait to spend more and more of it.

"I don't know," I say.

He holds out a palm. "It's just an idea. We're brainstorming here. Now back to his eyes. You said he—"

And then I remember. "He had this nasty scar near one eye."

"See?" Brent smiles, but there's nothing pleasant about the expression. "There you go. You remembered something else. A big scar near an eye is a good distinguishing feature."

"Yes," I say, not sure why he seems so happy right now.

"Tell you what," he says. "Tomorrow, I'll take some time off from the business to make some calls."

Tomorrow is Saturday. What does he mean he's going to take some time off from the business?

"Brent," I say, "it's your last weekend before you return to work. Couldn't we spend it together? I've really missed you."

He mulls it over. "I don't know, babe. I've gotta lot of momentum going. I don't want to stop now. How about we go out for dinner tomorrow night?"

I am at a complete loss. We literally just had an argument over whether we should go out to dinner tonight.

"I mean," he says, catching my expression, "why don't we go out for drinks? We can grab a few at the pub;, we could keep it really cheap. Maybe I could cook tomorrow night."

A horrible thought enters my mind: *This man is only*

interested in spending time with me if we're eating, drinking, or having sex.

But I dismiss the idea. Brent's a good man. He's not like that stereotypically bad husband who only acknowledges his wife's existence when she's cooking or naked.

"Alright," I say. "Sounds good."

He smiles. "Thanks, babe. I knew you'd understand."

8

BRENT – THREE MONTHS AGO – FEBRUARY 7

I haven't spoken to my parents in years.

The last time I saw them, I made it very clear I wanted nothing more to do with them. I mean, I'd already given them so many opportunities to prove they'd changed, or, at the very least, were working hard to become better, more loving, trustworthy people.

Mary and I had decided to take them out to dinner to share the news we'd gotten engaged. Foolish me, I was still trying to be the good son, to give them another chance to be part of not only my life, but also Mary's.

Big mistake.

At least Dad waited until the ladies excused themselves to go to the bathroom before he asked me yet another of his many rude questions. When Mom and Mary were out of earshot, he leaned over and gave me a funny look.

"Don't you think you can do better? She's not bad-looking, but she ain't real pretty either, is she?"

Up until that point in my life, I had never thought about

striking my father. But in that moment, I was ready to deck him.

I *should* have.

But we were in a nice restaurant, and I didn't want to get into a brawl with my old man. That would have only invited questions from Mary. I would have had to tell her what Dad said while she and Mom were in the bathroom. No woman should ever hear that her future father-in-law thinks she's not that good-looking. So I decided to keep quiet, pretend like it never happened, and just get through the dinner as quickly as possible.

I shouldn't have. What I should have done was leave with Mary right then. I don't know why I felt the need to be polite to my parents when they had never been that way with me.

"Mary's beautiful, Dad."

He shrugged, not picking up on the hard tone in my voice. Or maybe not caring to.

"It's your life," he said, as if I was making a huge mistake. "What are you going to do for money?"

"Remember I told you I was going to finish my degree? I'm going to be a coder."

"What if that doesn't pan out?"

"What's that supposed to mean?"

He gave me another of his condescending looks. "Brent, you and work are like oil and water."

"That's rich coming from you," I said.

He wasn't used to hearing me talk to him like that. I figured he was going to lay into me, but instead Dad smiled and looked at me as if for the first time.

"What about her?" Dad asked. "Her job pay well?"

"She has a name, Dad."

He rolled his eyes. "Quit being so damned sensitive. I wasn't trying to be rude."

"I told you already. Mary earns a good living."

"What about her old man?" he asked. "What does he do?"

"He's retired. He just sold his business a couple of years ago."

Dad's eyes lit up. "He must have some money, then."

I was not comfortable talking about money with Dad. It would only be a matter of time before he was asking me for some.

"And she's an only child, right? She'll get all of it, then." He apparently didn't think he'd tested my patience enough yet. "And so will you, huh, Brent?"

"That's *her* money," I answered, about to lose my temper. "Not mine."

"But you're marrying her."

I shake my head. "Forget it."

"Hang on, is she making you sign a prenup?"

"I said forget it."

Dad laughed. "That answers that question. Now I know who wears the pants in your relationship."

"Are you trying to be an asshole?"

Dad clamped his hand on my shoulder and squeezed hard. "You'll regret it if you ever talk to me like that again."

Dad tried staring me down, but I held his gaze. I was no longer a boy living under his roof. I was a grown man and not going to listen to his nonsense anymore. Finally, Dad shook his head and cracked a smile, like it was one big joke.

"You need to lighten up, Brent. I was just kidding around."

Lighten up, Brent. I had heard that phrase so many times

during my childhood. Like after Christopher pushed my head under the water in the creek. Like that time Christopher told the neighbor I'd stolen their sled, not him. *Lighten up, Brent.*

When Mary and my mother returned from the bathroom, Mary gave me a pained look, and I knew right away Mom had said something to offend her. Both women sat, and there was a moment of awkward silence. Mom gave Dad a wide-eyed look to let him know something had happened in the bathroom.

Dad didn't care. "So, Mary, tell me more about your job."

It looked like Mary was ready to leave, but she faked a smile and answered, "I analyze data for our healthcare clients to help them identify potential areas for cost savings."

"Computer stuff, then?" he asked.

My parents are not computer literate. They only just got email addresses.

"Yes." Mary sipped her wine. She does not like being the center of attention, much like me. "It's a lot of hours."

"A lot of hours *sitting*, I'll bet," Dad said.

"What is that supposed to mean?" I asked.

"Brent," Mary said, trying to keep the peace, "I don't think your father meant anything by it. And he's right. It is a lot of hours in front of a computer. I want to get a standing desk for the house."

"Sitting is really bad for you," Dad said. "Especially for your figure."

Mary and I froze. Mom continued to gnaw on a hunk of bread, like Dad didn't just insult Mary.

"It happens," Dad went on. "All that sitting and everything gets bigger. It affects women worse than men. Not fair, I know, but you can't argue with biology. All these women who spend their time sitting eight hours a day, it's no wonder they've got these huge hips and their asses get so wide and flat."

"Dad," I said, mortified.

"Your father's right," Mom said. "A young woman like her, she's gotta be more careful, or she'll be as big as a house."

Mary is not overweight. Not by a long shot. And even if she was, I wouldn't care. I love her no matter what she weighs.

"Mom, what the hell?"

Mary's face turned bright red. Her eyes were glued to the dinner plate in front of her.

"What?" Mom asked. She had always been thin and had zero sympathy for anyone who was not. It made me think about how Mom was so quick to point out how a friend or a neighbor had gained weight, like it was the mark of a character defect. "I just wanted to give her some advice. Trust me, I know what can happen to a woman's body."

"Alright." I threw my napkin onto my plate and stood. As if Dad's rudeness while they were in the bathroom wasn't enough, he's piled on even more appalling manners here. "That's it. We're done here."

Mary looked up at me with a grateful smile. Her eyes were teary. I could have killed my parents. I took Mary's hand, and she got up too.

"Where are you going?" Dad asks. "What's the big deal? We're trying to help you guys."

I didn't answer. As Mary and I walked out of the restaurant, Mom yelled at us about the check. They never had money and always expected me to pay whenever we got together.

When Mary and I got in the car, I apologized immediately.

"I'm sorry," I said. "I ... I keep giving them a second chance, and they always disappoint me."

"I can't believe they spoke like that to me," Mary said. "I'm so embarrassed."

"That's it. This is the last time." I shook my head. "I'm done with them."

Mary wiped away a tear. "Brent ... they're your parents."

I didn't care who they were. I'd cut them out of my life before. It was foolish of me to reach out to them when I got together with Mary, thinking that prison and all these years might have changed them. I was wrong.

"They haven't changed," I said. "They're probably still up to their old crap too."

By old crap, Mary knew exactly what I meant: criminal activity. Mom and Dad were constant scammers, always looking for dishonest ways to get their hands on money. Dad served some time for fraud, as a matter of fact, after I contacted child services and the whole house of cards came tumbling down. "I gave them a chance. I gave them so many chances, Mary. But that's it. No more. I can't do it anymore. I don't want them in our lives. I don't want them anywhere near you."

She reached across the car to take my hand. "Okay, honey. If that's what you want, then I support you."

Mary really tried to get to know my parents. But it was clear from their first meeting that they didn't care for her. She was too mild-mannered for Mom, and apparently she wasn't pretty enough for Dad. What an asshole. It was funny, in a very not funny way, that they were so disapproving of Mary, when she was an honest, caring, law-abiding person, and they were abusive criminals. Like they had any room to judge anybody, ever. Mary wasn't exactly upset by the fact I wanted nothing to do with them any longer. I don't blame her.

That was years ago, before we were married. After that dinner, I called my old man and told him, very bluntly, all the things I'd always wanted to say but never did. Of course he didn't take anything I shared seriously, either deflecting blame or actually blaming me for all the abuse I suffered. He cussed me out for getting him into trouble with the police and the county, then he blamed me for "screwing up his life," and he closed by saying he wished they'd only had Christopher for a son. Dad hung up on me before I could even tell him I never wanted to speak with him again.

I thought that was it. I thought I no longer had parents, and they no longer had me for a son.

But they've since reached out to me twice.

The first time was to tell me that my brother, Christopher, had died. They were vague on the details, and I didn't press them for too much information. I suspected, and still do, it was either drugs or, even worse, that he'd come to a violent end. Christopher was an addict who liked the hard stuff. He was also very much like my parents, a criminal through and through. He ran with some dangerous people doing who-knows-what. It's not only possible, but it was very likely he'd double-crossed or angered the wrong people and they'd killed him.

Though we were brothers, he and I couldn't be any more different, especially when it came to right and wrong. I don't even jaywalk. I always return my shopping cart to the corral at the grocery store. And I never go more than five miles per hour over the speed limit, not even on the highway.

Mom asked if I could attend the small service. She was so broken up, hardly able to get any words out over the phone, and, despite all the hard feelings between us, I really felt for her. I can't imagine what it must be like to lose a child. It violates every parent's sense of natural order.

Despite their seedy past and unrepentant criminal natures, my parents were religious. I was expecting a more traditional service, something involving the church they irregularly attended. But there was no mention of that, or even of a minister. My parents were basically going to hold the service themselves in the house I grew up in, and after, they planned to scatter Christopher's ashes in the creek behind the property.

The same creek where Christopher once "jokingly" tried to drown me.

I really felt like I should attend. I even talked it over with Mary, who encouraged me to go if I thought it would give me closure with my evil brother. But I couldn't bring myself to make that drive, seeing that old neighborhood, being in that house where I was constantly tormented, to spend time with people I never wanted to see again, to pretend to mourn for a brother who absolutely hated me.

I refused to attend.

I thought that would be the end of my relationship with my parents for sure. Dad had already made it clear, in our last phone call, that he blamed me for all the bad things that had happened to him. Surely my refusal to attend my own brother's funeral would be the final straw, in a long series of final straws.

But then an email came through this morning.

From Dad.

Son – Your mother and I miss you terribly. We've done a lot of soul-searching in the last two years, and we've come to realize just how terrible we were to you. Neither one of us were cut out to be parents, and we regret the way things turned out for you. I don't blame you for anything —you were right to escape the hell that our home must have been.

We've dedicated ourselves to becoming better people. Mom now works at the church and volunteers in the soup kitchen. I've gotten myself sober and have been earning an honest living as a garbageman. They call me a sanitation specialist, which is kind of a hoot, but really I'm just a guy who collects trash. It doesn't pay much, but it's the only job I could get.

I know you might not want to mend fences, and if that's how you feel, I understand. And I know if you're willing to try, I've got a long ways to go to prove myself to you, son, and earn your trust. I'm so sorry, for everything. For not being a good man, a good husband, a decent father. The truth is, Brent, that I'm broken. I'm not trying to pass blame here, but my parents weren't great either. They did a number on me when I was a boy ... but that's neither here nor there, and it's not an excuse for my own behavior. I look back over my life and regret just about everything I did. The only thing I don't regret is having you and Christopher. That was probably the best thing I ever did with my life.

Did you ever marry that nice woman, Mary? I'm sorry for what I said about her. I don't know what goes through my head sometimes. She's a very nice-looking woman and seemed like a sweetheart to boot. You two made a good couple.

Well, I know getting an email from me out of the blue like this must be weird and maybe difficult. I could go on and on, but I don't want to overwhelm you. Write me back if you want. I'd love to hear from you. But if you don't, I understand.

Your mother and I are getting old now. I'm really starting to feel my age. Mom was in the hospital last month for an infection and kind of had a close brush with death. That's why we wanted to reach out to you. We might not be around much longer, and I hate how I left things with you.

I love you, son.

I COULDN'T BRING myself to delete the email.

I also couldn't bring myself to tell Mary that my father had reached out. Until I decide what I'm going to do, I don't plan on saying anything to her about it.

I let it sit in my inbox. Throughout the day, I read it over several times, I pore over every word, like I'm a forensic linguist helping the police interpret a ransom note. My father has never talked like this before. He has *never* admitted to any wrongdoing whatsoever, not even when the state brought fraud charges against him and he, apparently, had no defense. The public defender eventually convinced him to accept a plea deal. The attorney must have known Dad had no reasonable chance of avoiding time in prison. But a plea deal is *not* an admission of guilt, as my father would go on and on about years after he served his time.

But I can't ignore the fact that my father is not only saying things he's never said before, he also sounds *sincere.* One apology for years and years of horrible emotional and sometimes physical abuse is not enough. But every atonement has to start somewhere.

I decide to sit on the email for a day. One day turns into two, which turns into three. Dad couldn't have reached out at a worse time, to be honest. I'm struggling at work, and my depression has come back, and all these bad things are bleeding into my marriage. Mary and I had a really bad argument last night, and looking back on it, I don't even know what started it. I think my poor state of mind and issues at work are beginning to wear on her.

I must have read the email a hundred times. I don't want to believe this is a sincere attempt at a reconciliation. It'd be easier, honestly, to pretend like I'd never got the email at all, and go on acting like my parents are basically dead. But I can't unring the bell. I did get this message from my father, and he *does* sound genuine.

So I write him back.

Dad – Got your email. I really don't know what to say to you, to be honest. I can't tell if this is real. I don't know what you want from me, or what you want me to say. You, Mom, and Christopher all abused me. It's taken years of therapy, and I'm still working through it all. Everything that happened has had a ripple effect on the rest of my life. I don't have a lot of friends. I get anxious and

*nervous around people. I suffer from periodic depression
that seems to come out of nowhere. I don't know if I can
forgive you, to be honest. Maybe I don't even want to. It's
a lot to process.*

Maybe it's better if we never speak again.

MY FATHER WRITES BACK within a few hours of my email. He's
utterly apologetic, almost to the point where it's embarrassing. I can picture him on his hands and knees almost,
begging me to forgive him for everything.

"Are you okay?"

I jump at the sound of Mary's voice. I didn't even hear
her come into the living room. She was upstairs folding
laundry a few minutes ago. Quickly, I close my laptop so she
doesn't catch sight of one word of this email from my father.

"Fine," I say, forcing a smile.

She gives me a dubious glance. "You looked ..."

"Like what?"

"*Pained.*" She sits beside me on the couch. "What were
you reading?"

I don't lie to Mary. Ever. We've always enjoyed an incredibly honest relationship. And I'm almost certain—as
anybody can ever be—that she's not in the habit of lying to
me either.

But I don't want to tell her I've been communicating with
my father. What with everything else going on right now, I
don't even want to get into it with her. I don't think she'd take
it well, and I don't want to add any fuel to the fire that seems
to be almost constantly burning between us.

So I lie to my wife for the first time in our relationship.

"Oh, just work stuff." I shake my head. I feel *awful* lying to Mary. It comes completely unnaturally to me. I'm sure she sees right through me. "Aaron sent me a nasty email about something that wasn't even my fault and—I don't really want to talk about it."

She rubs my shoulder. "That's fine, honey. We don't have to think about work right now."

I smile at her, but the gesture is so fake. What I just told her wasn't totally a lie. Aaron *did* send me a nastygram yesterday for something that wasn't my fault. The customer service representative told me the client wanted some coding tweaked, which I did, but then the client apparently flipped out because that change affected another process I wasn't involved with. According to Aaron, I should have foreseen a problem I didn't even know was a possibility.

"I'm sorry about last night," she says.

I reach for her. She leans into me. I put my laptop on the coffee table, and together we lean back on the couch. It's so good to hold her. We never do this anymore.

THE LATEST EMAIL from Dad is just as apologetic as the rest, but it's also different.

> *Son – I'm sorry to hear you're struggling at work and with your condition. It pains both your mother and I to know that your upbringing made you this way. We really want to help you, Brent, but we also want to respect your wishes and not meet in person.*

And I think there's a way.

Your mother and I were very fortunate. A friend of a friend started a wellness retreat business recently. Several members of the church had been and highly recommended it to your mother and me. We were reluctant. Or, should I say, I was reluctant because you know what I think about all that nonsense. Your mother was really interested, and she kept after me about it until I finally had to say yes.

It was the best thing we've ever done for ourselves.

Now, I didn't want to bring this up the first time I reached out to you because I know how it must sound. You're probably thinking that Mom and Dad went away for a few weeks and got brainwashed, and now they're wearing white robes and about to drink poisoned Kool-Aid, or something crazy like that. But, son, I swear it's nothing like that.

I thought it was going to be some silly talk about energy and the universe and all that, and that there was no way it could help me feel better.

But, son, I am not lying when I say it has turned my life around. Going on this retreat really cleared my head, made me see things for what they are, made me realize there was still time to make it right with you. I would never have emailed you if I hadn't gone.

Now I know I'm not the best person to give advice, especially considering how much I screwed up my own life

and yours as well. But here's the website and email
address. Take a look and give it some thought. They might
be able to help you out too.

I'm immediately skeptical. Mindfulness is a thing right now. Once, in a fit of desperation, I even downloaded an app on my phone to try it out. Maybe it works for some people, but it certainly doesn't work for me. I don't ever feel any better when it's over.

And my father is right: I'm the last person he should be giving advice to. I don't want his help, and I don't need it. I'm glad he seems to have gotten his own life back together, but that doesn't mean I want or need his assistance for improving my own.

9

SUNDAY – MAY 14

Brent is already gone when I wake up. He did actually cook last night, like he promised, and we shared a nice meal together that was low on carbs before grabbing a couple of drinks at the pub. But I hate waking up on a Sunday morning and finding he's not here. After putting on some comfy clothes, I check the room and find his laptop and backpack and gym bag are gone again. He must be working out, then heading out once more to work on his side business.

It's not like Brent is avoiding me. We've spent time together since he returned from his retreat. But he's different. He's changed in ways I can describe but also in ways I can't. He doesn't *smell* like he used to. I know, that's weird. Maybe he's just using new soap or a different shampoo, and I didn't even realize. But everybody has their own smell, you know? Brent's is different to how it used to be.

There are other things. He was always good at putting the seat down in the bathroom. But he doesn't do that anymore. Not that it's a big deal at all—I don't get why some women freak out about that. But I don't understand why he's stopped doing it. I'm trying not to read too much into everything, but part of me wondered if this is a subtle way for Brent to assert himself ... it sounds silly.

And then, last night, when we started kissing on the couch ... he asked if I wanted to watch some pornography to spice things up. I couldn't tell if he was joking. We've literally never discussed it before, and porn does not seem like Brent's thing at all. But he was serious, all right. He sat there, waiting for an answer. Talk about an awkward conversation. I'm pretty straight-laced when it comes to making love and was not at all interested in *that*. Besides, as far as I could tell, we were both already as spiced up as we needed to be. Brent could tell how uncomfortable I was, and quickly apologized before putting his lips on mine again. It turns out I was right: we didn't need any help spicing things up.

There are other differences. Over dinner last night, I brought up that time we went to the movies and watched the wrong film. We bought tickets to see that comedy with Ben Stiller but accidentally sat in the wrong theater. All the previews were for dramatic or scary films, and we sat there looking at each other, wondering what was going on. When the movie finally came on, it was one of those stupid slasher flicks ... but we ended up staying anyway to make fun of it. There was a teenaged couple in the back row making out for half the movie, which was kind of hilarious, given what was happening in the horror film playing on the screen.

It's one of those memories that really stands out for both of us. And I kept waiting for him to burst into laughter, like I was, when recalling it over dinner. But he just sat there, half-smiling and nodding his way through my retelling of the event. It was like it meant nothing to him, or like it had happened to somebody else.

I hadn't planned anything for today. It's his last day before returning to the office, so I assumed he would want to spend it with me, not running around everywhere. I'm all caught up on the laundry, and Brent, darling that he is, took care of the dishes after dinner, so there's not a whole lot to do around the house. I decide I'm going to surprise him at the gym. Hopefully he's still exercising by the time I get there.

I throw on some yoga pants and a top and check myself in the mirror. Those few pounds I lost while Brent was away are noticeable. I brush my teeth and use mouthwash, then pull my messy hair back into a ponytail. I'm so consumed with catching up to Brent at the gym, I nearly forget to take my lupus medication before I jump in the car. I woke up again this morning with a butterfly rash on my face and my joints feeling achy. I can't deal with a flareup right now. The last one had me in bed for a few days.

I usually do a group exercise class at the gym. Most of the time it's Zumba or yoga, but occasionally I'll try spinning or one of the others. You can go at your own pace, and everybody pretty much minds their own business. All the same, I usually take a spot in the back row so nobody sees how uncoordinated, out of breath, or inflexible I am.

Brent is not into any of that, however. He's usually in the weight room, so if I want to surprise him, that's where I have to go. I park in the fourth row and do a quick scan of the lot for Brent's car. The lot is nearly full; there must be hundreds of people exercising this morning. I could spend ten minutes out here looking for his car to make sure he's here, so I decide against it and head inside.

Normally, I avoid the weight room like it's a semicolon. I'm kind of a plain-Jane type of woman, decent-looking, I guess, but for the most part nondescript. I am definitely not in amazing shape or anything like that. I'm just, you know, average. But no matter what I'm doing, no matter what I'm wearing, even if it's loose, baggy sweatpants, there's always at least one creepy gawker in the weight room, and quite often more than one. It makes exercising in there uncomfortable, so that's why I normally avoid the room at all costs. I don't need somebody gaping at me in the mirror while I'm doing shoulder raises or whatever. It's ridiculous.

But today I force myself to enter that large, high-ceilinged space that is mostly men. It's Sunday morning, so the weight room is packed. Nearly every machine and rack and bench is taken. I don't see Brent anywhere. I walk through the free weight section, where several men are squatting hundreds of pounds and look like they're going to snap in half with every repetition. Several creepy gawkers latch onto me with their eyes, but I try to ignore them.

I wander through the weight room. I don't see Brent anywhere, but it is the biggest area of the gym. But then, over the loud rock music and various (somewhat comical) grunting of men trying to lift heavy weights, I hear his voice.

And it's angry.

"I've been waiting for ten damned minutes. How much longer are you going to be?"

At first I think I'm confused and just hearing someone who sounds like my husband. Brent doesn't speak to anyone like that, never mind in a gym of all places, where there is no shortage of testosterone or short-tempered alpha men. But then I spot him in the corner, by the dumbbell rack. He's standing over an obscenely muscular bald man who is pressing two dumbbells over his shoulders on a standalone bench. The bald man looks so strong, like he could probably throw Brent twenty feet using only one arm.

"Yeah," Brent says. "I'm talking to *you*, buddy."

The bald man drops his dumbbells and, red-faced, rises to glare at Brent. When the man comes to his full height, he's towering over my husband. I am stunned by what I'm witnessing. Brent does not talk to people this way. Ever. And it seems incredibly foolish of him to raise his voice at a guy who looks like he competes in bodybuilding competitions.

"Be humble," the bald man snarls. "Or be humbled."

I don't know what to do. I'm not the only person who's taken notice. One of the trainers is hurrying over.

Brent actually balls his fists. I can't believe this is happening. The other man has at least five inches on him and easily fifty pounds, all of it solid muscle. Does Brent want to get hurt? In the brief moment before the personal trainer manages to get between my husband and the other man, I consider the possibility. He *really* hates his job. If he gets injured, then that would put him out for a few more days ...

No. That's silly.

I shake my head. That's not like Brent. He wouldn't risk serious injury to avoid going to work. Where did I ever get such an idea?

Before any punches are thrown, the trainer and one of the other gymgoers have managed to separate my husband and the other man. I am, I hate to admit, totally embarrassed by what I've seen. Brent is not a violent man, at least, I never thought he was until this moment. Is this something he's suppressed all these years?

I'm beginning to wonder if I know my husband at all.

Too ashamed at the situation, I turn away before Brent realizes I'm here. As quickly as I can, and without attracting attention, I hurry out of the weight room. I don't want to confront him about his behavior in front of everybody else, and to be honest, I don't even know what to *say* to my husband. He looked like he was ready to hurt that man. Even if the guy was using the bench for a few minutes, so what? The gym is really busy today. It's always packed on Sundays. You just have to wait your turn when it comes to the equipment.

I don't know what to do with myself. I consider acting like I didn't witness his troubling behavior. Maybe I'll just go to Zumba. There's a class starting in a few minutes. But I don't think I'll be able to focus on the exercise or get much out of it today. There's something *off* with my husband. I need to know what's going on.

I decide to wait in the lobby for him. I take out my phone and try to distract myself while I'm waiting. I have no idea how long he'll be.

A few minutes later, I look up and see him coming around the corner. But he's not alone. There is a stunningly attractive blonde woman walking right next to him. She looks like a fitness model, with her incredibly toned, tanned body, and I catch myself wishing I'd put on a little makeup before throwing together this outfit and jumping into the car to surprise my husband at the gym. Not that I could compete with *her*. This woman is in a different league. There is not an ounce of fat on her body, *and* she's got these incredible, sleek curves.

The worst part is, they're walking pretty closely together. If I were just some random person watching them interact, I'd think they were in a relationship. Brent says something I can't hear to the woman, who tips her head back and laughs like he's the world's funniest man. Brent is many things, but he's not a comedian. I think I've heard him tell, like, two jokes in the whole time we've been together.

What could they be talking about?

Brent freezes when he sees me standing about twenty feet away in the lobby. The woman slows as well, then her eyes drift over to me, and she loses her smile really fast. It's almost like she knows who I am, even though we've never met.

"Nice talking to you, Brent," she says in a neutral voice before peeling away from him and heading for the water fountain.

Brent smiles as he comes over to hug me. "What are you doing here, babe?"

I step back before he puts his arms around me. "Who was that woman?"

"What? Jeanne?" He frowns. "She works out here a lot."

"You know her from the gym?"

His smile slips. "Yes, Mary. I know her from the gym."

"Why did she act so weird when she saw me, then?"

"Did she?" He looks over his shoulder in her general direction for a moment before turning back to me. "I don't know. I guess she's shy."

Shy.

He wants me to believe that woman who is flaunting everything she's got is shy.

That woman has never been shy in her whole life. I could tell by watching her for about five seconds. The way she's dressed says otherwise also. Those skintight shorts don't leave anything to the imagination, and her breasts are popping out of her half-zipped top.

"Mary," Brent says, putting his hands on my shoulders. "You know me. Do you honestly think I would *ever* betray you? Come on."

I'm being silly. So what if Brent was talking to another woman and she laughed at one of his jokes? Am I really that self-conscious? I've never been the jealous type before. But then again, Brent has never done anything to stir up jealousy …

"Mary." He stares into my eyes. "I love you more than anything."

I know he does. No matter how bad things got before he went away, no matter what, I always knew he loved me. And that has *not* changed.

"I, uh, wanted to surprise you," I say. "But it looks like you're done already."

"Yeah, got an early start. Did you just get here?"

Now is the time to address his behavior in the weight room. I almost completely forgot about it because of how he was behaving around that woman a moment ago. She's done at the water fountain now and gives us a wide berth when heading for the exit. Not once does she look in Brent's direction. It's conspicuous how much she's avoiding us.

"Yes," I say, not sure how to broach the subject. "I was—"

"Don't let me keep you, then," Brent interrupts. He holds up his laptop bag. "I wanted to get started. I had some more ideas last night, and you're never going to believe this, but … what's wrong, babe?"

"Oh, nothing," I say. I feel like, from one moment to the next, I don't know what Brent's going to say or do. I want to talk to him about the fight he almost got in, but I'm still trying to process what just happened between him and the woman. "What am I never going to believe?"

"I reached out to a potential investor last night, and the guy wrote me back this morning. He wants to meet. How cool is that?"

"Last night?"

Between making dinner, sharing a meal together, and then our wild nocturnal activities, I don't know when he had time.

"I was having trouble falling asleep. You get me so ramped up, you know." Brent squeezes my side. "I thought about waking you up for some more fun, but you were really tired, so I left you alone. I went downstairs and sent out a few emails. This is our first bite. It could lead to something. You never know."

"That's great, Brent."

Everything is happening way too quickly for me. I'm happy that Brent is taking action. I've never seen him exhibit this much drive before, about anything. Usually I'm the one who has to suggest things to do. I'm not used to my husband's newfound pep.

"I know, right?" He smiles. "I'm stoked. Even if it doesn't work out with this guy, the fact that he's willing to meet shows that people like him will be interested in my idea."

I take his hand. "I'm happy for you."

"Thanks, babe." He kisses me. "Now, you came here to work out. I'd better not keep you."

"You know, I really only came to surprise you. I wasn't crazy about exercising this morning." I move in closer to him. "Maybe I could grab a coffee with you at the shop? I won't bother you."

"Oh." He frowns, looks away. "I don't know, babe. I really have a lot of—"

"I won't stay long," I say. "Just for coffee. Then I'll get out of your hair."

He has to think about it. "Sure, great idea. Follow me over?"

I'VE NEVER BEEN to this coffee shop. It's pretty expensive, noticeably more than the place by the bank where Paige works. Brent orders avocado toast on wholewheat bread and a large coffee. I just get a drink. I haven't checked the credit card in a few days. I wonder if Brent has been eating here on all these long days he's spent in the coffee shop. The man waiting on us recognizes my husband and addresses him by name.

"How's the big idea coming along, Brent?" he asks.

"Pretty good," Brent says. "This is my wife, by the way. Mary."

The man turns his gaze to me. "Nice to meet you, Mary. Brent has told us all so much about you."

"Oh really?"

He nods. "And about his business. It sure sounds like a great idea."

I smile back. "Brent's very talented."

While waiting for our order, we find a table. I go to sit by the window because it's a beautiful day outside, but Brent asks if we can go in the back. He explains that's where he likes to work because there are fewer people walking by, fewer distractions. I follow him to the rear of the coffee shop, where Brent sits at a table for four and puts his back against the wall. He takes out his laptop and opens it in front of him. The computer is positioned between me and my husband.

"Do you have to work right now?" I ask. "I just wanted to talk for a few minutes."

He looks at me like I'm being needy. I see the judgment in his eyes. With a big sigh, Brent mutters, "Sure," and then closes his laptop.

"So tell me about this guy you might meet," I say. "Who is he, and what does he do?"

"You wouldn't know him," Brent says dismissively. "He's somebody I met once at Designed Solutions. He's the CEO for one of our vendors. I got the feeling when he came in, he was kind of looking for people to recruit."

"That's really exciting," I say.

Brent shrugs. "It's just the first step. We've got a long way to go yet."

"I know, honey." I reach for his hand. "You know, you don't have to do everything in a day, right?"

One corner of his mouth smiles. "I know. But I feel like I've wasted so much of my life. Do you know how much time I've spent at Designed Solutions? And before that, how much time I spent working jobs I hated? It makes me so angry when I think about it. Why did I throw all that life away? What was the point?"

"Hey." I feel like he's out of control. That sneaking suspicion of mania, or perhaps a narcotic, slips back into my mind. "You had to eat and pay rent. Everybody makes sacrifices. We do the best we can, honey."

"I know," he says. "But I'm done with all that. I want to *live*. You know? I don't want my life to be lived for me."

I know what he means, and I wish I were that passionate about something. If I were that ardent, if I felt like I had some amazing idea, then maybe I'd be in a manic mood as well. But I don't have any grand ambitions. I like my life. It's not too late to have children, if we want them, though Brent has expressed reluctance before. I'd love to travel as well. It'd be wonderful to see more of the world. We have a lot of years ahead of us.

"Hey," Brent says. "I completely forgot. But this morning I contacted a PI."

The man who waited on us calls out Brent's name. Our order is ready. My husband jumps to his feet to get our drinks and his toast.

"Why didn't you get something to eat?" he asks. "You must be starved."

I am a little hungry, but honestly, this place is expensive. Brent's avocado toast itself cost almost fifteen bucks. The whole bill was nearly thirty dollars, just for two drinks and one appetizer.

Now I'm wondering, though, if I really am cheap? We live comfortably, so what's the big deal if we overpay every now and then for some good food? Brent might be onto something here.

"Maybe I'll get something," I say, noncommittal.

I can't simply forget that we spent several thousand dollars on Brent's retreat, and he didn't earn a paycheck during that timeframe either. Brent, meanwhile, has started in on his avocado toast. As has become his habit with everything else, he now eats incredibly quickly also.

"The PI ..." Brent says, with half a mouthful of toast. "I found this guy, sounds promising. He's an ex-cop and still has a lot of friends on the force."

"Okay." I sip my coffee. For how much it cost, I was expecting better. "How did you find him?"

"I asked around," Brent says vaguely. He's already done

with his first slice of toast. There is avocado all over his fingers. "His name's Jim Smith."

I'd like to check him out for myself. "Does he have a website?"

"No," Brent says. "No, you won't find him anywhere on the web. He's really selective about his clients. He doesn't want to get all kinds of calls."

"That sounds kind of weird, to have a business but no web presence?"

"He's semi-retired," Brent explains. "He knows a ton of people and basically only takes cases on referral. I was lucky he even took my call, to be honest."

"How did you get his number?"

"Friend of a work colleague." He waves a dismissive hand. "It doesn't matter. He comes highly recommended."

"Hmmm." Of course, Brent hasn't mentioned money yet. And it looks like he's going to make me ask. "How much would this cost us?"

Brent shrugs. He's halfway through his next slice of toast already. "He works on a retainer, two thousand dollars."

I shouldn't have just taken a sip of coffee. I nearly do a spit-take.

"Two *thousand*?"

Brent nods. "Yeah, two thousand. Whatever he doesn't spend, he returns. He said a job like this, it should only take a week or so."

I hold out a palm. "Wait a minute, Brent. I don't even understand what we're asking him to *do.*"

Brent looks around the coffee shop like he's checking for eavesdroppers. "He'll find the guy and then, you know, give him a warning."

I wait for him to explain, but Brent is not in an expansive mood today.

"A warning?"

Brent gives me a look like I'm being childish. "Yeah, a warning. You should see this PI. He's *tough*. I wouldn't mess with him. If he has to get nasty, he's more than capable."

I'm gaping at my husband. "You've already met him?"

"He came by earlier. We talked for about fifteen minutes. The guy really impressed me."

My wheels are spinning. "What is this about him getting nasty? You don't mean—"

Brent cuts me off. "That's what we want, right? We don't want this creep bothering you anymore."

I am not comfortable with this. "Even if this guy is stalking me, I don't want anybody to get hurt. I'd prefer the police get involved, Brent."

He waves a hand at me. "You don't want to call the cops. I already told you the other day, all they're going to do is search in their database, make a call or two, maybe send a cruiser down the street one night. That's all. No, we need to *deal* with this, Mary."

What he's saying makes a kind of sense. Brent knows a lot more about these sorts of things than I do. He's had a lot more interaction with the police in his life than I have. I trust him to know better here.

But all the same, I can't shake the bad feeling I'm getting about this.

"Look, hon," Brent says. "This guy is really good, and he's not going to mess around like the cops will. A cop needs to worry about what his sergeant is going to say, who's gotta worry about what the lieutenant and captain are going to say, who have to answer to the chief ... it's one big cluster-you-know-what, honey. Trust me. The police department is one giant bureaucracy. This guy, he answers to nobody but us. He can do what needs to be done."

"I don't know, Brent. Like I said, I don't want anybody to get hurt."

"Nobody will," he says. "This guy is a pro. He explained that most stalkers are cowards. The minute somebody gets in their face, they bug out and look for somebody else."

That doesn't make me feel any better. I don't want to scare this man away so he can stalk another unsuspecting woman.

"So what do you think?" he asks.

"Could I talk to him?" I ask.

He gives me a look. "Why? I already told him everything he needs to know. He'd just be repeating himself."

I feel very pressured here to spend a lot of money for a service I don't fully understand, provided by a man I've never met. I really don't like how pushy Brent is being here.

"Babe," he says, "your safety is more important than two thousand dollars, isn't it?"

"I'd like to talk to him at least once before I pay."

Brent has to think about it. I have no idea why. It's not an unreasonable request on my part.

"I'll get you his number," he says. "Okay?"

I let out a breath. Brent's right. When it comes to my safety, I shouldn't balk at spending a little bit. What good will all that money be if I wind up in the hospital or worse?

"Thanks, Brent."

He puts his hand on my face. "Sure, babe. What kind of husband would I be if I didn't make sure you were safe? I love you, Mary. You mean everything to me."

10

Brent is late coming home. And he forgot to text me the phone number for the detective. By the time I hear his car pulling into the driveway, we should be eating dinner. But I haven't prepared anything because he didn't answer any of my texts from this afternoon.

There must be a look on my face, because he is immediately apologetic. "Did I miss texts from you again?"

He gives me puppy-dog eyes. I've never seen him use that expression before. To be honest, I didn't even know it was within his acting range. But he pulls it off. He looks so darned cute that I feel my anger melt away.

"Yes, you did. Now would you get in here and give me a kiss?"

Brent meets me in the kitchen, where we embrace. Things start to heat up, but I pull away. We have to eat dinner.

"I was trying to reach you," I say, "because I wanted to make you something really nice before you went back to work tomorrow."

His face darkens. I shouldn't have mentioned work. Brent hasn't talked about his job much, but I'm sure he must be very nervous about returning to the office after a leave of absence. I never told him what Paige shared, but surely he must be expecting that his coworkers were talking about him and that rumors must have flown.

"Yeah," he says. "Thanks for reminding me."

"Sorry." I try giving him the puppy-dog-eyes look. But it has no effect. Apparently that expression is way outside *my* acting range. "So, what do you think?"

"You know, I'm not really hungry," he says, rubbing his stomach. "Not feeling great right now."

I immediately palm his forehead. "Are you sick? Coming down with something?"

He removes my hand, and our fingers intertwine.

"I'm fine," he says. "I'm not sick. Just not looking forward to going back to that damned place."

"I know," I say, biting back tears. I wish he didn't have to go back, to be honest.

We put our arms around each other.

"I feel like quitting," he says. "Now that I've spent all this time on my own business, it's like I can't get motivated about my job anymore."

"I'm sure," I say.

He lets go of me and grabs a beer out of the fridge. His shoulders sag as he takes a long drink from the bottle. All that energy from the last few days is gone. This is as low as he's been since he came home. I've seen this haunted look in his eyes before. It usually precedes a period of depression.

"If I quit," he says, "I could focus *all* my time on the new business. I'd be much more likely to succeed if I weren't juggling a full-time job at the same time. Don't you think?"

Wait, is he serious?

"I wish you could, honey," I say.

He nods gravely. I'm really worried. The retreat was supposed to teach him mindfulness, which would help keep him from falling back into negative patterns of thought. But right now, he seems like the old Brent, anxious and brooding.

But suddenly, his face brightens, and he perks right up. "I'll be alright. I don't know why I'm so worried. I can do this job. We already know *that*. I'll be fine."

I'm dumbfounded. I've never seen Brent rebound so quickly before from a dark mood.

"I know you'll be fine," I say. "I believe in you."

"Thanks, honey."

We kiss again. I can taste the beer on his breath. I wonder if it's not his first of the night, with how strong the smell of alcohol is on him. Did he stop at a bar on the way home from the coffee shop? And if so, why didn't he ask me to meet him?

Brent finishes his beer and goes for another right away.

"Hey, Brent," I say. "While I'm thinking about it, could you give me that detective's number?"

He continues his long sip of the beer, puts the bottle down when he's finished, and looks over at me. "You want to talk to him still?"

"Is that a problem?" I ask.

The words come out sounding a lot harsher than I want.

Brent shrugs. "Suit yourself, but he's just going to tell you what I've already relayed. Let me get it for you."

He leaves the kitchen and re-enters the foyer. Brent left his backpack out there by the front door. He unzips it and roots around, finally pulling out his cell. No wonder he didn't notice my calls or texts, he kept his phone in his backpack.

"Sorry," he says. "I was in the zone and didn't want to be disturbed. You know how it is."

I get it. I don't like to be bothered by a flood of steady texts when I'm trying to work, and I've always extended him the same courtesy. So we tend to keep our texts to a minimum during the workday. We usually only trade a few notes, asking each other how everything is going, and to figure out dinner. I'm fine with that, and he was too.

But making it so your wife can't contact you on the Sunday before you go back to work after being away for a month is not okay. I want to give him a piece of my mind, but I don't want to ruin the evening because I know he has a lot on his mind about tomorrow.

Brent returns to the kitchen, scrolling through his contacts for the number.

"Here it is." He starts reading me the number, but realizes I don't have my phone out. "Do you want it now or what?"

What is his problem? It's not my fault he forgot all about it and made my reminding him until this moment impossible. I give him a displeased look, which he doesn't even seem to notice as he stands there impatiently with his phone out.

"Hold on," I say.

I pick my phone up off the island counter.

"Okay, what is it?"

He reads the number off quickly to me. Without so much as a goodbye or a word about dinner, he strides through the kitchen and plops down on the couch in the living room. I peer out to see what he's doing. His head is down towards his phone as he bangs out a text to somebody. Who in the world is he writing? Brent is not a texter. Other than myself and one of his college buddies, I don't think he regularly messages anybody. Maybe he's communicating with one of his potential investors.

I take a deep breath. His attitude tonight is not acceptable, but I also don't want to upset him. Brent is acting like he's not bothered by his imminent return to work, but I know better. He must be really nervous.

I've got the number entered in my phone. I hit the call button. It's not really surprising, the more I think about it, that this man keeps a low profile. Being semi-retired and having made some enemies as a cop, he wouldn't want his phone number out there.

It rings a few times before a man with a throaty voice answers. He sounds like an old smoker.

"Is this Mary?" he says, like he's been expecting my call.

He sounds a little familiar, but I can't place the voice. He must just sound like someone I know.

"Hi, Jim," I say. "My husband gave me your number. I was wondering if this is a good time to talk?"

"Sure," he says. He sounds friendly enough. "You must have a few questions for me."

"I do," I say. I peek into the living room. Brent is no longer looking at his phone. He's just lazing on the couch. I get the feeling he's listening in on my conversation, though I don't know why that bothers me so much. "Brent talked to you about the, uh, man?"

"About your *stalker*, yes."

"Well," I say, feeling uncomfortable, "I don't know if he's a stalker—"

"From everything your husband told me," Smith interrupts, "I am absolutely certain he is. This is how stalking starts, believe me. I worked a lot of those cases. I know the signs."

"Right," I say. "But—"

"Even if it's *not* stalking," he cuts in again, "you have to treat it as such. Caution is the parent of safety."

I haven't heard that phrase in a while. Most people use the cliché *better safe than sorry.*

Smith goes on. "I saw this happen a lot, Mary. A woman gets a funny feeling about a man. She doesn't want to be rude, because years and years of acculturation demands she be polite, so she talks herself out of her bad feeling. She just hopes it will go away. She tells herself over and over that it's nothing, the man is maybe a little off, but he's not a psychopath, and then, fast-forward a week or a month, and something terrible happens. I've seen it so many times. You don't want to be a victim, Mary. We humans developed these emotions for a reason; they're one of our survival mechanisms. When you get a bad feeling about something, you really gotta listen to yourself."

I don't have a great feeling about *him* right now. Should I listen to that sentiment?

He says, "You really can't take a wait-and-see approach with this type of behavior. You need to nip it in the bud immediately."

What he's saying makes sense. Women are taught from an early age to be polite and agreeable. That's what happened to Gwen about ten years ago. One of her coworkers wouldn't leave her alone until finally she just had to get really nasty with him. This was before #MeToo was a thing, so a lot of people thought she overreacted, of course.

"Okay," I say.

"Great," he says. "I'll get started tomorrow, then."

"Whoa, hold on," I say. "I just meant, okay, I understand what you're saying."

"Mary," he says, and again his voice sounds familiar to me. But I cannot place it. It's not somebody from work or the gym. Maybe he knew my parents? No, that couldn't be it. He would have done his research on me and realized we had a connection. He would have said as much. "What's holding you back?"

"I don't want ..." I don't know how to put this tactfully. "If you find him, I'd like to get the police involved."

"Of course," he says. "Look, I'm not some heavy who's going to bust down his door and kick his teeth in."

I could have done without the imagery.

Smith continues, "I'm going to find him, follow him, and get some proof he's stalking you. Once I have that, the police will be forced to do something about it, or I'll contact a local reporter I know and trust with my life."

"Okay."

This is starting to sound better.

"Trust me, Mary. You won't regret it. You owe it to yourself to make sure you're safe."

He's supposed to be a private detective, not a sleazy used-car salesman. But he sure sounds more like the latter as opposed to the former.

"It'll be the best money you've ever spent, believe me. Can you put a price on being able to sleep easy at night?"

"Okay," I say. He's right. You can't put a price on your own safety. And I have the money. "Alright. So how does this work?"

"I'll sit on your house," he says. "Don't look for me, though. I don't want this creep knowing you've hired somebody."

"Okay."

"You and I won't meet face-to-face. I'll be in the background, waiting, watching. When I have what I need, I'll let you know, and we can proceed from there. If you spot him, you just text this number and let me know."

It seems odd not to meet this man in person, but I understand the need for secrecy. "When can you start?"

11

BRENT – TWO MONTHS AGO – MARCH 11

The wellness retreat is run by a gray-haired couple who describe themselves as "ex-members of the rat race." The short biography on the About page of their website is scarce on details, but both of them appear to be in their late fifties, maybe early sixties, and they worked in real estate and finance. About five years ago, worn out by the endless grind of American capitalism, they quit their jobs, learned meditation from a guru, took up yoga, and found "their true calling." They realized they wanted to help others "get unstuck" from the machinery of the lives they were told all along they should want.

So they bought an old farm that was no longer being worked and began what must have been the expensive process of converting it into a retreat. They've only been in operation for a couple of years, according to the website, which Dad confirmed with me. He and Mom were one of the first groups to go through there, so they got a heavily discounted price.

I can't deny the fact that Dad sounds like a totally

different person. He can't go more than a few sentences in our email exchange without apologizing or expressing regret over how he handled yet another aspect of parenting. His remorse seems heartfelt, earnest. Mom has written me a few emails now as well. She was never great with words and had a difficult time expressing any emotion other than anger toward me, but she too seems very different. She's as apologetic as Dad and swears up and down that this retreat changed her life.

I want to believe them. But giving them another chance is a lot to ask. I can't forget all the times Dad hit me, or all the times Mom made excuses for Christopher's terrible behavior, or all the times I came home from school, biting back tears, and they blamed me for whatever happened ...

And I haven't told Mary that I started talking to my parents again. At first, I didn't want to bring it up because I feared it would be another sore subject, and right now we have enough of those. But the longer you hide something, the more difficult it is to share. Now I feel like I can't tell Mary at all because she'll be upset I kept it from her.

As usual, I've made a complete mess of things.

―――――――――

MY BOSS, Aaron, is looming behind me. I can always tell when he's there, even if I don't see him come out of his office. The man makes a lot of noise when he moves around, either clearing his throat or cracking his knuckles. I can't tell if he does this to attract attention or if these are subconscious tics he's not even aware of.

"Hi, Brent," he begins. "Could we talk for a moment?"

As a salaried employee, I don't have to punch in and out

for lunch. But this is the time I normally take a few minutes at my desk to eat. I wrap my sandwich back up in tinfoil before swiveling around in my chair to face him. I can tell from his tone and demeanor this isn't going to be a pleasant conversation.

"Hey, Aaron. What's going on?"

He points behind him. "In my office."

Oh boy.

He had to have noticed I was eating, but he obviously doesn't care. I start to get that bad feeling that I'm about to be fired. I screwed up something last week that Aaron wasn't happy about. In my defense, I caught the error myself before it went out to the client, but he was angry I didn't identify the issue before I sent it to QA for testing. He called my work sloppy and said that it also reflected poorly on him as my supervisor.

I follow Aaron into his office, feeling the furtive eyes of my coworkers follow us.

"Close the door," he says.

Not good. I don't know what this is about or if it's going to be a long meeting. I sit opposite Aaron and try to look relaxed.

"It's come to my attention that you left early a couple of days ago," he says.

That means somebody told him.

I think back. All the days here run together. I'm usually in by eight o'clock and out by five. I don't remember leaving early recently. And even if I did, I'm a salaried employee. If my work is done, I can go. I don't need to check in with my boss if I want to call it a day at four thirty.

At least, I never had to before.

"You left, and it wasn't even five o'clock," Aaron adds.

I rack my brain. I really don't remember leaving early this week. "Two days ago?"

"We had something come up after you were gone." His lips grow thin. "It ended up not being an issue. Rich stepped up, like he usually does."

I do my best not to make a face. There have been plenty of nights where I was the only one in our group still around when something came up late and I helped out. I don't make a big deal out of it. I don't broadcast it so everybody knows how wonderful I am, like Rich does.

"Aaron," I say, "I honestly do not remember leaving early, but also, I never go before four thirty and only when my work is done for the day. That's never been a problem before."

With my schedule and given the odd emails that come through at night or on the weekend, I'm working about fifty hours a week. Assuming I did leave a little early one day, what is the big deal? I'm getting my work done.

"Brent," he says, "the quality of your work has been questionable recently. It's not a good look for you—or for the department—to leave early when we have all this work. You really need to think about how your actions are perceived."

Of course. Aaron's worried about how this makes him look. There is no love lost between us. He'd probably be happy to fire me, but he can't because I haven't done anything egregious. Sure, I've made a few mistakes this year, but so does everybody.

"I'm sorry," I force myself to say. "I don't remember leaving early, but, like I said, my hours have never been an issue before."

Aaron puffs his lips out. "Well, Brent, maybe they *are* a

problem, considering all the quality issues that have come up recently."

There was one thing—*one thing*—a month ago. Before that, the last mistake I made was a few months back. I feel like everything is being blown way out of proportion.

"From now on," Aaron says, "I want you to check in with me before you leave for the day."

My eyes almost pop out of my head. I'm not some kid fresh out of high school working a cash register in the mall, who spends all his time scrolling through TikTok on his phone when he should be working. I'm a professional in my thirties, and I work hard for this man and this company.

"I expect you to be here till at least five o'clock," he goes on. "I'd prefer later, actually, because the CIO works till six."

The CIO also makes about ten times what I do. His children are set up for life, maybe even his children's children. Expecting me to keep his hours is absurd, especially when I'm not on the C-level track. Heck, I don't even want to be a manager.

"And if I'm not here," Aaron goes on, "then check with Rich before you leave."

Now that is a slap in the face. Rich and I are peers. Even worse, he's no better at this job than I am. It's just when he messes something up, he's better at talking his way out of it than I am. I cannot believe what is happening.

"I like you, Brent," Aaron says unconvincingly. "I think you have it in you to be a valuable contributor to this organization. But you have to show me something. Alright?"

I CALL Mary on my way home from work. I was planning on going to the gym to exercise after I got off, but I don't have the motivation for it after my lousy day.

"I don't even think I left early," I say after relating my conversation with Aaron.

"Brent," Mary says, "don't you remember? You left around four thirty a couple of days ago."

"I did?"

"Yes." I can hear how frustrated she is. "You went in early, remember? And by four you were wiped."

How did I not remember this? God, the days really do run all together. It doesn't help that I'm in the middle of another bout with depression. The condition really messes with my memory. I'm not clear-headed. I feel like I'm constantly moving through a fog.

"I should email Aaron and tell him," I say. "Four thirty was never a problem before, anyway. This guy has it out for me."

Mary hesitates. "I don't care for him either, but he is your boss. If he wants you to stay until five, then that's what you should do."

Is she taking Aaron's side? "I don't care about that. It's the checking-in part. I'm not a baby. I get all my work done. I feel like they're—"

"Brent, I'm sorry. But I can't do this tonight."

"Do what?"

"Have another conversation about your boss and how much he hates you. It's all we ever talk about. I had a rough day too."

I take a deep breath. She's right. All I do is complain about work. But in my defense, I've been trying to change things. I've been casually looking for another job while developing a plan for my side business. I need to get cracking on both. It's probably time to move on. Once your boss sees you a certain way, especially if it's in a negative light, it's really difficult to change their mind. I could be the perfect employee for the next year and Aaron would still prefer Rich to me.

"I'm sorry, hon," I say. "See you at home?"

"No, remember I told you? I was going to meet Paige and Gwen for dinner."

"I thought you weren't leaving till seven?"

"I wanted to run an errand before we meet up."

I suspect that Mary wants to leave early so she doesn't have to see me right after I get home from another miserable day at the job. I don't blame her for wanting to avoid somebody in a bad mood, but it hurts all the same because that someone is me.

"Alright, well, I'll see you later."

The house is dark when I get home. I heat up some leftovers and pick at my food, but I don't have much of an appetite. My life is circling the drain. I'm not happy at work, Mary and I aren't in a good place, and ... who am I kidding about starting my own business? I'm not an entrepreneur. The thought of picking up a phone and calling people—investors, potential clients, vendors—is daunting. Considering that I'm already working over fifty hours a week (and now probably longer), where will I find the time to do all this?

I'm absent-mindedly checking my email for the hundredth time today when I see the latest note from Dad. I almost scroll right past it because I don't know if I can deal with him right now, but I open it up.

Son — I don't know if you've had a chance to look into this retreat, but I called the fella who runs it to see if he could fit you in. Now, they're normally booked six months in advance, but it turns out somebody cancelled on them last minute. They have a spot open next month.

They have a long wait list of people, but he and I became friends while I was there, and I asked if he could do me a favor and offer you the slot. He's willing to do that, but he needs an answer in two days. Like I said, they're doing a business, and there are a lot of people trying to get in.

Please call me when you get this so we can discuss it. I really think this would be a good thing for you.

Oh, right. Like I can take thirty days off from work right now. Like I can just ... I haven't spoken to Dad over the phone in years, but I'm so angry I dial his number from memory because I want to give him a piece of my mind.

"Brent!" he answers. "Oh my God, it's so good to hear from you, son."

"Dad." The word sounds foreign to me, I haven't said it out loud in so long. "I appreciate you're trying to help, but I can't—"

"Is it the money?" he interrupts.

I don't even know how much this retreat would cost, but I'm sure it's expensive. "That's part of it, yeah. But only part."

"Like I said," Dad goes on. "Me and the guy are buddies now. He's offering you a discount."

I shake my head. "Dad, it's not just the mo—"

"They're charging people twelve grand."

I nearly fall out of my chair. Twelve thousand dollars?

Mary and I live comfortably, but we don't have that much sitting around. I couldn't imagine spending that amount just to learn how to meditate. It's crazy.

Dad is still talking. "... was only four when your mother and I went. So yeah, they're doing a business, but you can tell they're onto something when they're able to charge that much."

"I can't afford it," I say.

"He's offering you a discount because you're my son. Only ten thousand."

"Oh, *only*?" I laugh. "Dad, I'm not going to pay ten thousand dollars to spend thirty days on a farm."

"Son, it's going to change your life. You have to trust me."

Sure, Dad. I trust you.

"No, not happening," I say, rising to pace the dining room. "Even if it *could* help, we don't have the money—"

"Your mother and I will pay for most of it."

That stops me dead in my tracks. My parents have never paid for *anything*. When I was a kid and my sneakers were falling apart, they'd grumble about buying me a new pair, and even then we'd shop at the Goodwill store. I was never good at sports, but I remember wanting to try Little League one year. They refused because it was too much money, and they didn't want to waste it on someone as clumsy as me. They found the money for Christopher, though. He always got what he wanted. He got to play every sport, because he was naturally good at them and my parents could brag about it to everybody.

"It's the least we can do, son." Dad's voice grows thick with emotion. "We don't have much, but we can scrape together about seven thousand dollars. You'd only have to pay the difference."

"Dad ..." I'm at a loss. "You don't have to do that."

"We want to," Dad says. "We wish we could pay the whole thing for you. We've treated you very badly, Brent, and we know this wouldn't make up for everything. But it's something."

"I don't know," I say. "I'd have to take a leave of absence at work, and then Mary ..."

"Did you and she get married?" he asks.

In our email exchange so far, I haven't talked about her at all. I kept her out of the conversation because I didn't want to let my parents fully back into my life.

"Yeah, Dad. I married her."

"I'm happy to hear that, son," he says. "She's a good woman."

"Then why did you and Mom treat her so horribly?"

Dad takes his time answering. "I'm real sorry about that. I ... I'm not making excuses, Brent, but I was raised a certain way. I had ideas put in my head, about how a woman should be and how a marriage should operate. Looking back now, I see how wrong I was, how stupid. That's one of the many things this retreat helped me with. I see everything a lot more clearly now."

He really sounds sincere. And I have to admit: being able to see everything more clearly would be great. Ten thousand dollars is a lot of money, but Mary and I could afford three thousand. The hardest part would be taking a leave of absence from work, but ... what if this retreat helps? Maybe if I get my head right, I'll find a better job. Maybe I will be able to start a side business, which can grow into something.

"Son," Dad says, "you owe it to yourself."

"I have to talk it over with Mary."

12

THURSDAY – MAY 18

I'm happy that Brent's return to work has seemingly gone well. He came home Monday night, his first day back, with a bounce in his step. We enjoyed a nice dinner with some wine, and for the first time since he's come home, he didn't leave the house to work on his side business. It was wonderful. We watched one of our favorite old movies, and then we made love. The next morning, he was gone when I woke up.

I keep waiting for the other shoe to drop. I'm imagining the angry call from him, either during his lunch hour or his drive home, about how terrible Aaron was to him or how Rich is now acting like he's the new boss. I'm expecting the worst, which, I know, isn't a great attitude to have, but old habits die hard. Before Brent went away, I was beginning to think he'd soon be out of a job. Once your boss doesn't like you, it's really hard to change their opinion of you and your work. It's difficult to succeed anywhere, even if you're doing a good job.

But it's been a few days now, and I haven't heard him

complain once about Aaron or Rich or anybody else, or anything that's gone on there. I'm just finishing up early for the day and plan to meet Paige for coffee, but then I hear Brent's car pull into the driveway.

I check the time, and my stomach drops. He's home *early*.

The panic sets in. Brent is not supposed to leave the office before five. Aaron made that very clear. So what's he doing home already? My mind goes immediately to a very bad place. I can't help but assume he was—

"Hey, honey." He flies into the house, all smiles. "How was your day?"

"Uh, fine?"

He gives me a funny look before swooping in for a kiss. "You don't sound so sure about that."

I check the time again on my phone, just to make sure I'm not going crazy. "It's four fifteen."

He nods. "Yeah?"

"I thought Aaron didn't want you leaving before five."

He frowns. "When did he say that?"

"Brent." I give him an incredulous look. "He called you into his office two months ago, remember? It was a really big deal to you."

For a moment, Brent says nothing. I try to read his expression, but I can't. Again, I have no idea what's going on in that head of his.

"You should call him," I say. "You were supposed to check in with him before you leave the office."

"Oh, it's fine." Brent waves a hand dismissively. "Don't worry about it. Aaron and I are on the same page."

"You are?"

"Yeah." He puts his arms around me and kisses my neck. "It's all good."

"I still think you should call him," I say while he goes to work on my neck. "Or at least text. This was a huge deal two months ago. You thought you were going to be fired."

"Aaron's not going to fire me," he says. "Relax, honey."

I pull away from him. Brent looks into my eyes with a confident smile. He really *has* changed. I still haven't gotten over it, even though he's been home more than a week now.

"Okay," I say. "If you think it's fine ..."

"Don't be a worrywart," he says, touching my face. "I've got it all under control. That asshole isn't going to run my life anymore."

Before I can respond, his lips press against mine. I forget all about his job.

He puts his lips next to my ear and whispers, "How about we take this upstairs?"

"Oh, Brent," I say. "I can't. I'm supposed to meet Paige. How about later?"

He shakes his head. "Sorry, hon, but I wanted to take some time and work tonight. I just wanted to come home, see you, and recharge before I head out."

Now that is disappointing. He's gotten me all fired up. "How late are you going to be?"

"Real late," he says, pulling away. I follow him into the kitchen, where he opens the fridge and gets a beer. "Oh, crap, I almost forgot. This one guy I've been talking to? He wants to meet tomorrow night for dinner."

"Really?" I want to jump for joy. I won't lie: Brent has spent a lot of time on his side business. I wish he were home more. But it already looks like it's paying off. Maybe once it's up and running, he'll be more available. "That's amazing, Brent. I'm so proud of you."

"Thanks, babe." He chugs his beer down. "I made a reservation for seven thirty at the Blue Star."

"The Blue Star?" I ask.

We've never been. It's this really expensive restaurant in the city. I don't even think I have a dress nice enough to wear. For the three of us, or four if this gentleman brings a significant other, the meal will cost hundreds of dollars. I'm assuming we're going to pay, since Brent is the one trying to win this guy over to become an investor.

"Yeah," Brent says. "You can't meet a guy like this at McDonald's, hon."

"I didn't say anything."

"Yeah." He smirks at me. "But you were thinking something."

Okay, he's got me there. Still, though … "Couldn't we do Rindella's? That's a nice restaurant."

Brent has gotten another beer out of the fridge. I don't know how he manages to stay in such fantastic shape, drinking this way. And why does alcohol no longer seem to bother him the way it did before? Gosh, *I'm* actually considering going on this retreat. If I could come back looking as good as my husband and feeling like I can conquer the world …

Brent puts his beer down on the island counter and takes my shoulders in his hands.

"Look, honey. We can't do this halfway. We're either in or we're not. There are no half measures when you're trying to start a business. So we go big, or we go home."

The old Brent never spoke in strings of clichés. But the new Brent can't go more than a sentence without using one. It's kind of funny, given how much people speaking in clichés used to drive him crazy.

"Who are you, and what have you done to my husband?"
I ask.

He laughs, turns back for his second beer. "I know what I want now. I can see everything really clearly. Life is so much easier."

"How late are you going to be?" I ask, winking at him. "Because maybe I'll wait up."

He tosses his head back and laughs. "You can't make it past nine forty-five."

I know. I'm kind of lame.

"Then wake me up."

I give him a kiss I know he'll be thinking about the rest of the night, before turning away and heading out of the kitchen.

PAIGE IS WAITING for me at our usual table in the coffee shop. She's dressed as provocatively as ever, in a low-cut blouse and a short skirt. I order my coffee and meet her at the table.

"Look at you," she says.

"What? Do I have something in my teeth?"

"No."

I look myself up and down. I'm wearing an old pair of pants and a top that's been through the dryer too many times. I've got my hair pulled back in a ponytail, and I didn't bother with makeup.

"You're practically *glowing*," Paige says, checking me out.

I do many things. Glow is not one of them.

"I am?"

"Yeah." Paige leans in and lowers her voice. "You look like you and Brent just ..."

"No," I say quickly, feeling my cheeks heat up. "Not this afternoon, anyway."

"Ohhhh." Paige laughs. "So things between you are still cooking?"

I feel like everybody in the coffee shop is listening to our conversation and watching me. But of course, when I look around, nobody seems the least bit interested.

"You could say that."

"Do tell, girl," Paige says.

I fill Paige in on the latest. I don't share details of my sex life, but I paint enough of a general picture for her to understand that Brent and I can't keep our hands off each other.

"All that being said, I wish I saw more of him," I say. "He's either at work, or working on his side business, or we're in bed. We haven't done much talking."

"Sounds terrible," Paige says mockingly.

"It's not." I chuckle. "But a month is a long time away, and I still don't know a thing about his retreat."

"Not one thing?"

I shake my head no. "Not really. I know they worked on mindfulness, and he performed a lot of manual labor, and they exercised and went on a lot of hikes. But other than that, he hasn't shared anything."

"But is that so strange?" Paige asks. "Brent wasn't the biggest talker before he left."

That's true. On the other hand, Brent is a very different person now. I guess the retreat didn't change that aspect of him, however. "He says he made a lot of friends there, but I don't know any of their names."

Paige shrugs. "I don't know, Mary. I think you're looking for something to worry about. Because to me, it sounds like things are going really well, for him and for the two of you."

"Hold on," I say. "Last week, wasn't it you who were warning me about these retreats? Remember?"

"That was last week," Paige says. "And besides, what do I know?"

We both laugh at that. Paige talks for a few minutes about her dating life which is, to put it mildly, a bit messy. There are two guys, and sort of a third, she's either talking to or seeing or doing other things with. It's so funny how night-and-day different the two of us are, yet we're somehow good friends. I guess in our case, opposites really do attract.

"You haven't seen that creep again?" Paige asks.

My eyes drift past her and take in the parking lot. He's not out there. I haven't seen that scary man driving the gray SUV since that day he followed me to the store, then drove down my street. Thank God. Though I have been keeping an eye out. A few times this week I woke up in the middle of the night in a cold sweat when I heard a car going down the street at an odd hour. But it wasn't the guy.

Though I've promised not to, I've also kept an eye out for Jim Smith. He was supposed to periodically watch the house and follow me around, but he must be very good at what he does because I haven't seen him once. I'm beginning to regret paying a private detective two thousand dollars when it looks like I might not have a stalker.

"No, not once," I say.

"That's good," Paige says. "Men are so horrible, aren't they?"

"Brent's pretty great."

She pretend-gags and rolls her eyes. "Not all of us are lucky to have a man like Brent."

I playfully swat her hand. "Don't be jealous."

She makes a face, and for a moment, I think something

so incredibly ridiculous, I'm embarrassed to even acknowledge it. For the briefest of moments, I believe Paige is going to admit she is jealous that I'm with Brent.

"Speaking of that," she says, "I've got some more office gossip for you."

Now it's my turn to roll my eyes. The last time she shared juicy gossip, it was disconcerting to say the least.

"Don't worry, this time it's good," she says. "Mostly."

"Mostly?"

Paige can't wait to share whatever she has to say. "Two of the women who were in here before with Rich came back. I overheard them talking again."

"Do I really want to know?"

"Well, they both couldn't stop talking about how hot Brent is."

"What?"

She nods. "They said he's like a new man since he came back. They were gushing about him."

For the second time in a week, a feeling of jealousy overwhelms me. Who are these women? Does Brent work closely with them? Has he flirted with either of them, like he did with that blonde woman from the gym? Why are they talking about a married man like they want to jump his bones?

"You should take it as a compliment," Paige says. "Your husband is hot. Which reminds me, when was the last time you had me over?"

I force a smile at Paige's joke, but my insides are churning.

Before Brent went away, never in a million years would I think him capable of infidelity. And I still don't think he would cheat on me. But at the same time, I can't get the image of him and that woman out of my mind. If an attractive woman propositioned him, if there were no strings attached, would he turn her down?

I've never even had to think about this before ...

"Earth to Mary, hello? Are you there?"

Paige is waving her hand in my face.

I tell her about the woman at the gym. Paige shrugs it away.

"It's the twenty-first century. Women hit on men now. I do it all the time. I don't think you have to worry about Brent."

"I guess."

But I *am* worried.

"If that man was even *thinking* about stepping out on you," Paige continues, "then he wouldn't have his hands all over you, every night, since he got back."

"You're probably right." She has a point there. "Did these women say anything else about my husband, other than how hot he is?"

"Oh, that's what I really wanted to tell you," Paige says. "He apparently put that guy Rich in his place."

"What?"

"One of them mentioned how Rich tried to steamroll a meeting they were in, but Brent was having none of it. From the sound of it, things got pretty heated."

Why didn't Brent mention any of this?

"They were both impressed," Paige adds, picking up on my confusion. "I'm guessing it came as a surprise to everyone there."

"Yes," I say absently. I'll bet they were as surprised as I am right now.

Paige checks the time. "Oh, crap. I have to get back. Hey,

do you wanna grab dinner tomorrow night? Maybe you could invite me over to check out your hot husband?"

I manage a weak grin. "Can't. We're having dinner in the city with a potential investor."

"Investor?" She gives me a knowing look. "See what I mean? You guys are doing great, girl."

We hug and say goodbye. This time, when I watch Paige hurry across the parking lot to the bank, I'm relieved to find there's no gray SUV parked next to my Prius. I throw out the rest of my coffee. If I have any more caffeine at this hour, I'll be up all night. Before I reach my car, my phone buzzes with a text.

It's from Brent.

> Thinking of you.

I'm touched. That is so sweet of him. Brent is a kind man but wasn't the most demonstrative guy before. With a smile on my face, I get behind the wheel and hit the road. I don't really have anywhere to be since Brent is out, so I swing by the grocery store to pick up a few things and buy him some more beer. We were really concerned he might have a problem before he went away, but now it seems like all those worries were for nothing. Sure, he has a couple of beers every day, but so do a lot of people. They don't seem to be affecting him at all. Brent just worked eight hours and is now headed off to his new favorite coffee shop to do more work. If he had a problem, would that even be possible?

At the grocery store, I grab a basket from the bin and take my time going up and down the aisles. Brent needs more fruit already, so I bag some red and green apples, grab another bundle of bananas. While I'm looking over the grapes, I get a feeling that someone is behind me.

"Hey, sweetheart."

I know before I turn around that it's him, the creep driving the gray SUV around. I put the box of grapes into my basket and reach into my pocket for my phone before turning around.

He's two feet away, dressed in the same fashion as the other day: hat, sunglasses, and dark clothes. He's not holding a basket or pushing a shopping cart around. His hands are empty. It's pretty obvious he's not here for groceries.

I can feel my lip trembling before I manage to squeak out the word: "Hello."

One side of his mouth curls into a wicked grin. His smell hits me. This time I'm more certain: it's definitely marijuana. He smells like he just got sprayed by a skunk.

"You shop here too?" he asks.

I don't answer. Instead I start walking down the aisle quickly. He follows right along. Where are all the employees? The registers are the other way. I should have turned left. But I wasn't thinking. I was just reacting. The deli is a few aisles away. There will be a guy there, hopefully two, working. I don't care how it sounds, the first employee I find, I'm going to tell them this man is bothering me and ask if they can contact the police.

"Why are you in such a hurry?" he asks, staying right behind me.

"Get away from me."

"Oh, sweetheart," he says in a threatening tone. "You don't think it's going to be that easy, do you?"

Where are the employees? Not finding anybody that can

help, I stop and hold up my phone. I'm texting Jim Smith; then I'm dialing 9-1-1. I want him to see what I'm doing.

"Your husband is a dangerous man," he utters.

I haven't finished my text to Jim Smith. But his words stop me dead.

"You already knew that, didn't you?" he asks.

"What are you talking about?" I say.

He sneers. "He's not who he says he is."

"You don't even know my husband."

I'm about to go back to my text, but then his next words stop me again.

"I've known Brent for ten years."

Ten *years*? It has to be a mistake. Or he has to be lying. My husband would never associate with a guy like this. I've known Brent for almost a decade myself, and I've never met this person before. Brent doesn't have a lot of friends. The few he does are very close, and I know all of them.

"I'm calling the police," I say.

"You don't want to do that," the man answers. "I'm sure Brent doesn't either."

My hands are shaking. "Who are you? What do you want?"

His sneer turns into a devilish smile. "Oh, you're good, sweetheart. You're real good. You've got the suburban housewife act really down."

I am *not* a housewife. I work a full-time job myself. Not that there's anything wrong with being a housewife, of course. But I don't want to tell this man anything, so I let him go on thinking he knows something about me.

"You and your husband, you play pretend. You pay your taxes and say hello to Mrs. Ryers. You keep a nice house. Once a week, Brent mows the lawn and you do the gardening. You go for walks around the block and hold hands, I'll bet. You act like you're good, law-abiding suburbanites. But I know better."

"Who are you?" I repeat.

"I'm the truth," he says. "I'm what's real."

I have no idea what he means, and I don't care to understand. It'd be easy to dismiss him as some kind of lunatic, but that's not the vibe I'm getting at all. There is an intelligence behind this man's eyes.

"What do you want?" I ask. "Why are you following me?"

"I don't care about you, sweetheart," he says, and for a moment I believe him. "*Brent* and I have unfinished business."

"What business?"

"He knows." He looks me up and down. "No offense, but you don't seem his type. *Brent* prefers the wild ones ..."

"What did you just say?"

"You mean you didn't know?" He puts a hand in front of his mouth. "Oops. I guess I shouldn't have said anything."

I shake my head. "Get away from me."

He pulls down his sunglasses. While he speaks, his eyes rake over me. "*Brent* loves the ladies, alright. But none of them have ever looked like you, sweetheart. He mostly goes for the blondes. And they're usually, um, a little more *fit* than you."

If I weren't so terrified of this man, I'd slap him right across the face.

"I think I touched a nerve," he says. "Sorry. But I thought you already knew that your husband gets around."

My head is spinning. I don't want to believe a word this man says, but the problem is, he's really convincing. Am I on someone's sick, twisted version of candid camera? Will Brent suddenly appear at the end of the aisle with a film crew, and we can all have a laugh?

Nope.

"Brent's not a cheater," I say, unable to help the tears forming in my eyes. "He's a good man, and he loves me more than anything. Now I want you to leave me alone, or I will call the police."

"Tell your husband." The man leans in. His teeth are yellow. "That Joshua wants what's his."

I take a step back, but he moves forward, staying right on top of me. The only thing between us is my basket of groceries.

"Alright," I mutter, "I'll tell him."

The man smiles and pushes his sunglasses back up his nose. "And tell him that if I don't get what's mine, I'll take *you* instead. You got it, bitch?"

My whole body is trembling. "I got it, I got it."

"Ma'am!" someone calls out. "Is this man bothering you?"

A young male employee is coming up the aisle fast. Joshua, if that's even his name, ducks away. I can't move. With my hands shaking so badly, I have to put my basket down on the floor. The employee rushes over to help me.

"Ma'am, are you okay?"

I don't know how to answer that question.

13

O nce I get my breathing under control, I text the
private detective, Jim Smith. He writes back immediately to say he's in the area and will move on this
guy, assuming he can locate the gray SUV. I don't know how he
plans to do that exactly, but I can't think about it right now.

The manager of the grocery store offers to call the police
for me, but I decide against it. I don't know if I can believe a
word this man calling himself Joshua just told me, but if
there's any truth to it, I'm not sure I want to get the police
involved. He didn't come out and call himself a criminal, but
the implication was there. I don't know what to think about
anything, for that matter.

I leave my groceries in the basket right on the floor. The
manager offers them to me for free, and I think I answer
him, but I don't even know what I say. Instead, I stumble out
of the store and rush to get inside my car and lock the doors
immediately. I get the car started, but I don't pull out into
traffic. Instead, I sit there and try to control my rising panic.

Another text comes through from the detective. He's tailing the gray SUV and confirms the creep is not headed for my house. He looks to be heading into the city.

I breathe a sigh of relief, then call Brent. It rings through to voicemail. I try again. Same result. I curse a few times and even slap the steering wheel. I need to get a hold of him right now. I text and ask him to call me. A few minutes later, though, I haven't gotten a response.

Really angry now, I pull out into traffic and drive across town. It's slow going at rush hour, and it takes me nearly twenty-five minutes to reach the coffee house near the gym. I don't see Brent's car anywhere in the lot. I peek inside. He's not here.

I send him another text:

> Where are you?

Nothing.

I get back in the car and stare out vacantly into the night. With nothing to do but wait, I have a good opportunity to go over in my head all the strange things this Joshua character said to me.

According to Joshua, my husband is both a dangerous man and not who he says he is. What can that possibly mean? I can only come up with one answer: Joshua thinks my husband is a criminal who is pretending to be a solid citizen.

I want to laugh at the idea, because it's ludicrous. I've known Brent for almost ten years, and he doesn't have an illegal bone in his body.

And dangerous? Not a chance. Brent is not a pushover,

but he is a gentle man. I've never seen him become aggressive with any—

Except the other day at the gym.

Seriously, dangerous might be the best way to describe the Brent I saw at the gym. He was ready to fight that hulking bodybuilder. There was no fear in his eyes. Quite the opposite, in fact. He looked *eager* to get into a physical confrontation.

But that was the first time in ten years I've ever seen him like that. I can count on two hands the number of times he's raised his voice at anybody. Joshua is wrong about my husband. Brent is not a dangerous, violent criminal.

Then why was Joshua dead-on when he suggested Brent wouldn't want me calling the police? The man intimated that Brent has something to hide. Is that why my husband preferred to hire a private eye instead of getting the cops involved?

I don't know what to think anymore. So much has happened in the last week—

Brent is calling me.

"Hey, honey," he says. "I just saw your texts—"

"Where are you?" I blurt out.

"Whoa, take it easy. I'm sorry I missed your call, but you know I don't get great reception with this new phone."

"I want to know where you are."

"I'm ... at the mall, honey. Why do you ask?"

"Why are you at the mall?"

"I realized th—Mary, what's wrong?"

I can't help it. I start crying again.

"That man approached me in the grocery store," I say between sobs. "I let Jim know, he's following him right now, I tried calling and texting you, Brent, and—"

"Honey, please slow down, okay? Where are you? I can meet you, wherever you are. Okay?"

"I'm at your coffee shop," I say.

"Don't go anywhere. I'll be there in fifteen minutes."

"Okay."

It takes Brent longer. He parks next to me twenty-three minutes after the call. I'm out of the car before he's turned his engine off. As he opens his door, I start in on him.

"Where *were* you?" I shout. "Why can I never reach you anymore? What are you doing, all this time away from the house?"

Brent gets out of his car slowly and regards me like I'm paranoid and possibly deranged. Holding his palms out, he says in an irritatingly calm voice, "Honey, let's calm down and talk about this. Okay? Can we go inside?"

"I don't want to go inside!" I shout. "I want to know where the heck you were!"

"I just told you, I was at the mall."

"Why?" I ask, the tears streaming again. "Why were you at the *mall*, Brent? I thought you'd be here. You told me this is where you go."

He opens the rear driver side door and unhooks a clothes bag. Holding it out in front of him, he says, "I needed a new suit. I have to make a good impression tomorrow night at dinner."

Great. He went out and bought himself a new suit while I was being terrorized by this Joshua character. I know it's unfair of me to expect Brent to be on call, but I can't help it. I'm still spooked by the encounter earlier.

Brent hangs the suit bag back up in the rear of his car and closes the door. "Sorry, honey, but I tried some of my suits on the other day. They don't fit me well anymore. And we need to look good tomorrow night."

I know how much this dinner means to Brent. But I can't even think about going anywhere tomorrow night. Heck, I don't even want to go home right now because Joshua knows where we live. This cannot be happening. The worst part? What if this man *actually* knows Brent? He could be lying, of course, but what if just *one* of the things he said was true?

"He said he knew you," I say.

Brent leans back against his car and puts his hands in his pockets. "What?"

"Joshua, the guy, when he cornered me in the grocery store, he said he knew you."

"Joshua?" Brent's mouth twists as he thinks. "I don't know anybody named Joshua."

"He said he knew you," I repeat. "He said that ..."

I can't even look at my own husband. I start crying into my hands. A moment later, Brent is wrapping me in a hug.

"Come on, honey. Let's go home and talk about this. Okay?"

I've got a terrible feeling in the pit of my stomach. But where else can I go?

I MAKE Brent go into the house alone. He checks every room and turns on all the lights, then meets me at the front door before I set one foot inside. There is no worse feeling in the world than being terrified of entering your own home.

Brent sits me down at the dining room table and goes to work in the kitchen. While he's cooking, he brings me a bottle of wine and pours me a generous glass. He sits with me and holds my hand while the food heats in the oven. He's got a beer, but he hardly touches it. Instead, he's focused completely on me while I tell him what happened.

"Joshua said he's known you for ten years. He also said ..." I look down, unable to meet my husband's eye. "You like women. Particularly blonde women."

Brent takes it all in while he grips my hand.

"He threatened me. Us. He threatened us. He said he wanted what was his. That's what he wanted me to tell you. If he didn't get it, he'd take me."

"Take you?"

"I don't know if he meant kill me or kidnap me."

Honestly, I don't know which would be worse. I don't even want to think about it too much.

"That son of a bitch," Brent mutters, shaking his head.

"I threatened to call the police, and he, um, he warned me that wouldn't be a good idea."

"Why not?" Brent asks.

His hand grips mine a little more firmly.

"He said you wouldn't want the police involved. Kind of like, you had something to hide, in other words."

Brent's breathing has gotten shallow. "Did he say anything else?"

"He said you weren't who you said you were."

"Oh, Jesus ..."

Brent lets go of my hand and rises from the table. He gives me his back. Everything about him gets incredibly still. My heart is racing. I get the sense he's about to admit something to me, something terrible and awful that no wife would ever want to hear. He's about to tell me the last ten years have all been a lie, that he's living some kind of double life, which means I've been so monumentally naïve and stupid. How could I not have known? We occasionally watch those true crime shows, and it always drove me crazy when the wife of a man who turned out to be a serial killer would look into the camera and claim she had no idea. I never believed them, not for a second. Who could be that gullible? That credulous?

Apparently, I can.

When he turns back to me, there's a desperate, almost pleading look in his eyes. The timer in the kitchen suddenly goes off to signal the food in the oven should be done. But neither of us make a move to fetch it. I've lost my appetite, and so has he. My husband is about to tell me something that will completely change our lives forever, I just know it. Now I understand what this retreat did for him. It didn't change him—

It brought his *true* self to the surface.

Brent shakes his head. "It's Christopher."

14

BRENT – ONE MONTH AND THREE WEEKS
AGO – MARCH 18

"Hey, hon," I say. "Could we talk?"

Mary looks up from her novel.

"What's wrong?"

"Nothing," I say.

I hate that this is the state of our relationship: I ask Mary if we can talk, and she assumes something is wrong. This has to change.

Mary dog-ears the page she's reading and puts the book on the coffee table in front of her. I sit beside her on the couch. I've been working up the nerve all day to talk to her about this. She has one leg folded over the other and regards me cautiously, like I'm about to deliver bad news.

I take her hand. "So I've been thinking ..."

She squeezes my hand. "Brent, you're worrying me. What's going on?"

I look away. I don't know where to start. I've always found it very difficult to share my feelings, partly because I never seem to have the right words at my disposal, but also partly because I don't understand what I'm feeling myself at critical moments. Right now, I'm nervous, excited, fearful, concerned, uncertain, hopeful, and troubled ... all at the same time.

"My life has gotten out of control," I say.

Merely saying it out loud, I feel like a huge weight has been lifted off my chest. I'm already feeling better. Mary rubs my back. She knows how hard it is for me to get the words out sometimes.

"I'm really struggling," I say. "At work, at home, and I'm worried about my drinking. I think ... I think I might have a problem."

Mary keeps rubbing my back.

Now's the time to tell her I've been talking to my father again. Now's the time to tell her the resumed relationship is dredging up a lot of unresolved things from my past, which is making everything more difficult.

"Are you okay?" Mary asks.

I nod.

"Maybe you should take some time off work," she says.

I look over at her, wondering if she's read my mind.

"I was thinking about it, actually."

"You've been working hard," she says. "With the pandemic and everything else going on with the company, you haven't taken any time. What's it been, three years?"

I nod again. "I want to, uh, take a leave of absence, actually."

Her hand stops in the middle of my back. "Oh?"

I force myself to look her in the eye. "I found this place, it's like a retreat."

"Okay."

Her voice is totally neutral. I can't tell what she's thinking, if anything.

"They call it a wellness retreat. It's supposed to be really good. They teach you meditation and do mindfulness throughout the day. They've helped people with depression and anxiety, and people with addiction too. You should read some of the testimonials on the website. And I've been in contact with the couple who run it. They seem like they could help me."

"That sounds really good, Brent," Mary says.

She sounds like she means it.

"It's thirty days long, is the thing." I grimace. "I'd have to take a leave from work, and also, I'd be gone for a month."

We haven't been apart that long since we've been together. I don't know how she'll feel about that, though, to be honest, she might actually enjoy a little time away from me. Maybe that's what she needs too.

Mary puts her head on my shoulder. "I think it'd be good for you, Brent."

"I think so too," I say.

"I'd like to read more about it," she says. "What's the web address?"

I tell her. Mary pulls it up on her phone while we sit together on the couch. The website comes up. I see the familiar images of the farmhouse and sprawling acres of land.

"My God, it's beautiful," Mary says. "Where is it?"

She scrolls through the website. I direct her to the testimonials, and then she reads up on the program itself.

"All that meditation and exercise could really benefit you," she says. "Though I have to say I'm surprised. You never wanted to try mindfulness before."

I turn fully to face her on the couch. "I'm at the end of my rope."

She closes her eyes. When she opens them, they're a little moist. "I'm sorry, Brent."

"It's not your fault."

"Some of it might be," she says. "I haven't been a great wife recently."

"You have." I rub her thigh. "The problem is, it's not cheap."

She smiles. "It doesn't look like it would be. How much is it?"

Now is the time to tell her about my parents. It's the perfect moment. I can tell her that Mom and Dad went there, have totally changed their lives, and now, for the first time ever, they're offering to help me pay for something important.

"Three thousand," I say.

Mary makes a face. She recovers quickly, but there is no missing her sudden change in expression.

"We could make that work," she says. "But what about your job?"

"I'd need a doctor's note from my therapist," I say. "But that won't be hard to get, honestly. I had a panic attack the other day in the parking lot before I went in."

"Oh my God! Brent, why didn't you tell me?"

"I didn't want to worry you."

She puts her arms around me. "I think this would be good for you. But what about after the leave? Do you think you could just return to your job?"

I've thought about this a lot. I want to lie to Mary and tell her I'm sure everything will work out. But I don't know that with any certainty. This retreat might help, or it might not. Even if it does, when I get back to work, things might not get any better with my job. Aaron isn't the most understanding of bosses. He might hold it against me for taking a month's leave and find more ways to make my life there miserable. He almost certainly won't consider me for any promotions in the future. By taking this leave, I might be shooting myself in the foot at work, but then again, there are other companies out there. Maybe I'll start somewhere fresh, or maybe I'll finally start my own coding business.

"I'll have to," I say. "And we'll just see how it goes. There's nothing else I can do. But I'll tell you what, I can't keep going on the way I have."

She nods. "I think you're right."

I knew she'd understand.

Mary leans into me, and we sit back against the couch together. "It's funny, though, I never imagined you going on a retreat like this."

"Yeah. Me neither."

15

A fter I take a moment to grasp what Brent just said, I respond, "You told me Christopher was dead."

"He *is*," Brent says, sighing heavily. "But I have to hand it to him. The guy is still finding ways to make my life miserable, even though he's been gone for years."

Now I'm even more confused.

"Brent, you're not making any sense."

He returns to the table and offers his hand. I take it, reluctantly.

"There's no other explanation," he says. "It has to be Christopher."

"I don't understand."

"We looked alike." He nods. "Think about it."

I never met Christopher, but I have seen a couple of old photographs from their childhood. People had trouble telling them apart, especially when the two boys were young. When I looked at one photograph and Brent put me to the test, I studied the picture for a long while before pointing to the boy with the bowl cut on the right. He was very happy about that, naturally, because most people he showed the photograph to would admit they didn't know.

I never told him the truth.

I just guessed and happened to be right. Fifty-fifty shot.

Okay, well, I kind of cheated. Brent's parents always preferred Christopher, and in the photograph, that too was obvious. My mother-in-law is standing behind Christopher, and my father-in-law is half-turned in his direction and has a hand on his shoulder. Brent, if you take a moment to look, seems like an afterthought in that family photo. That was why I picked the boy on the right.

"When we were kids, Christopher used to pretend to be me," Brent says. "He rarely got caught doing anything wrong, because he was really sneaky, but on those rare occasions when he did, he'd claim to be me. Or he'd claim later it wasn't him. I remember when we were fourteen and he vandalized some school property after hours one night. Somebody out late walking their dog saw him and was able to identify him for the police. Christopher denied it was him, and then, when the school searched my locker, they found all the empty graffiti cans he'd used. I got into a ton of trouble for that. I swore to my parents that it wasn't me and found the courage to point the finger at Christopher, even though I knew I'd catch a beating for it later. Mom didn't believe me."

"What about your father?"

"I think he knew it was probably Christopher. But he didn't care. He was livid that I'd even think about ratting my brother out, *even if* Christopher was responsible. Dad hit me that night. I still had a black eye when I went back to school after my suspension."

"My God," I say.

Brent has shared a few details from his childhood. They were enough to paint a horrible picture of what his life was like. But I'd never heard this story before.

"I'm sorry," I say.

He looks down. "It wasn't long after that I called child services. I just ... I couldn't take it anymore."

There are tears in his eyes. I squeeze his hand.

"I never told you this." Brent looks back up at me. "But not long before we met, the police showed up at my apartment one night. They'd come to arrest me."

"What?"

His face is turning red. "I ... didn't tell you because it was too embarrassing. I mean, I hadn't done anything wrong. Let me explain. They took me down to the station and started questioning me. I didn't understand what they were after or where any of it was going. I should have asked for a lawyer straight away, but then again, I didn't have anything to hide, so I wanted to cooperate. I thought it would help. Trust me, that is *never* the right thing to do with the police. But you know, hon, I've never broken a single law in my life. So I went along with their questioning, and eventually they came around to the heart of the matter. I was implicated in some kind of credit card fraud and identity theft. They had followed an electronic trail, and it led back to me. That's when I asked for an attorney."

"It was Christopher, wasn't it?"

He nods. "Once I got my lawyer, and we shared my personal computer with the police, we cleared it up pretty quickly. I showed them a picture of my brother, and it turns out he was forging my signature—I still don't know how he got it—and writing checks and opening up credit cards in my name. He was part of some elaborate scam where he was working with other criminals. He posed as me, all in case he got caught."

"What did the police do to him?"

"They never arrested him. The evidence implicating *me* was circumstantial, and Christopher was another step removed. It was easy to prove I hadn't done anything but hard to prove he had. Regardless, he left the area before they could bring charges. None of the men he worked with ever came forward either. Like I said, this was all before we met. I should have told you, but the truth was, I was afraid. I didn't want to scare you away. My parents were awful enough. I thought if you knew I also had a sociopath for a brother, you wouldn't want anything to do with me."

"Oh, Brent."

I squeeze his hand. A single tear escapes the corner of his eye.

"I'm guessing this is some guy my brother used to run with. He probably told this Joshua—I doubt that's even his real name, by the way—that his name was Brent, or that he pretended to be me, you know? This creep somehow found us and thought I was Christopher."

It all makes sense. Now I feel awful for even considering Joshua was telling me the truth. I know my husband. He's a good man.

Brent is not a criminal.

"He threatened me," I say, "to put pressure on you."

Brent nods. "Who knows what happened between this guy and Christopher? It's all conjecture. But I'm willing to bet they were involved in a scam, and then Christopher screwed him out of the money or whatever. That's probably what Joshua wants, his share of the loot."

"This is all unbelievable."

I'm as straight-laced and law-abiding as they come, and honestly, I kind of live a boring life. I get up, go to work, keep the house tidy, occasionally exercise, see my friends a couple of times a month. That's it. I haven't been to a party in ... gosh, has it been that long? I don't even do *bars* anymore. Friday nights, on the couch, watching a movie with Brent, that's good enough for me.

This admittedly minor brush with the criminal world has been utterly terrifying. To think, there are people whose lives are touched by it every day, who actually *choose* to live in constant danger; it's incomprehensible. Like this Joshua character. There was nothing stopping him, no internal brakes, from threatening me, some woman he's never met before, in the middle of what should have been a busy grocery store.

"Hon." Brent squeezes my hand. "I'm so sorry. I hate that my family has put us in this position. I ... God, I hate them."

He looks ashamed.

"It's not your fault," I say. "You're not your parents, and you're not your brother."

"I know, but ..."

"Hey." I wait till he meets my eye. "You gave them so many opportunities, and they never changed. You cut them out of our lives years ago and never talked to any of them again. There's nothing more you could have done. This is not your fault."

Friday – May 19

THE FOLLOWING NIGHT, I'm in the middle of getting ready for
our fancy dinner with the potential investor when I get a text
from Jim Smith. I quickly put down my makeup and open
the message.

The private detective sent the text to both Brent and me.

> Please call me when you get this. I have
> information to share.

"Brent!" I call out.

He pokes his head in the bathroom, where I'm getting
ready. His eyes bulge when he sees me in the new dress I
picked up this afternoon. It's a black gown that's really
classy.

"Babe," he says, "you look *amazing*. We might be late to
dinn—"

I swat him away before he gets his paws on me.

"We got a text from the detective. He wants us to call."

We step into the bedroom. Brent doesn't have his phone
on him—he never does anymore. So I use mine to call
Smith. I activate the speakerphone.

"Hi, Mary," the detective says, his voice bright.

"Hey, Jim," I say. "I'm here with Brent."

"Great. There have been a few developments. I managed
to find the SUV last night, as you both know. I got his plates
and ran them. They're registered to a guy called Josh Petri.
He's got a rap sheet, alright, been in and out of the clink a
few times.

"I followed him back to his place. He's staying at this
seedy motel about thirty minutes away. It's the kind of place
that advertises hourly rates, if you catch my drift. I stayed on

him for a few hours last night, but there was nothing doing when he got home, so I left off. Anyway, I got into his personal background. He went away for armed robbery about fifteen years ago. After he was released, he played the part of good citizen for a little bit, but it wasn't long before he was brought up on fraud charges. The witness who was going to testify against him turned up dead before trial, so Josh walked. I hate to be the one to tell you this, Brent, but there was another man being investigated under those fraud charges as well, it was—"

"My brother."

"Yep." Smith sighs. "Sorry, I really do hate to be the bearer of bad news."

Brent makes a pained face. I rub his shoulder.

Brent says, "It's alright, Jim. Was there anything else?"

"Now that I know where he's holed up, it's only a matter of time before I obtain evidence of stalking. Once I have that, I'll let you know, and we can discuss next steps."

"Sounds good, Jim," Brent jumps in. "We appreciate all your hard work. Now I hate to cut you off, but we have to—"

"Wait," I say.

Brent gives me a look and points to the clock on my nightstand. It's taken me a little longer than anticipated to get ready for our dinner. That's because it's been a while since I had to get gussied up for an evening out like this. But I don't care if we're a few minutes late, and quite honestly, I'm a little annoyed that Brent seems to care more about our being on time than having this conversation about the guy who's been stalking me.

"What do we mean by *next steps*? I thought we all agreed we should go to the police."

Brent looks down at the phone, as if he wants Smith to dictate the course of action for us. That's a little odd to me.

"That is certainly a possibility," the detective answers. "And probably the best one. But the situation is fluid. Why don't we wait till we have good evidence and then decide how to play it?"

"I think that makes a lot of sense," Brent says. "Good talking to you, Jim."

"Have a nice evening."

Before I can interject again, Smith ends the call. I just stand there and gape incredulously at Brent.

"It would have been nice to talk to the man for a few more minutes," I say.

"I know." Brent offers an apologetic smile. "But we *are* running late, babe. I really don't want to keep this guy waiting. Tonight is all about impressions."

"Fine, Brent," I say curtly. "I'll finish getting ready, then. See you downstairs."

"Mary," he says, "don't be like—"

I shut the door to the bathroom before he can finish. Staring into the mirror, I try to get myself under control. I'm *annoyed* with my husband right now, and that's not the best emotion to be feeling when we're about to meet another couple for the first time for dinner in the city. I'm already really anxious, and this isn't helping. After taking a few deep breaths and reminding myself how much this means to Brent, I get back to putting my makeup on.

Before I'm finished, there's a tentative knock at the door.

"It's open," I say.

Brent opens the door and stands in the doorway, admiring me. Normally it'd make me feel sexy, but I'm in no mood.

"I'm almost done," I say.

"I'm sorry," he says.

A few more swipes of eyeliner and then I'm ready. I check myself in the mirror one more time. It's been a long time since I wore this much makeup.

"You look beautiful," he says.

Since he's been home, I've tried really hard not to confront him unnecessarily. Brent is in a really good place, and I didn't want to bring him down. But the last nine days have been really difficult for me. Brent has changed a lot, and while that's mostly a good thing, it is an adjustment for both of us. He's also been working really hard, which, again, is mostly a good thing, but it means he hasn't been around as much as he used to be. That too is an adjustment.

And while all this has been going on, a violent criminal has been stalking me.

I've tried to keep everything in, as best I could, but now I can't hold back anymore. This is a *big* deal, and Brent is more worried about our dinner date, it seems. It's not right.

"Brent," I say, "I—"

He's gotten down on one knee.

"What are you doing?" I ask.

He reaches into a pocket and pulls out a small black jewelry box. My heart is immediately in my throat.

"What are you doing?" I repeat.

"I didn't want to do this in the bathroom, babe. I was hoping we could get to the restaurant a few minutes early and I could surprise you before they showed up. But I couldn't wait anymore." He opens the box and holds it out to me. There's a beautiful, glittering ring inside. "I bought this for you. I know, you're looking at me like I'm crazy, but I ..."

I can't help it. I start crying. I'm going to ruin all the

makeup I just spent a long time putting on. I wipe away my tears quickly.

"Things have been really hectic recently," he goes on. "I took all that time for myself; then when I came back, you must have thought I had completely changed. I've spent too much time recently on the new business. You deserve better, babe. I wanted to give you this—actually, I wanted to ask you, would you like to renew our vows?"

I step forward and take the box. The ring really is gorgeous.

"Brent," I say, having trouble finding my voice, "you're supposed to give me this at the renewal ceremony."

He laughs and comes to his full height. I look up into his eyes, and all my anger is gone. I don't even think about how much this ring must have cost us. I don't even care at this moment. This man really loves me.

"Of course I would," I say.

16

The Blue Star is the nicest restaurant I've ever been to. I feel like a movie star when the valet opens the car door for me and I step out onto the sidewalk. Brent hands the young man wearing a shirt and bow tie the keys, then offers me his arm before he whisks me inside. The lighting is soft in the restaurant, and the other diners waiting for tables in the lobby are all dressed elegantly. The maître d' seats us immediately. We're a few minutes late, so I'm really nervous and expecting the other couple to already be here, but our table is unoccupied.

Brent pulls out my chair for me and, like a true gallant, waits for me to sit before he does. The maître d' hands us big, oblong menus printed on very expensive cardstock, while a wine server appears immediately and offers us the house blend. The man pours Brent a little. My husband examines the wine, checking its legs, then smells it before taking a sip. I didn't even know Brent knew how to taste wine, but he looks like an old pro. Where did he learn how to do this?

"It's good," he says neutrally, like he's being parsimonious in his praise. "Please leave the bottle."

The server pours us two full glasses, then deposits the wine bottle in a bucket of ice next to our table. I sip the wine carefully because I don't want to spill any on my new dress, and I don't want to have too much before the other couple arrives. I don't want them thinking ... I don't know. I want them to think Brent and I are the perfect couple, completely well-adjusted, responsible individuals, worthy of investing in.

Brent leans over. "You really do look *hot,* babe. I might have to take you into the bathroom for a quickie."

I blush and focus on the menu. All the entrées sound delicious. And they're all ridiculously expensive. I'm trying really hard not to think about how much everything costs—but it's especially difficult when I've got this new ring on my finger. Not to mention my dress or that dashing suit Brent is wearing. By the way, he looks *amazing.* Those broad shoulders and that tapered waist of his are almost tempting enough to take him up on his offer. I mean, not really. I'd never be caught dead making love in the bathroom of a restaurant. But the minute we get home, now that's a different story.

"What do you think?" He looks around. "Pretty nice."

"Um, *yeah.*" It's by far the nicest restaurant I've ever been in. "I wasn't sure places like this existed in real life."

He laughs, and his hand finds my thigh under the table.

"Love you, babe," he says.

"Love you too."

All this is a lot to take in. Before Brent went away, we were arguing a lot, and he was in danger of losing his job. I didn't know what the future held for us as a couple, to be honest. A separation almost seemed inevitable.

But now here we are, sitting in this ridiculously expensive restaurant, about to meet with an investor. I've got this new ring on my finger, and we have plans to renew our vows. It really is amazing how quickly life can turn around.

Brent begins to rise. "Here they are."

On the way over, I repeated their names over and over in my head. I'm really bad with names. Dorian and Katya. Dorian and Katya. Dorian and Katya.

I get up also. Dorian is a big, hulking man in a dark suit with salt-and-pepper hair that looks like it was just cut a few minutes ago. If I had to guess, I'd say he was in his mid to late forties.

The woman he is with, Katya, is *not*. She looks about half his age. She has wide-set, icy blue eyes, the high cheekbones of a runway model, big, pouty lips, and quite the body. Her breasts look fake, not that there's anything wrong with that, and she has long Barbie-doll legs. Her strapless dress is provocative and, honestly, a little risqué for this place. Her body is toned and tanned.

"Dorian!" Brent says, extending his hand. "Great to see you."

Dorian isn't as enthusiastic as Brent. He offers my husband a polite smile and a handshake. "Hi, Brent."

"This is my wife," Brent says, "Mary."

Dorian offers me a cool smile. I shake his beefy hand. It looks and feels manicured.

"Hello, Mary," he says. "Very nice to meet you. This is my wife, Katya."

Of the four of us, his wife is the tallest. Even without the heels, she'd probably still have an inch or so on Brent, who isn't short.

Katya leans in and brushes her big, pouty lips on my husband's cheek. I can't help it. The greeting drives me insanely jealous. This woman is obscenely attractive. She looks like she just stepped off the cover of a fashion magazine. Then she turns to me with a dazzling smile and offers me a kiss on the cheek as well.

"Hello," she says, in a noticeable accent. She sounds Eastern European. "It's very nice to meet both of you."

"Please." Brent motions at the table. "Sit. You have to try this wine. It's very good."

Dorian sits next to Brent. Katya takes her place next to me. The woman gives me an indecipherable look.

"Sorry we are late," she says, not sounding sorry at all. "Dorian is always on the phone. Always this, always that, always a deal."

"Oh, it's no problem," I say. "Brent and I were just sitting down. I've never been here before."

"Oh really?" Katya sounds truly surprised. "We come all the time."

I'll bet. Dorian just *looks* wealthy. And he's got the, forgive my cynicism, trophy wife to boot.

"It's pretty good," Katya says.

Pretty good? For ninety-nine point nine percent of the people on this planet, the Blue Star would qualify as the best restaurant they'd ever set foot in. But Katya is kind of flippant about it, like this level of fine dining is run-of-the-mill for her.

"Seriously," Brent is saying, "you have to try this wine."

Dorian pulls the bottle out of the ice bucket and reads the label.

"Ehhh," he says. "They did it again."

He holds the bottle out for Katya to see. She makes a face, then shakes her head.

"Did what again?" I ask.

"This house blend," Dorian says. "It's not very good. They try to push this on their diners because the margin is better."

Dorian snaps his fingers. Literally. Snaps. His. Fingers. A server hurrying by to wait on another table stops and backtracks.

"Could you bring us something better?" Dorian asks him. "I'd like a Merlot."

Though Dorian isn't my husband, I'm completely embarrassed by his behavior. Katya doesn't seem fazed at all. Brent, for his part, is doing his best to hide what must be shock. He would never talk to a server like this.

Dorian and the server get into a back-and-forth about what brands of Merlot the restaurant has. Once the server names a brand Dorian deigns to drink, the man then grills the server about vintage. They finally settle on an acceptable wine, and the server hurries off. Now, I like a glass of wine as much as the next woman, but I'm not very knowledgeable about any of it. Dorian, on the other hand, seems to be the stereotypical wine snob and very arrogant about it.

"You come to a place like this," Dorian says, once the server is thankfully out of earshot, "and they try to give you third-rate wine."

"You're right," Brent says, surprising me. He's not a wine snob either, but I guess he's trying to get on this man's good side. I have to admit, I don't like it. "I'm glad they have a Merlot you like."

Dorian waves the comment away. "So, Brent, how's the development coming along?"

Brent descends into what I politely call technobabble. He's explaining the functionality of the app he wants to develop that will drive his business. When Brent told me about his idea for a side hustle before he went on the retreat, it was a much more modest proposal, involving the development of a fairly straightforward app. This business idea he's discussing with Dorian is not that. Now Brent is talking about an app that itself will create *other* apps through machine learning. I might be a data analyst, but all this coding is a bit over my head. I look over at Katya. She seems bored. She's already got her phone out and is texting away.

"So," I say, "how long have you and Dorian been married?"

"Two years now," she says, putting her phone down. "We met when Dorian traveled to Ukraine for work."

"You're from the Ukraine?" I ask.

She laughs. "It's not *the* Ukraine. Just Ukraine. Americans always say *the.*"

"I'm sorry," I say, blushing terribly. "I was only repeating what I'd heard others say. I didn't know."

"I know, but it is wrong," she says.

Okay, we're not off to a great start.

"Where in Ukraine are you from?"

"Would it mean anything to you if I told you?"

Oh boy.

Katya smiles. "I joke. Sorry. I didn't mean to make you feel awkward. I am from Kyiv."

I force a laugh.

Katya turns to face me. Her dress is so short that I get to see a lot of her legs. A few of the men sitting nearby are stealing glances at her, but she either doesn't notice or doesn't care.

"How long have you and Brent been married?"

I tell her our story. She listens with a surprising amount of interest. I realize while I'm speaking that she's judging us as well, that later she and Dorian will discuss what we shared, so I make sure to really talk Brent up.

"He's a great guy," I say. "He works really hard, all the time. He's very reliable, very dependable. You can always count on him. And he's always got these great ideas."

"Yes." Katya smiles. "I know what you mean. With Dorian, it is always go-go-go."

I find myself relaxing a bit. "Yes. Exactly."

The server returns with a bottle of Merlot. Dorian repeats the same process Brent performed in tasting the wine. He sips and lets it sit in his mouth for a long moment while our server waits anxiously. Finally, he swallows.

"It's not bad," he says. "We'll take it."

The server puts the bottle down and is about to go, but Dorian grabs his wrist.

"Wait a minute," he says. "I'm ready to order."

Dorian has neither consulted the menu, nor asked any of us if we're ready. I really don't like this guy at all. I make a face at Brent, who pretends like he hasn't seen it. Katya quickly picks up her menu.

"When my husband is ready," she says, "he is *ready*. If you know what I mean."

I almost point out that the world does not revolve around Dorian, but Brent shoots me a wary look as if he's read my mind. He gives me a subtle shake of the head. I bite back what I really wanted to say. I understand why Brent is treading carefully here, but does he really want to do business with a guy like this? They are going to have to interact with each other for a number of years.

I consult the menu. I wasn't ready to order, but when the server looks to me, I just pick one of the things I was interested in. Katya takes her time reading the menu, and Dorian grows impatient while we wait for her to order. In the end, she just asks for a salad.

Putting a hand on her nonexistent stomach, she gives me a sheepish look. "I am trying to watch my weight."

This woman has no weight to lose. As a matter of fact, she could stand to put on a few pounds.

The server leaves us once more.

"So, Brent," Dorian says, "I know dozens of men just like you, all of them claiming to have the next big idea. Tell me why I should invest in you and not them."

I'm expecting Brent to get that deer-in-headlights look. He's usually uncomfortable when someone puts him on the spot, as this guy has just done, and incredibly rudely, I might add. I feel Katya watching me intently too, but I keep my eyes on my husband.

Brent does not freeze, however. He just smiles easily.

"Come on, Dorian. We've been over this. You've seen the numbers, and you know what the projections are. If you didn't take me seriously, we wouldn't be having dinner right now. You like what you've seen, and I think you've already made your mind up in general. Now it's just a matter of getting down to brass tacks."

I cannot believe those words just came out of my husband's mouth. This retreat has turned him into this uber-confident man.

For a very charged moment, Dorian does not respond. Then he cracks the slightest of smiles.

"Alright," he admits. "I like what I've seen. But you're not in the end zone yet, Brent. You've still got some convincing to do."

"Oh, business, business." Katya rolls her eyes. "So boring, don't you think?"

Not really. I mean, maybe it is to her because she doesn't need to think or worry about it ever. She lives a life of luxury, without a care in the world. But to me, Brent starting his own business would be life-changing.

Brent begins. "There's a huge market out there. I think, inside one year's time, we can capture ten to fifteen percent of that market. Fifteen percent of a lot is *a lot*." He laughs at his own joke, but Dorian doesn't find the humor. "Anyway ..."

"I have to use the bathroom." Katya gives me a look. "Would you like to join me?"

I really wanted to hear the men talk about Brent's new business, but I feel like it'd be impolite to turn Katya down. I put my napkin on the table and rise.

"Be right back," I say.

Brent and Dorian barely register our departure. They're too busy discussing metrics, trends, market share. I have no idea how Brent figured all this out, but now I understand why he's been working so hard. He really knows what he's talking about. I'm impressed.

I just hope Dorian is too.

"The bathroom is this way," Katya says.

I follow her as we snake our way through the restaurant. We could have proceeded to an aisle and then walked along the wall to reach the hallway leading to the restroom. But instead, Katya decides to cut diagonally across the floor, weaving and strutting her way between tables. Just about everybody we pass stops to gawk at her. I feel like an afterthought, following along behind Katya.

There is an attendant in the bathroom. Women leave her tips before exiting. I make a face that I hope Katya doesn't see. I didn't bring any cash with me to the restaurant. Will it look tacky if I don't leave a tip? I don't want to come off as cheap or impolite in front of her, not when her husband is considering investing a lot of money.

Katya stops in front of the first set of mirrors to study herself. She fusses over an eyelash for an inordinately long time.

"I cannot get my makeup right," she says.

"I think you look great."

Still hunched over the sink, Katya looks over her shoulder at me. "Do you think?"

I nod. "Yes. You're beautiful."

She shrugs, like she's used to hearing compliments. "I used to be model in Ukraine. They always tell me my ass too big. Do you think?"

She sticks her rear end out and wiggles it back and forth. Another woman who's finishing up at the next sink looks over, surprised.

"Uh," I stutter, uncomfortable that I have to offer a perfect stranger an opinion on her rear end. I mean, I would feel awkward if Paige asked me the same question. "No, no, not at all."

I'm not used to offering my opinion on another woman's derriere. But Katya is watching my reaction intently in the mirror.

"I can tell you were a model." I'm not sure what else to say. "You look, uh, really beautiful."

The other woman who couldn't help but eavesdrop on

our conversation shakes her head as she leaves the bathroom, apparently offended by Katya's brazen question.

Katya opens her expensive-looking clutch and fishes out a tube of lipstick. She applies another layer to her lips.

"Dorian paid for these." She wiggles her shoulders, but I know she's not talking about her shoulders. "He likes a woman with big breasts."

"Oh?"

My face is a million degrees now. Katya finishes with her lipstick, then suddenly turns to me.

"Your husband has mental problems, I have heard."

"I'm sorry?"

She makes a sad face. "It is okay. I do not mean to judge. I heard Brent has mental problems."

There are other women in the bathroom, and every single one of them, including the attendant, is now turned our way. I'm blushing terribly.

"I don't know who told you that," I say, "but Brent is a good man. He—"

"He took leave of absence, yes?"

Oh no. No, no, no, no, no. I did not expect this to come up. But it has. Why didn't I anticipate it? Why didn't Brent? We sort of game-planned for this evening, outlining the things we wanted to say and how we wanted to say them. But we did not plan for this.

"He took some time off work," I admit. I don't want to be caught in a lie. "In part because he wanted to spend some time getting his new business off the ground."

It's not an outright lie. But it's not exactly the truth either.

Katya regards me skeptically for a moment before nodding. "I understand. Men, they can be so selfish, you know?"

"Not Brent," I say. "He's a wonderful man."

Katya purses her lips. "We heard that he was going to be fired and went away to keep from being fired."

"What?"

"In this country," Katya says, "all you have to say is you're depressed or have condition, and they cannot fire you. Right?"

That's not exactly how it works, but I'm not an attorney and don't feel like getting into a legal discussion with this woman who is being quite rude.

"That's not what happened," I say. "I don't know who told you that, but that is not at all the truth."

Katya gives me a doubtful look.

"Brent took some time off work. Outside of a few days here and there, he hasn't taken a vacation in, gosh, nearly three years. He's a good man. Your husband can count on him."

"Has he ever run business before?"

Now I see what's happening. While Dorian pumps Brent for more information on the business idea, Katya is going to pump me for more private information.

"No," I say, "but he's really good with people. And when he's passionate about something, like he is this idea, then he's unstoppable."

"First time for everything," Katya says. "Not everybody is like my husband, a born leader."

Or a born jerk, I don't say.

Katya thinks it all over. Then she smiles conspiratorially. "I should not be telling you this, but Dorian is really interested in your husband's idea." She lowers her voice. "Very much. I should not say a word, but I like you. Dorian likes a man who is assertive. Tell your husband to be more so."

"Okay ... thank you."

Katya rubs my shoulder. "Dorian *wants* this to work out, he really does, but he will ask you for something in return. He does not know you at all, and he does not know Brent that well, so he will ask for more than words, promises."

I'm confused. What more can we do other than discuss our planning and strategy?

Katya looks me up and down. "Your husband is lucky man. You are really sexy."

Only one person on this planet has ever called me sexy, and that's Brent. He's my husband, so it doesn't really count.

I'm blushing again. "Oh, thank you."

"You are," Katya says. "Brent loves you very much."

How can this woman tell? We've just met, and she only saw the two of us together for a few minutes. I don't think Brent and I even interacted in that time other than a few discreet looks.

As if she's read my mind, Katya answers, "He talks to Dorian about you. He tells my husband how great a woman you are, how you will be able to help the business because you are data scientist."

Me, help the business? Brent and I haven't discussed this yet. And I'm a data *analyst,* not scientist. They're not really the same thing, but I don't correct her.

"He told Dorian that you and he would run business together, that you were really smart."

Wow.

"Your husband is a lucky man," Katya says. "Are you ready to go back out?"

I haven't gotten a chance to fix my makeup. After a quick check in the mirror, I tell her I'm ready.

"Oh, before we go," she says, "text Brent and tell him to be more assertive."

"Oh, right." I get my phone out. "Thank you so much, Katya."

She smiles prettily at me. "I shouldn't say these things, but I like you."

I text Brent as quickly as I can, urging him to be more assertive. Katya checks her phone while I'm doing this. When I'm done, Katya holds out her palm.

"Let's give them a minute to talk," she says. "Let Brent be more assertive."

"Alright."

She puts her rear end on the edge of the counter behind her. "You really think my ass isn't too big?"

"No."

"Would you tell me the truth if you thought yes?"

I don't know what to say. I must look like I've swallowed a canary. Katya bursts into laughter.

"I joke with you, sorry."

"Oh. Right."

"What is Brent like in bed?"

I'm immediately put off by the question. That is none of her business. Though the woman has just shared what could be really helpful information.

"He's ... great."

She laughs. "I embarrass you. Sorry. In Ukraine we speak frank with friends."

"Yeah, we don't. I mean, I'm not used to that."

"You see how Dorian is?" she asks, edging closer to me. More women have come and gone from the bathroom now. Not one went past without sizing Katya up, then looking quizzically at me. They're all wondering what we're doing here together, the runway model and the plain Jane.

"How Dorian is?" I ask.

"Yes," she says. "Very aggressive. He knows what he wants and asks for it right away?"

That's one way of putting it. "Yes."

"In bedroom, he is opposite. He lets me be in charge."

I laugh nervously. All this bedroom talk is making me uncomfortable. I enjoy sex as much as anybody, but I don't even discuss my exploits, for lack of a better word, with my best friend, Paige. I've known Katya for less than fifteen minutes, and she already wants to know what Brent is like in the bedroom.

"I love it," she says. "I let him be the boss everywhere else, but in bedroom, he answers to me."

I don't know what to say. Katya must be able to tell how uncomfortable I am, but she doesn't change the subject. I force myself to smile up at her.

"You two must love each other a lot," I manage to say.

"We do," she says. "But if he ever cheats on me, like he did with other wife, I will take all his money and go."

Wow.

"Katya, you said a moment ago Dorian was going to ask us for something," I say. "Do you know what that is?"

She smiles at me. "I already said too much. How about we go back to the table?"

BRENT AND DORIAN are deep in conversation as we cross the restaurant. Brent is very animated, his hands moving almost as quickly as his mouth. By the time we reach the table, he's just finishing up his point.

"If we move quickly," he says, "we'll have at least two, maybe three years of lead time. That's a lot of runway. Any potential competitors will be playing catch-up for nearly thirty months."

Dorian thinks it over. "You've got a point there, Brent."

As we take our seats, Katya gives me a knowing look. Dorian eyes his much younger wife.

"You were in there forever. What do you women *do* in the bathroom?"

Katya takes his hand. "You wish you knew."

We all have a good laugh at this. While Dorian and Katya are busy looking in each other's eyes, I steal a glance at Brent, who gives me a discreet wink. Apparently, things went well with Dorian while we ladies were in the bathroom. I'm excited for him, even though I don't much care for Dorian. Hopefully he's going to be, as Brent put it, an angel investor, someone who puts a lot of money into a business but doesn't interfere much. Brent might be able to get along well with this man during a dinner date, but I'm not sure he'd thrive if Dorian, or somebody like him, was constantly looking over his shoulder.

Dorian pours his wife a glass of the Merlot, then offers it to me. "Would you like to try?"

"Thank you."

I have to admit, the Merlot is *much* better than the house blend they brought us. Maybe there's something to what Dorian said, and the restaurant is just trying to increase its profit margins by pushing its own wines. And, to be fair, if you're going to pay this much money for a meal and drinks, then shouldn't you only get the best stuff?

I'm relieved when the food arrives. I'm ready for this night to be over. Poor Katya's salad is really small. There is no way I could subsist on that for even one meal. But she doesn't seem bothered at all. Brent and Dorian tuck into their steaks right away. I take my time, wanting to savor every bite of my lobster ravioli.

When we're about halfway through our meal, Dorian gets a call. He checks the caller ID.

In his gruff manner, he announces, "I have to take this."

Dorian heads outside. We continue to eat quietly. I'm getting full, but Brent isn't slowing down. Katya, on the other hand, has barely touched her meager salad, though she is drinking a lot of wine. Dorian returns, but when he sits this time, he puts his phone on the table next to his plate, like he's expecting another call.

"So, Mary," Dorian says, "a man is only as good as the woman behind him. Tell me what you bring to the table."

"Excuse me?" I say, offended.

Dorian peers at me from across the table, not saying a word.

"My wife does *not* stand behind me," Brent says. Dorian shoots him a nasty look, like he's somehow overstepped by defending me. "Mary and I are a partnership. You will not speak to her like that. I don't care how much money you have to offer."

Nobody moves. Nobody says anything. I was really offended by what Dorian said, but I fear Brent has gone too far here. He might have just shot himself in the foot. Not that I particularly want him to work with a guy like Dorian, who seems like a real jerk, but angel investors are few and far between.

"I want you to apologize to my wife." Brent shakes his head. "Or we're done here."

My hero. If it was appropriate to swoon right now, I totally would. But we're in the middle of what has become a very heated conversation. All eyes are on Dorian now, including Katya's.

His lips form a thin line, and he nods appreciatively. "I respect a man who won't take crap from anybody. A business owner needs to be assertive."

Katya shoots me a quick look. I pretend not to notice. I don't want Dorian catching on.

"I only wanted to see how you'd both react," Dorian answers. "That was important to me. I don't want to do business with people who can be pushed around."

"You could have found a more polite way of going about it," I say, not able to help myself.

He smiles. "You're right. Sorry, it's just my nature. I cut right to the chase."

Katya shakes her head. "My husband. Deep down he is big teddy bear. You will see."

I doubt that very much. And, honestly, I don't want to get to know this man any better. If he wants to bankroll my husband's business and then be hands-off, that's fine with me. But he'd better not expect to be invited over to our house. I won't be sending him a Christmas card.

Dorian gets another call. After checking the number, he shakes his head.

"I'm sorry, Brent, but something has come up. I'm going to have to cut this dinner short." He holds up a finger and answers his phone. "I'll call you back in ten minutes."

Without waiting for a response, he hangs up. Dorian pockets his phone and nods at Katya, who gets up from her chair. Dorian finishes his glass of wine in one heaping gulp, then sets the glass down on the table.

"You have to leave?" Brent asks.

"I'm afraid so," Dorian says. "I really enjoyed meeting you, Mary."

He offers his hand. This strange evening has certainly come to an abrupt end. I shake his hand. He squeezes a little too hard, like most guys do. Katya leans in to give me a kiss. I expect her to go for the cheek, but instead her lips home in on mine, and she lingers a bit too long.

"Nice meeting you. Let's get together sometime," she says.

"I'd like that," I say, still reeling from the more-than-friendly kiss she gave me.

Brent gets up. Katya kisses him full on the lips, which makes me a little nuts.

"I'll be right out, hon." Dorian hands the valet ticket to his wife, along with a hundred-dollar bill. "Have them bring the car around."

She playfully blows him a kiss, then struts her way out of the restaurant. Dorian watches her go.

"She is something, isn't she?"

"Your wife is very beautiful," I say.

Dorian nods. "I know." Then he turns to Brent. "Now look, Brent. I want to move forward with this."

Brent's eyes light up. Though I have some misgivings about this man, I'm really excited about the prospect. Even if it doesn't work out with Dorian, it shows that *somebody's* interested. That means other investors would be too.

"The way I see it, to do this right, you really need a million dollars of start-up capital," Dorian says.

My jaw almost hits the floor. Where did this figure come

from? When Brent first had this idea, he didn't think he'd need to pay for anything other than a website and email service provider. That's it. We were talking hundreds of dollars—at most a few thousand. I have no idea how we got from four figures to a *million dollars.*

But that's not the most surprising part of this. Nope.

What's more surprising is the fact that Brent is nodding his head.

He's agreeing with Dorian that he needs a million dollars.

"The more I think about it, the more I agree," Brent says. "I'm not sure we need a million, but certainly—"

"You absolutely need it," Dorian says. "And that's the bare minimum. Look, Brent, I've been around the block a few times. I've invested in a dozen businesses like yours, so I know what has to happen and what's going to work. The guys who can't commit, who want to hedge their bets from the beginning, they're the ones who fail. In fact, they don't even *get the chance* to fail. They don't get off the ground. That's not my game. I want somebody who's all in. If you can't commit, then I'll take my money elsewhere."

"No, Dorian, hold on. Mary and I are very serious about this."

Dorian looks him dead in the eye. I'm watching a stare-off, and I know if Brent looks away, he'll lose out on this deal.

My husband stands his ground and does not look away.

Dorian nods. "Yes, I think you are. That's why we're having this conversation. So let's do something. I'm not here to screw around. I want to know you're serious."

I hold my breath. This is what Katya warned me about. Her husband is going to ask us for something now.

"You need a million dollars to make this work," Dorian

says. "I want more than your word that you're committed. I want you to show me this is for real."

"How do we do that?" Brent asks.

Dorian pretends to think it over, but I can see right through the act. He already knows what he's going to ask. He's probably known since before he sat down to dinner tonight. Dorian is one of those rare, very fortunate people, who always knows right away what they want and can think several steps ahead.

"You need a million dollars of start-up capital," Dorian says, like he's laying down a proclamation. "I will invest five hundred K. But I want *you* to put up the rest. That way, I know you're invested, both literally and figuratively."

"Dorian," Brent says, looking overwhelmed, "I don't have—"

Dorian holds out a palm. "I don't want to hear *I don't* or *I can't*. If you want to do this, come up with half the money. That way, I know you're serious and not just looking to bilk a wealthy guy with too much money on his hands and not enough expertise in his brain. Come on. Let's do something here."

Brent looks over at me. I don't know what he wants me to say. We don't have a half million dollars. I don't even have that much from what my parents left, not that I'd tap into it. That money is supposed to be part of our retirement savings. Putting it all toward a business venture is incredibly risky. I believe in Brent of course, but there are no guarantees. Most start-ups, from what I hear, fold inside a year. The thought of putting all that money at risk is a nonstarter for me.

"We'll have to think about it," Brent says.

"Don't think too long," Dorian says. "I've got other

people, just as qualified and more committed than you, asking me for money."

He offers his hand. Brent shakes it.

"Thanks for meeting with us," he says.

"Thank *you*, Brent," Dorian says, then turns to me. "It was a pleasure meeting you, Mary. Your husband is a lucky man."

And with that, Dorian is gone.

17

BRENT – DAY ZERO – APRIL 11

I wake early, while it's still dark out. Carefully, so as not to wake Mary, I slip out of bed and take a long, warm shower. I'll definitely be sharing a bathroom while I'm away on the retreat, so this might be my last long, steamy shower for the next month.

I packed last night, but I take a moment to go through my things again. Two pairs of sneakers, jeans, sweats, under-wear, socks, undershirts, T-shirts, long-sleeved shirts, two pairs of gloves for working on the farm, a pair of boots, two towels, toiletries. It's all there. When I zip the luggage bag closed, Mary stirs in the bed.

"Are you leaving already?" she asks.

"Not yet," I say.

Carrying my bag, I tiptoe downstairs and make myself some oatmeal and coffee. I hate fruit, but I force myself to eat an apple. On the farm, I'm going to be forced to eat healthy, so I might as well get started now. I sit in the darkness of our house and look around. I'm really going to miss not being here. I'm as much a homebody as Mary is.

When I'm done eating, I get up and walk around. I don't have to leave just yet, got another twenty minutes or so. Mary wants to see me off too, so I don't want to get on the road early. I peer out the bay window in our living room and look across the street to Mrs. Ryers's house. Despite the hour, there's a light on in her first-floor window. She has trouble sleeping.

There's an unfamiliar gray SUV parked in front of Mrs. Ryers's home. I don't recognize it as belonging to anybody on the street. The lights are off, but it looks like the car is running. Curious, I watch the vehicle for a moment. I think there's a guy sitting behind the wheel.

The front door to Mrs. Ryers's house opens, and the older woman appears. Her porch light activates, and she steps outside. She must have noticed the car also.

Mrs. Ryers stares openly at the car. It looks like she's holding a phone. The SUV suddenly pulls away from the curb and heads down the street. Its lights are still off. I wonder if that was an oversight or intentional. Maybe the driver doesn't want anybody getting his license plate.

Mrs. Ryers goes back into her house.

"What are you looking at?" Mary asks.

She has quietly come down the stairs and stands in the foyer in one of my old T-shirts, her feet bare. My shirt is big on her.

"Nothing," I say, not wanting to worry her. Mrs. Ryers probably took photos, and by now I'm sure she has already contacted the police. I really like her, but she is the busybody of the street. "Just wanted to take a look at the neighborhood before I go."

I meet Mary in the foyer. We embrace for a long time. The longer I hold her, the less I want to leave. I begin to wonder if I could do all these things myself, at home. If I could just get a better mindfulness app and work on my anxiety and exercise more regularly and eat better ... I *could* do all this on my own. I don't need to go away.

Mary kisses me. "I'll miss you."

"I'll miss you too."

She lets me go. I should really tell her about my parents. It's not right, keeping something like this from her. I've never done it before. But I don't want our last moment together to be awkward. I want to go out on a high note.

"I love you," I say.

"I love you too."

We kiss, and then I pick up my bag. I stop in the doorway to give her one last look. She has puffy, tired eyes, and her hair is a mess from sleeping, but she's beautiful. I love my wife terribly.

"Bye."

Outside, I pop the trunk and toss my bag inside. Then I get behind the wheel. I can see Mary standing in the doorway, watching me. All she has on is my T-shirt, and normally she'd be worried about one of the neighbors catching sight of her, but she doesn't seem to care right now. Mary slowly raises her hand and waves. Then she palms the glass of the outer door.

I blow her a kiss and then back out of the driveway. The sun is just coming up now. A fog covers most of the road as I pull away. Once I'm in the street, I wave to her one more time. The temptation to turn around and go back inside the house and forget all about this retreat is almost overwhelming. I'm nervous and don't know what to expect, and I don't want to be away from Mary for this long. My coworkers are going to talk about me and be weird when I get back, and that might actually make the job worse than it already is.

But I need to do this.

I drive away.

IT'S ABOUT TWO HOURS' drive to the retreat. First I drive from one suburb to the next, passing homes and strip malls and chain restaurants and office complexes. Then there are no office complexes. Then there are fewer and fewer strip malls and no chain restaurants. Then the houses grow more distant, bigger, set farther away from the road.

My mind is racing. I can't help it. There are supposed to be seven other guests attending the retreat, and the couple running the business have hired a few people to help. I'm not great at meeting new people or making small talk. What am I going to say? How much should I share? What will the other people on this retreat be like? Will they be better off than me, or worse? I don't know, and it's too much to think about.

Mom and Dad did this, which means I should be able to do it, right? Compared to them, I'm a well-adjusted saint. I shouldn't be worried.

But I am.

The closer I get to my destination, the more tightly I grip the steering wheel. The bad feeling in the pit of my stomach won't go away. The website provided an overview of the program, and the owners gave a little more detail in our email exchange, but the truth is, I don't really know what to expect. Will I have any time to myself? Or will I be working or meditating or exercising at all times? I'm really anxious and can feel my heart racing. I'm having trouble breathing.

I have to pull over and get out of the car.

I'm in the middle of the countryside. Long, green gently sloping hills stretch out away from me. Silos stand like obelisks beside commercial farms. A tractor plods along slowly past me on the road. The driver gives me a little wave. I manage to return the gesture, even though I can't catch my breath.

Get yourself together. You can do this. You *have* to do this.

I focus on all the positives. Mom and Dad seemed to have completely changed. The owners have shared a few success stories also, of people turning their lives around. One of their former clients just got her dream job; another has finally published a book; still another started her own business. If things can change for them, things can change for me too.

I put my hands on top of my head and breathe. The fog is worse out here. The tractor hasn't gone more than a few hundred yards up the road, but I can't see it even though its four-ways were on.

You have to do this.

For Mary.

I get back in the car. My heart has slowed, and my breathing is under control again. I'm about six miles away now, very close.

I have to take it slowly the rest of the way because of the poor visibility. It's turned into a cloudy day, not bright or warm enough yet to burn away the fog. The next six miles tick away, bit by bit. My hands are shaking when the GPS tells me to turn ahead. I'm driving along an old wooden fence. The fog covers the grounds to my right. Like a phantom in the mist, the farmhouse appears as a looming gray structure in the distance. The GPS tells me to turn right here. I don't even see the entrance till I'm past it. I have to slam on the brakes, back up, then turn in.

The dirt road leading to the farmhouse is bumpy. I only see one other vehicle, parked near the home. Am I the first person here? Maybe. I don't know whether that's good or bad. Maybe neither. I pull up to the other vehicle and park beside it. The farmhouse is old and massive and a bit more run-down than the pictures online.

Actually, it's a *lot* more run-down. What the heck? I wonder if part of the work I'll be doing consists of repairs to the home. Great. I am *not* handy at all. If they expect me to replace shutters or mend a roof, they'll be in for a bad surprise.

I pop the trunk and get out of my car. I'm actually a few minutes late, so I wonder why I'm the first one here. Maybe the other guests parked their cars somewhere else, out of the way? I don't know. They didn't say anything about that in the email they sent around with all the information. Now I'm really freaking out. Did I get the day wrong? No, that's impossible. I must have read the email with the information a dozen times. Mary did too. Today is the day. I was supposed to be here fifteen minutes ago. I shouldn't be the only one, unless all the other guests are also late. Maybe they arranged for alternate transportation.

That bad feeling I had on the drive here is only getting worse. I'm starting to get *scared*. I don't like the look of the farmhouse. The eerie landscape, shrouded in fog, isn't helping either. I can't see more than twenty feet away. I'm all alone out here. I take my phone out. My reception bounces back and forth between none and one bar. I should leave. I don't like this.

The front door of the farmhouse groans open.

18

SATURDAY – MAY 20

The next morning, Brent is up early again. He's got his gym clothes on, and he's already packed his bag for the day.

"Brent," I say, trying to wake up, "are you leaving already?"

"Yeah," he says. "I want to get a quick workout done at the gym before I get down to work."

"Okay ..."

I sit up in bed. We haven't even talked about the dinner last night with Dorian and Katya. We spent a fortune on it, and then on the way home, Brent didn't want to discuss it. He said he needed the night to decompress and think everything over.

"I'll call you later," he says. "Maybe we could do something fun tonight?"

"Brent," I say, rubbing the sleep from my eyes, "can we *talk* about last night before you go running off?"

He makes a hurt face. "I'm not *running off*, honey. I'm just going to the gym."

"Yes, to the gym, then to the coffee shop or wherever. I've hardly seen you since you got back."

I am shocked by his reaction. Brent literally rolls his eyes and looks up at the ceiling for a moment, like I'm being completely unreasonable. But I don't care. It's *Saturday*. We haven't spent a day together since he returned from the retreat. Things can't go on like this.

Like it pains him, Brent comes over and sits on the edge of the bed. "You're right," he says, trying to sound patient. "We should talk about it."

"Wait ... now?" I ask.

"You wanted to talk," he points out.

"Brent, I just woke up. Could you let me get situated first?"

"Honey, I really wanted to get an early start. I have to run the numbers again. Dorian sent me an email with some different ideas late last night. I want to come up with a slightly different proposal."

I hold my palm out. "Slow down. We haven't even discussed whether we want to be in business with that man."

Brent purses his lips. "I don't see why we wouldn't. You heard him; he just offered us half a million dollars."

"Not exactly," I say. "He said he'd give us the money if we came up with that much ourselves. That's not really the same thing."

"Yeah," Brent says. "But look at it from his perspective, honey. He has to be careful. He can't just invest in anybody and everybody and hope they're on the level."

"Brent." I pinch the bridge of my nose. "We don't have half a million dollars."

"But we almost do." He gives me a look like I'm being thick-headed. "The money your parents left."

I want to point out that my parents left that money to me, but I stop short. Things are getting heated right now, and I don't need to draw such a hard line in the sand.

"That money is for our retirement."

"It's not enough to retire on, Mary. Shouldn't we at least consider using it to grow our wealth?"

I made it clear early on that money was only for emergencies, and that I didn't plan on touching it until I was actually retired. "Brent, we *are* growing our wealth. We both have a 401k and savings. We have enough money. I'm—"

Brent shakes his head. "Look, if we want this guy—or anybody else like this guy—to take us seriously, then we've gotta show up and be willing to put our own money on the line. Otherwise, why would anybody else take us seriously? No investor is doing this out of the kindness of their heart."

I take a deep breath. I love my husband. Dearly. And I can tell how much he wants this to work out. But I'm not willing to put all that money at risk. And I don't appreciate how he's pressuring me into doing something he knows I'm not comfortable with.

"But what about Dorian?" I ask. "He was a jerk. I mean, do you want to partner up with somebody like that?"

"None of these investors are going to be Boy Scouts," Brent says. "They didn't get to the top by being nice, Mary. They got there by not taking no for an answer and willing things to go their way. That's how we have to be if we want to get anywhere."

"Brent, I like my life. Just the way it is. I don't want to uproot everything and—"

"Well, I *don't* like my life the way it is," he snaps. "That's why I went away on this retreat and did all this work. I don't want to work for somebody else the rest of my life. I don't want to grind my life away so somebody else can make all the money. I want to make a name for myself. I want to build *something*. Can't you understand that?"

"Of course I can." I'm trying to stay very calm. "And I want that for you. But I don't like that man. I mean, the way he talked to the servers and you and me? It was ridiculous. I don't trust him."

"You're just not used to dealing with people like him. He didn't inherit a penny. He wasn't born with a silver spoon in his mouth. He had to fight for everything he's got. That's why he's so aggressive."

"Brent, the way he spoke to me was unacceptable."

"It was just a test," Brent says. "And besides, I put him in his place. He will never talk to you like that again. I'll make damned sure of that."

It's true that Brent defended me. But the fact that he's willing to overlook this man's boorish behavior now, even if it was a test like Dorian claimed, is troubling. I think Brent wants to quit his job so badly and also wants this business to get off the ground so much, that he's not thinking clearly. There are some huge red flags, but he's not seeing them.

"Brent," I say, "I don't like him, I don't want to do business with him, and, to be honest, I'm not willing to risk our entire retirement savings on him."

He stiffens and looks away. For a moment, I consider taking it all back. I can tell I've upset him. But I have to stand firm here. He probably thinks I don't believe in him, but that's not the problem at all. Brent's idea can be brilliant, his business plan can be sound, and he can work harder than everybody else—and he can still fail. There are too many things that can go wrong. It'd be foolish to put all that money at risk.

"Well, then I'd better get going," he says, in a flat voice. "If it's not going to work out with this guy, I've gotta find somebody else who's willing to just hand over a million dollars to us."

"Brent, wait—"

He's already up, crossing the room in a hurry. He snatches his bag off the ground.

"Brent, please—"

He whirls in the doorway.

"I thought you believed in me."

"I do!"

"You know what, Mary, an opportunity like this doesn't come along often. This is our chance to really do something."

"Brent, please don't leave. Let's talk about this. Let's, actually, start from the beginning. This idea of yours has changed completely since we started talking about it. At first, all you wanted to develop was an app to help people pay their restaurant bills and bar tabs electronically to save the wait staff the time and trouble. It was something you were going to do in your spare time, here and there, and it wouldn't cost us anything. Then it grew into this, I don't even fully understand what, this thing involving machine learning and AI, and you introduced the idea of angel investors. Now you're telling me we have to show somebody we've got half a million dollars. Can't you see that it's all a bit much to take in?"

His shoulders sag. His face softens.

"You're right, honey."

Like a guilty man, he puts his bag down and returns to the bed. We give each other a big hug. He smells nice. But I can't get over the fact that he also smells different. He doesn't have the same Brent odor as before. Not that I'm one to talk right now, since I probably have terrible morning breath.

"I'm sorry," he says. "I've been living this nonstop ever since I got home. Actually, I spent a lot of time thinking about it while I was away too. I'm excited, and I got carried away. I'm sorry."

He's sorry, but he's also disappointed. I hate being the proverbial fly in the ointment.

"Look," I say. "I don't think we should transfer all the money from our retirement savings. That would be really risky."

"You're right."

His eyes are filled with hope.

I say, "Maybe we could afford a little bit, though."

"What are you thinking?" he asks immediately.

Slow down, Brent. Please.

"I have no idea. This Dorian guy sprang this idea on us last night over dinner. I haven't had time to process it, and you and I literally just had a conversation about it. All I'm saying is, let's think about it, okay?"

He smiles. "He's not that bad, you know."

I guffaw. "Are you kidding?"

"He's not," Brent says. "Once you get to know him."

"How have you gotten to know him so quickly, Brent?" I ask.

He's taken aback by my rather direct question. "I told you before. I've known him for a few years, actually. He's done business with my company. You have to trust me on this."

I don't remember Brent saying he'd known Dorian for years. Regardless of the length of their acquaintance, Dorian rubs me the wrong way.

"Look, Mary, I've been around the guy, and people I trust

at work speak highly about him, alright? I've got a good feeling about this."

Normally I trust my husband's judgment when it comes to people. He's usually good at seeing others for who they are. With Dorian, however, I'm afraid he's not thinking clearly because he so badly wants his new business to get off the ground. But I don't know how to put that delicately, so I let it go.

"Could we spend the day together?" I ask. "Do you really have to run to the gym at six o'clock on Saturday morning, then spend eight hours at the coffee shop?"

Brent looks away and thinks about it.

"Tell you what. I'll be home for lunch. Then we can spend the rest of the day together?"

"Deal," I say.

Sunday – May 21

THE NEXT DAY I wake up with a smile on my face. Brent came home as he promised, and we spent the whole of Saturday afternoon and evening together. We went to a movie, and then he cooked dinner at home. It was the perfect day. We haven't had one of those in a long time.

Brent's gone early again, but I don't mind. We had a wonderful time yesterday. We haven't laughed that much in a long time.

I make myself some breakfast and then don workout clothes. I might catch up with Brent at the gym, but even if I don't, I really want to start exercising more regularly again.

Now that he looks so amazingly hot, I want to push myself to get in the best shape of my life too.

I don't see my husband at the gym, but that's okay; maybe I'll surprise him at the coffee shop. After a killer spin class (I'm proud of myself for going to spin and not water aerobics), I get a quick shower at the gym and then head over to the coffee shop. Before I pull into the parking lot, though, I can see Brent's car is not there. I'm a little disappointed, but I try not to let it get to me. It'd be silly to get low after the amazing day we had yesterday.

I stop in anyway to grab a coffee. The man who waited on us the other day is there working the counter and recognizes me.

"Hey, Mary." Big smile. "How's it going?"

I have to read his name tag. "Hi, Terry. Nice to see you again."

"What can I get you?"

I place my order, wincing at the price. While he's tapping his computer screen, I glance around the place. "I was hoping to run into Brent."

Terry finishes with the order. "Oh? He hasn't been around today."

I frown. "Really?"

Terry nods. "I opened this morning and haven't caught a break since. Haven't seen him."

"Okay."

Terry asks, "Say, how did his big meeting go? He told me about it a few days back."

"Pretty well." I smile, but behind that smile, I'm wondering where Brent is.

"Great."

I don't want to share too much information about the

business. But now Terry has me thinking about it. While he moves on to the next customer, I recall our conversation yesterday morning. I wish I hadn't suggested to Brent that we could move *some* money out of our retirement savings for the business. Call me risk averse all you want, but I don't feel great about it. I'm trying to think of ways to walk that back, convince Brent that we need to be more cautious, when Terry loudly calls my name.

"Mary! Here you go."

I give him a rude look. He wears an apologetic smile.

"Sorry," he says. "I called your name about three times ... is everything okay?"

"Oh, sure. Sorry." I come over and take the coffee. "I was just in my own world for a minute."

"I know exactly what you mean." Terry winks. "Tell your hubby I said hello, alright? And tell him to swing by when he gets a chance. I haven't talked to him in a few days."

I'm halfway to the door when what Terry said hits me. I turn, and the woman behind bumps into my shoulder.

"Hey, watch where you're going," she snaps. She's acting like she almost spilled coffee all over herself, but her cup has a lid on it.

"Sorry," I say.

She passive-aggressively mutters a few more words on her way out, while I move out of the doorway. The line to the counter is long. Terry is busy trying to get through all these customers. I should let him be. But that bad feeling is back in the pit of my stomach. I have to ask. I just have to.

When Terry sees me coming, he frowns. He asks the next customer to give him a moment. The lady is not happy. She thinks I'm jumping the line.

"Something wrong with your order, Mary?" Terry asks.

"Oh, no. I wanted to ask ... um ..." I lean toward him. Terry looks confused. And I feel stupid. How will it sound if I ask this man about my husband?

"Mary." Terry lowers his voice. "Are you sure you're okay?"

"Did you see Brent yesterday?" I blurt out, much more loudly than I would have liked. "He was here in the morning."

Terry shakes his head no.

I feel queasy. Brent definitely told me he would be here in the morning, after his workout. I'm certain of it. And I'm pretty sure he mentioned it yesterday afternoon ... yes, he did, right before we went into the theater.

"I was off," Terry says. "First Saturday I've taken in months."

"Oh." A tidal wave of relief washes over me. "Oh, I see."

Terry gives me a concerned look. "Are you sure—"

"I'm fine." I plaster a smile on my face. "Really. Don't ... please don't tell Brent I was asking you ... I'm just being silly. Could we pretend like we didn't have this conversation?"

Terry nods very slowly. "No worries, Mary. I won't say a word."

I don't know that I believe him. "Thank you."

AFTER LEAVING, I sit in my car and try to talk myself out of the bad feelings I'm having. Almost twenty-four hours ago, my husband and I were enjoying the best day together we've had in years. Now here I am wondering, once more, if there's something wrong. Has he really been spending all this time away from me working on his business? Or is there something else going on?

Brent has his issues, but laziness is not one of them. He is not afraid of hard work or long hours. The last few years, since his company steadily increased his department's workload but naturally refused to bring on more help, fifty-plus-hour weeks have become the norm, as opposed to the exception. He wasn't happy about it, but Brent didn't cut corners. He put the hours in and made sure he got his work done.

But this newfound work ethic is almost, I hate to say it, unbelievable. After his first full week back to work, I thought he'd need this weekend to recover. But instead he worked about four hours yesterday, and today he's—supposedly—going to work even longer, even though tomorrow he'll be back in the office.

I know that starting a new business requires a ton of work, especially in the beginning, but all the same, I'm really starting to wonder if he's used some of this time out of the house doing other things. I don't even want to specify what those other things might be—I *can't*. But I am wondering, in a general, and ominous, sense.

I know it sounds ridiculous in light of how much sex we've had since he's gotten home but I can't help thinking ... is Brent cheating on me?

I mean, what else could he be doing? He was supposed to be at the gym, and I reasonably assumed he'd be at the coffee shop after, but he's nowhere to be seen.

I hate how suspicious I'm being. It's not like me.

Then again, Brent has never given me any reason to be.

I shoot him a text:

> Missed you at the gym. When do you think you'll be home?

Five minutes later, I'm still parked outside the coffee shop and haven't gotten a response. Sighing, I start the engine and drive off.

Though Jim Smith now knows where this Joshua character is staying and is, presumably, surveilling him, I still can't help but constantly check my rearview to see if there's a gray SUV following my car. I just want this—I don't know what to call it—thing with Joshua to be over. There are too many other things going on right now to deal with a stalker.

Not that there's ever a good time.

When I get home, Brent's car isn't in the driveway. As I head inside, I check my phone. He hasn't texted me back.

I spend the rest of the morning catching up on some house chores. Brent normally cleans the bathrooms on the weekends, but I don't know where he is, haven't heard back from him, and despite his boundless energy, I know he'll be tired after he's been out all day and has to get up for work tomorrow. So I get to work scrubbing the showers and toilets.

I forgot how much I hate cleaning the bathrooms. Brent has been doing it forever, all by himself. But for some reason, I get the feeling that the new Brent doesn't have time for this sort of thing—if he even remembers to do it.

I hate how nasty I'm being. I should get out of the house and do something fun, but when I contact Paige, she can't meet up. Her text is short:

> On a hot date with a dreamy guy.

I don't know what to do with myself. When I hear a car coming up the road, I pull the curtains aside and peer out the window. It's not Brent. But looking out at our front yard, I realize how long the grass has gotten. While Brent was away, I paid the kids across the street to take care of it. I didn't arrange for them to come back this week, since I knew Brent would be home. But the grass really is long, and I have no idea when he'll be back.

On the list of chores, mowing ranks pretty low for me, only slightly above cleaning the bathrooms. I should have had a glass of wine before I started all this. It would have made the work a little more fun, I think.

Outside, I fire up the lawn mower. It's an unseasonably hot day. The last time I mowed the lawn, I think we had a different president in the White House. I forgot how cumbersome this thing is. Dad bought it, probably fifteen years ago. Now that I think about it, I'm amazed it still works.

It takes me a good thirty minutes to mow the front and back. I've worked up a sweat by the time I'm pushing the lawn mower back into the shed. I come around the house to admire my handiwork. I missed a spot over by the sycamore tree. I should really hit it with the mower, or at least the weed whacker. But I've been doing chores ever since I got back, and honestly, I'm starting to get really annoyed with Brent. He can get that patch later. And now it's late Sunday afternoon, almost time to figure out what I guess *I'm* going to make for dinner.

I sit on my front steps in the sun, too tired to move. That's when Mrs. Ryers's front door opens.

Great.

I don't really want to talk to her. Not because of what Brent said when he came home, but because I'm just really tired and in a bad mood. Despite the warm weather, Mrs. Ryers is wearing gray pants and a red sweater that looks like it'd be really scratchy and uncomfortable. She waves at me from her porch. I wave back.

For a moment, I think I've dodged the bullet. But then she starts down her steps.

Mrs. Ryers doesn't get around so well anymore. She has to turn almost sideways and step down with her good leg before carefully placing the other on the next step. Seeing her struggle merely to ambulate makes me feel bad for her. She obviously wants to talk to me, and despite how painful it clearly is, she's making a point to come over. The least I can do is get up and meet her near her porch.

"Are you alright?" I ask, hustling over.

That short, painful trip down the stairs has winded her. She clutches at a hip and takes big breaths.

"I'm fine, dear," Mrs. Ryers answers. "Just old. Just very old. But I have to talk to you, Mary. It's important."

Her cheeks are red from the exertion. And I don't think that heart of hers is in great shape either. I feel rotten for not wanting to talk to her a moment ago.

I offer her my arm. "Why don't we sit on your porch, then?"

"Oh, that would be nice," she says.

With my help, she navigates the porch steps a little more easily. She sits in her favorite rocking chair, and I take the patio seat next to it.

"It really is time for me to move," she says, fanning herself.

Hearing her say that makes me sad. I've known her my whole life. She's lived here for *decades*. I can only imagine how the prospect of moving into a home or assisted-living facility must make her feel.

"Are you alright?" I ask, not liking her coloring at all. "Can I get you some water?"

She's about to politely decline out of habit, but then she relents. "That would be very nice of you, Mary. Please go inside and do get yourself a drink while you're in there."

I haven't been in Mrs. Ryers's house in years. Today, apparently, is a day where I do things I haven't done in a long time, like clean bathrooms and mow lawns and enter my neighbor's home. It's a bit like stepping into a time machine. She and her husband never bothered to install central air, and the carpets look about thirty years old. All the furniture on the first floor is exactly the same furniture she's always had, ever since I was a little girl. Old family photos decorate the walls. I see a very young and very beautiful Mrs. Ryers in many of them, here standing next to her husband, and there standing behind a knot of children, and later grandchildren.

The kitchen is really outdated too. I don't see a toaster oven, and the microwave looks about forty years old, very big and bulky. I open her cabinets and find a glass that reads Walt Disney World – 1980. At least, that's what it used to say. Most of the lettering has worn away in the thousands of times it's been run through the dishwasher. I find a companion glass that reads Epcot – 1980. Its lettering is more intact. After filling both from the tap, I return to the porch, where Mrs. Ryers's coloring has improved a little bit.

"Thank you." She takes a long sip from the glass. "That's just what I needed."

I sip from mine as well and then put the glass on the little wooden table between our chairs. "Feeling alright?"

"Much better," she says.

"I'm glad."

"Have you noticed that blue Chevy?" she asks.

I frown, looking up and down the street. I don't see a blue Chevy anywhere. "No."

"It's not here now," Mrs. Ryers says. "But the last few days, I've noticed it going past. It always drives by a few minutes after you get home."

Leave it to Mrs. Ryers to notice something like that.

"It's probably just a coincidence," I say, hiding my true feelings. I don't want to worry the old woman, who seems to be looking for any excuse *to* worry. But it's got me thinking now ... has this Joshua switched cars? Is he stalking me in a different vehicle now?

It's *possible*. But it does seem far-fetched. The private detective has been sitting on the guy's motel. Jim Smith would have noticed if Joshua had switched cars.

"It's always a woman I've never seen driving it," she says. "She looks old. Well, not as old as me. Few people are."

She laughs at her own joke. It makes me feel a little better that it's not Joshua driving this car.

"What is it?" Mrs. Ryers asks, picking up on my silence.

"Nothing." I smile politely. "Just tired from all the yard work."

"It is tiring." Mrs. Ryers leans forward in her rocking chair. "But there is something I have to discuss with you."

"Okay."

Mrs. Ryers looks across the street toward my house. "It's going to sound crazy, but I think it's important."

"What is it?"

She watches the house for another moment, then looks up and down the street like she's checking for vehicles. I wonder if she too has seen the gray SUV. Is that what this is about? It's exactly the sort of thing Mrs. Ryers would notice.

"Your husband is not the same man," she says.

"You're right. He's not. He went on this trip and—"

"No." She holds up a hand. "I don't mean he's *changed*. I mean *he's literally not the same man.*"

Oh boy. I don't even know what to say to her. Nobody on the street has suggested that old age has gotten the better of her, and maybe her mind is starting to go. But Mrs. Ryers is, I hate to say it, really old now. I wonder if she's suffering from dementia. Does that cause paranoia? I think so.

"I can tell you don't believe me," she says.

I want to find a polite way to tell her she's imagining things, but I can't think of one.

"What do you mean?" I ask.

"I mean just what I said," she answers.

"But ..." There's no polite way to tell somebody they're off their rocker. "What are you saying, that some man who looks exactly like him has assumed his identity?"

"Not exactly like him," Mrs. Ryers says, a bit defensively. "I told you when he came home that he looked a little taller."

Taller? That's what she's basing this suspicion on? It's ludicrous. The more reasonable explanation is that Brent is no longer slouching. He has a poise about him now. He projects confidence and stands tall, literally.

She shakes her head. "You think I'm crazy. You think I've got the Alzheimer's probably."

"No, I don't think that."

Mrs. Ryers looks me dead in the eye. She doesn't seem confused or doubtful or muddled. "He *walks* differently."

I've decided the best thing I can do is humor her for a few minutes. "How so?"

"Brent used to take these little steps." She mimics the alleged gait with her hands, putting one in front of the other. "Now he takes *strides.*"

She exaggerates the difference by moving her hands farther apart.

"Oh?" I ask.

She nods vigorously. "It's unusual for a person to change the way they *move.* That'd be like changing your handwriting, you know?"

"I guess. But don't actors do it all the time?"

"Yes, they do," she says. "I'm glad you brought that up, in fact. It seems like Brent's acting now."

I don't know what to tell her.

"You know, you just gave me an idea," she says. "Have you seen him write anything down since he's been back?"

"You're asking me, have I checked his handwriting?"

"Well ... not *checked.*" She seems to realize, all of the sudden, how bizarre her claim is. "But it would be interesting to see, wouldn't it?"

"Mrs. Ryers." I can't help it now. "Brent is Brent. He's my husband."

"Have you—"

A car comes screeching around the corner. It's probably that teenager who lives on the next block. He's always driving way too fast considering this is a residential area with young children only a few houses down the block. I have half a mind to knock on his door and have a conversation with his parents, but then I see whose car it is.

It's Brent.

He hits the brakes and swings his car into our driveway, much too quickly. Brent has always been a careful, conscientious driver. He was in a bad accident when he was eighteen, driving much too quickly around a bend of a rain-slicked road. He flipped his car, nearly totaling it. He should have been badly hurt, but walked away without a scratch. Ever since then he's been very responsible. Our friends make jokes that he actually drives *too* slowly.

Needless to say, I'm surprised.

Mrs. Ryers is watching me. No doubt she's waiting for me to admit that this too is evidence that supports her outlandish claim. Does she really think it's not him? Does she believe, I don't know, that there's a lizard or something underneath that skin, wearing the most realistic Brent-sized costume ever?

My husband throws his door open and jumps out of the car. He's wearing a button-down shirt and khakis and doesn't see me right away as he heads toward our house. But with that sixth sense we all possess, he must feel our eyes trained on his back. Before he reaches the top of the porch stairs, he turns.

"Hey, honey!" I wave to him. "Over here."

He offers me a tentative smile and an even more tentative wave. Mrs. Ryers continues to watch him, but she does not greet him. Brent's eyes drift over to her, and the two of them exchange the strangest of glances. They're looking at one another like they're mortal enemies.

"Mary," Brent says, in an authoritative voice, "could I talk to you for a moment?"

Oh, he wants to talk now? After I texted him hours ago and didn't hear anything back? As much as I don't want to engage with Mrs. Ryers any further today, I also don't want to go running across the street because my husband, who was nowhere to be found all day, demanded it.

"I'll be over in a minute," I say.

Clearly unhappy with that answer, Brent hovers on the steps for a moment longer. He shakes his head reproachfully before heading inside.

Mrs. Ryers has been waiting this whole time for him to disappear, so she can say, "See what I mean?"

"Mrs. Ryers," I say, as pleasantly as I can muster, "that's my husband."

I stand and take another sip of my water. Then I put the glass back on the table between us.

"You know," I go on, "if you ever need help around the house, or—"

"Ask him something only the real Brent would know," she says suddenly.

I'm thrown off by her startling interruption and the desperate look in her eyes.

"You know, like they do in the movies," she explains. "Ask him about some date you went on, see if he *really* remembers."

I give her a smile. "I'll see you later, okay?"

Mrs. Ryers does not say goodbye to me. She is angry that I'm not taking her seriously. I can feel her eyes on me the whole way across the street.

When I get inside, Brent is waiting for me in the foyer. I know he's upset that I was talking to Mrs. Ryers, but I don't care. I'm pretty upset too. He's ignored me all day. It'd be one thing if we'd spent the last week constantly in each other's company—every couple needs a healthy break from time to time. But he's been gone from the house so much since he got back.

I'm going to give him a piece of my mind.

But Brent has other plans.

He rushes right at me before I can say anything.

19

"I told you I didn't want you talking to that woman anymore!" he shouts.

I freeze. For a moment, I really thought he was going to ... to ... do what? Hit me? Grab me? No, that's stupid. Brent has never laid a hand on me. And he never would.

But at the same time, he *is* furious. His anger is scary and unprecedented. Brent never spoke to me like this before the retreat. I move backward till my back hits the front door, and hold my hands out. I need to put some space between us.

"I don't know why you're so angry," I say, trying to get my heart rate under control, "but do *not* yell at me like that ever again."

Brent's face is red. His eyes bulge. A vein throbs on the side of his neck.

"Mary." His voice still has an edge to it. "That woman is *poison.*"

He takes a step toward me, and I quickly dart around him, putting more space between us.

"Stay back," I say, trembling.

When he sees, finally, how panicked I am, the fight immediately goes out of him. Brent makes a pained, apologetic face.

"God, Mary, I'm sorry. I didn't mean to blow up like that."

I continue to back away from him. If this moment weren't so terrifying, I'd think of it as surreal. I've never been afraid of my husband before.

Brent holds his hands out. "I'm sorry, Mary. I'm really sorry."

My voice quavers. "Why di-did you get so angry?"

He closes his eyes and rubs his forehead. "Dorian called me. He made some more demands, which just came out of left field and ... I won't lie, trying to get this business started has been very stressful. I guess I just took it all out on you. That's no excuse, though. Do you forgive me?"

My hands are still trembling. "You spoke to Dorian this morning?"

He nods. "I was at the gym, working out, and he called me out of the blue with some ideas. I was in the middle of a workout, and he just went off, about this and that. Anyway, I asked if we could speak later today, but he couldn't. He basically made it sound like it was now or never to talk, so I agreed to meet with him."

Okay. That explains why I didn't see him at the gym or the coffee shop.

Now that I'm starting to calm down, I get a better look at my husband. He's got a Band-Aid on one side of his face, along the jaw.

"Are you alright?" I ask.

He touches his face. "Oh, this? I cut myself shaving this morning. No big deal."

I take a deep breath. I'm feeling a little better. Brent has apologized, which is appreciated, but that does not mean I can forget about how he just acted.

"Brent," I begin, trying to find the right words, "I understand that getting your business up and running is very stressful, but—"

"I'll never speak to you like that again," he says, looking miserable. "I'm sorry. There's no excuse. Dorian threatened to pull his money, and made all these other demands. I was in a bad mood. It won't happen again."

"Yeah." I tilt my head. "Maybe Dorian is not the right man to partner up with, Brent."

He shakes his head. "No, he absolutely is. The thing is, he might be a little bit of a jerk, but all his ideas are great. I really think we have something here. This time next year, you might be able to quit your job, Mary. In five years' time, if things go the way we think they will, we'll have so much money, we won't know what to do with it."

He's really high on this idea, but I don't share his enthusiasm. I also don't know enough about the industry to reasonably determine whether it's a good idea or not. I kind of have to take him at his word about this.

Brent gives me a proud smile. "I also talked him down."

"You did?"

"Yes." That smile widens. "I told him we could only invest four hundred thousand, and that he'd have to come up with the rest."

"Brent." I've gone from terrified to angry to calm all the way back to furious in the span of a few minutes. Why is my married life like riding a roller coaster? "We *don't* have four hundred thousand dollars to invest. I am *not* willing to risk my inheritance."

"Oh, I get that," he says quickly. "Trust me, I don't want to use *all* the money. That would be stupid. But it goes to show, I can get the guy to move. He's not going to push us around."

My head is spinning. Right now, I don't want to use *any* of that money.

"Why did you call Mrs. Ryers poison?"

Brent's smile slips. His manner changes from relaxed to a bit stiff.

"She's a gossip," he says. "I don't like gossips."

"She's *harmless*," I say.

"Oh yeah?" His anger is rising again. "What were you two just talking about?"

"We were ..." I don't want to tell him. It'll make the woman sound a little off her rocker, and Brent will use it to prove his point. "... only saying hi, Brent. You know, catching up."

He does not believe me.

"About what?"

"The usual neighbor stuff."

"Like what?" he demands.

I hold out a palm. "I don't appreciate being interrogated, Brent."

"Oh yeah?" he asks. "Well, I don't either. Anyway, it seems like you're constantly asking me where I've been, what I've been up to, like I'm some sort of criminal. It's getting *old*, Mary."

Where is this coming from? "I've been pretty understanding, Brent. You were gone a month, and you've spent a lot of time away from home since you got back. I am your wife, after all."

"I can't deal with all this negativity right now." He folds his arms. "I'll be upstairs for a bit, resting. After I'm recharged, I'm going back out to work."

"Brent, please calm down. We need to talk, I think. About everything. I really don't like this Dorian guy—"

He marches upstairs before I can finish.

WHEN I'M ALMOST FINISHED dinner an hour later, I hear him coming down the stairs. I pretend not to notice him, however, as I work over the stove.

"Hey," he says.

I don't turn around.

"*Hey.*"

I stir the pasta, even though it doesn't really need any more stirring. I'm so angry with him that I can't even turn around and give him the courtesy of a look. The timer on the oven beeps. I open it, and the smell of warm Italian bread washes over me.

"Smells good," Brent says.

"Did you come down for dinner?" I ask.

"No."

He moves behind me, but I still haven't turned around. I fuss over the sauce, which is, honestly, done. I turn down the burner so it doesn't start popping.

"I came down to apologize," he says.

I turn off the burners. Using potholders, I lift the bread out of the oven and put it on the cutting board next to the stove on the counter. I still haven't turned around.

"I'm really sorry," Brent says.

I start cutting the bread. It's a little too hot, but I don't want to look at him.

"Honey." His hands are gentle on my shoulders. "Would you please turn around?"

I put the serrated knife down on the cutting board next to the steaming bread. I bite back the tears in my eyes and face my husband.

His hand goes to my cheek.

"I was *way* out of line," he says. "You deserve better than that."

"Brent ..." I look down. "Ever since you got home, things have been so *extreme*."

"I know." He nods. "You're right. You're absolutely right. I'm still learning how to manage this."

He motions in front of himself.

"I've got all these new thoughts," he goes on. "This whole different way of being, and I'm still learning how to be. It's an adjustment. For both of us."

He looks ashamed of himself. I rub his sides. "It's okay, honey. I'm so happy you got the help you needed. But it is *a lot* for me. Is there any way we can slow, like, everything down?"

"Of course," he says.

His hands are on my neck. For a moment, I panic, recalling how angry he was earlier and how it seemed like he was going to ... but his hands are gentle now, caressing. He knows how much a light touch or a kiss on the neck drives me crazy.

"Brent," I say.

He leans in and kisses me. He's such a good kisser. Has he always been so good? It's enough to make me forget about everything that happened earlier. His hands slide up and down my body. As things are starting to heat up, I gently push him away, smiling.

"Let's eat dinner, okay?" I ask. "And maybe talk some more about your business."

He smiles. "Sounds great. But I am looking forward to dessert."

It's such a cringey line. But it makes me laugh.

Brent forces me to sit, and he brings the food, silverware, dishes, and wine out. He pours me a glass, and while we eat the pasta and bread, I ask him about work and the new business. He goes into more detail than usual, speaking with obvious knowledge about the industry. The app he's envisioning won't literally come up with ideas for new apps, but it will develop the coding language for new apps much more quickly and cost-effectively than human coders. It sounds a bit like science fiction to me, but Brent insists AI technology like ChatGPT is already doing some of this. Just when we're finishing up, both our phones buzz.

It's a group text from Jim Smith, telling us to check our email.

> Good news. I was able to access Joshua's room today and obtained evidence that he's been stalking you both. There was a written journal, listing dates and times of your comings and goings, with handwritten notes about your cars, license plates, phone numbers. There are also a few notes about your friend Paige, as well as your neighbors. Apparently, there's an old woman who lives across the street from you and noticed him. She even chased him away once. I'm preparing my report now, along with all the evidence. Once I have it all together, I'll file the police report. In the meantime, I will continue to monitor Smith's activities.

"Wow," I say. "I wonder how he got into the room."

"He probably bribed a maid," Brent says.

"Can he do that, legally?"

"I guess." Brent shrugs. "Either way, I'm happy."

As scared as I am of Joshua, I didn't want the detective to do anything illegal.

Brent can tell I'm not thrilled. "Look, it's a *motel room*. It's not like it's the guy's house. He doesn't own the place. Maids can go in and out as they wish, pretty much. Jim probably told the owner this guy was up to no good, and the owner *let* him snoop around. It's all on the level."

"Are you sure?"

"Honey." He reaches for my hand. "This is a good thing."

He's right, of course. I'd rather we had evidence of this guy stalking us than not have any.

20

BRENT – DAY THREE – APRIL 13

I've made a terrible mistake.

    I should have known better. God, the one time I'm really stupid, the one time I decide not to be skeptical, is the one time I get into serious trouble. It just goes to show that all it takes is one bad decision and your life is ruined.

    I don't know what time it is, but it feels early. Maybe four or five o'clock in the morning? I don't know. I can't tell. I'm in a windowless room, and there's no light filtering in under the door.

    I should have known ... I should have known. Now I'm stuck here.

    The room I'm in is small. There's a tiny cot pushed up against the wall. The room is narrow. In two normal strides, I cover the distance from one side to the other. The room is a bit longer than it is narrow. I can cover the length in less than four steps.

    Other than the bed, there's no other furniture in the room.

    The bucket is in the other corner. It's amazing what you

can get used to. How adaptable the human sensory experience is. I don't even smell my own waste in that bucket anymore. But I haven't gotten used to the *idea* that it's right there, only a few feet away from where I'm sleeping, from where I eat.

They brought me an apple for dinner last night.

One apple.

That's it.

Even if they don't have any other food, even if they couldn't afford to buy anything else, they could have certainly given me more apples. After all, this is a farm, and they've got an orchard on the property. I saw it. I know it's there. I know it's real, unlike everything else about this place. It's not like they're going to run out of apples any time soon.

I get a bad feeling that from here on out, however long this goes, all I'll be eating is apples. If my situation weren't so dire, Mary would find it humorous that I'm going to be forced to eat fruit, and nothing but fruit. She knows how much I hate it.

At least apples are nutritious.

That gnawing sense of hunger hasn't gone away, though. Since I got here, they haven't fed me enough. An apple here, a slice of bread there, that's it. But I can't say I'm surprised. In fact, I'm not surprised at all. Honestly, it's surprising they've given me anything at all to eat.

I don't know why I'm still alive.

They haven't told me why I'm here yet. They're trying to break me, obviously. This is the same thing the police do—though obviously without these extreme measures—to suspects. Put them in a room by themselves, cut them off from the rest of the world, don't tell them anything. This is probably exactly what they do to terrorists or suspected terrorists. Lock them away, barely feed them, don't let them see the sun, wait till they're starved and aching with thirst, force them to sleep horribly for days on end, make them psychologically vulnerable. Then they'll do and say whatever you want.

I force myself to stand. The room wobbles. I'm lightheaded. They haven't given me enough water. Putting a hand against the concrete wall, I steady myself. A few breaths later, the room stops spinning.

It's so cold down here. They only left me with one old blanket. If I were trapped down here in winter with just my clothes and this blanket, I would probably freeze to death. It's a terrifying thought.

Right on cue, a shiver runs through me. I don't want to think about being down here in the winter. I *can't*. By then ...

By then, what?

The truth is, I don't know what's going to happen. And that's the most terrifying part about this entire experience. I'm completely cut off from the world. They took my phone. I am all alone in this tiny, soundproof room in this sprawling basement, on this farmhouse in the countryside. Nobody will even *start* looking for me for another four weeks.

And no one else is coming.

It's just me.

And them.

There's a slot in the door, large enough to pass a tray of food and small thermos through. That's how they'd been giving me my meals. I tried grabbing his wrist the first time dinner came, but it was just out of reach.

My wrist is chained to the far wall of this room. When the chain is fully extended, I can just reach the door.

The sound of the slot opening wakes me later. It could be

fifteen minutes, or it could be a couple of hours. I have no way to tell time down here.

"Brent, you awake?"

The light streaming in through the slot is weak, but also blinding. I've been living basically in darkness for the last three days.

I raise a hand to shield my eyes. Do they finally want to talk?

"What do you want?"

"How's your bucket, is it full?"

"What do you want?" I repeat.

"Check your bucket first."

I get off the bed, more slowly this time. But I still get light-headed.

"I need more water," I say.

"First check the bucket."

I can't see it that well. I lift it into the light from the slot in the door. The bucket is about half full. Up close, the smell hits me.

"I need it changed out."

"We'll change it out," he says.

"I need water," I say. "And more food."

"You'll get it. So long as you behave."

I laugh mirthlessly. "What the hell else am I going to do in here? How can I not behave?"

"We're going to ask you questions," he says. "And you'd better answer them."

"Or what?"

"I think you already know."

I shake my head. "I want to hear you say it."

"Come on, Brent," he says. "It doesn't have to be like this."

"You're right. You can let me out."

He laughs. "Not happening. Not *yet*, anyway."

"I need another blanket," I say. "It's too cold in here. And food and water."

"You're in no position to make demands."

I'm trying really hard not to break. I don't want to give him the satisfaction of seeing me cry, or witnessing me beg. But with each passing moment, I can feel my resolve crumbling. I can't go on like this forever, maintaining a stiff upper lip. I'm not Superman. I'm not James Bond. I'm just a regular person, like everybody else.

"Are you ready to answer our questions?"

"Let me out," I say. "And maybe we'll talk."

"Hmmm. Not yet, I guess. You need another day or two, I see."

"Wait—"

The slot slams back into place, plunging what has become my cell once more into darkness. I pound on the door and cry out for him to come back, but he doesn't. I sit back down on my cot and force myself not to cry.

21

MONDAY – MAY 22

The next day, Brent is late getting up. He's normally at the office by eight o'clock, but at seven forty-five, he's still in bed, lightly snoring. I usually don't wake him up for anything, but I don't want him going in to the office too late. Despite how great he made his first week back at the office sound, Aaron isn't going to be too happy if Brent starts strolling in late and also leaving earlier than usual.

"Hey, honey," I say, gently laying a hand on his shoulder. "It's almost eight o'clock. Don't you think you should get up?"

He doesn't seem alarmed by the hour. Yawning, Brent sits up in bed and stretches. "I'm going to sleep for another few minutes."

I think he should get a move on, but Brent is a grown adult, and I don't want to mother him. So I let it go. I head back downstairs to heat up some oatmeal and start my own workday. But a few minutes turns into nearly a half hour. When I realize how much more time has passed, I stop what

I'm doing and listen. I don't hear Brent moving around upstairs.

I *really* don't want to be his task manager. We've never had to do that with each other before. But Brent is going to be *late* if he doesn't get up right now. I go back upstairs and, less gently than before, touch his shoulder.

"Brent. It's late."

He opens one eye. "What time is it?"

"Almost eight thirty."

He waves a hand. "I'm going in late this morning. I need the rest."

His one eye closes. I stand there like an idiot. I shouldn't have to pester him about punctuality.

"Do you think that's a good idea? You left early last week, and it's only your second Monday back in the office after your lea—"

"I'll get up in a few minutes, Mary," he says dismissively.

I back away from the bed. I was afraid this was going to happen. Brent has been burning the proverbial candle at both ends ever since he got home. He was bound to crash like this. All these long days and long nights and stressful exchanges with Dorian have finally caught up to him. Now he's going to be late to his *actual* job, and he doesn't seem the least bit concerned.

"Okay, Brent."

I force myself to go back downstairs. A few minutes turns into another half hour. Instead of paying full attention to my own work, for the last hour now I've been distracted by Brent. Every few minutes I stop whatever it is I'm doing to see if he's finally gotten up. It's killing me to let him sleep in like this, but I just can't go in there again. I don't want to turn into a nag.

I'm also angry that it's even come to this. I shouldn't *have* to pester him to get out of bed for work. A few minutes after nine, I hear him finally moving around upstairs. I hear the shower come on. He doesn't really have time for one, but Brent needs one to wake up in the mornings. He always has. I expect it to be fast, but he takes his sweet old time in the shower. It's almost nine thirty by the time he comes down-stairs, at last dressed for work.

Or should I say, overdressed. He's wearing a suit and tie this morning.

"Alright, hon," he says. "I'm headed in."

"Brent, I don't want to tell you what to do, but—"

"I know, I know." He comes over to give me a kiss. "I slept in too late. But it'll be alright. It won't happen again."

"You need to get more rest," I say. "And you need to give yourself time to relax. You've been doing too much."

"You're right." He smiles sweetly at me. "I'll work late tonight to make up for it. Aaron won't mind."

"Are you sure?"

"Yeah. No worries."

"Okay, honey."

We kiss goodbye, and he's off. By the time he reaches the office, it'll be after ten o'clock. That's two hours later than he typically gets started. Aaron is not going to be happy.

But I can't worry about that too. I've got my own job to do. With Brent finally up and gone, I focus for the next several hours on generating some new reports for the company. Work takes my mind off everything else that's been going on, and the next thing I know, it's one o'clock in the afternoon. I take a break to make myself a BLT, which I eat on the couch in the living room, switching on the TV as a distraction.

I scroll through Netflix, not really interested in anything I'm seeing, and eventually settle on an old TV show I've watched a million times just to have some background noise. My phone buzzes. It's another group text from the private detective.

> I've put my report together and made copies of the evidence. I've forwarded them to your email addresses. I will head to the station tonight to file a report, once my colleague can take over surveillance at the motel. More to come. Stay tuned.

I exhale. At least this whole stalking fiasco is almost over. I'm about to put my phone down, when it buzzes again. Brent responded to Smith's text immediately. I wish he were that attentive to my texts.

> Thanks for all your help, Jim.

I put my sandwich down on the coffee table and open my email on my phone. Sure enough, there's a message waiting for me from Jim that includes several attachments. I scan the report, which is attached to the email as a PDF. There's not a lot in here that I don't already know. The report includes a lot of the minutiae of Smith's work so far. Dates and times of Joshua's movements. I scroll through until I reach the copy of the man's arrest record. Smith already shared this information with us, but I'm still shocked by everything I read about this criminal. There are also JPEGs attached to the email. I open them one at a time. They're all photographs of Joshua's gray SUV, but in a few of them, the vehicle is parked on our street.

I get chills.

I don't want to think about this right now. I close the attachments and email and put my phone down. It's all being taken care of. Brent was right to hire a private eye. I can't believe, looking back now, that I hesitated for one second to pay this man two thousand dollars. It's been worth every penny. As soon as the police have this information, they'll arrest Joshua, and he'll be out of our lives for good.

I hope.

I DON'T BOTHER Brent at work about dinner, knowing he's going to work a long day to make up for his late start this morning. It's a mild day, so I sit on the porch and eat while the sun goes down. My eye catches that patch of lawn near the sycamore tree that I missed with the mower. I really don't feel like getting to it, but I also know I won't be in the mood tomorrow either. So I finish dinner and set my plate down on the small, round glass table on the porch and head into the backyard. I'm just about to start trimming the grass when I hear a voice call my name.

"Mary!"

Startled, I nearly drop the weed whacker and trip over a jutting root in my front yard. Looking across the street, I see Mrs. Ryers. She has risen out of her rocking chair and is palming the banister of her porch.

"Look!"

She points to my right, farther down the street. It's getting dark out now, so I can't really see what color it is, but there is a Chevy sedan parked on the other side of the road, facing our way. Its engine is on.

"She's back!" Mrs. Ryers says. "See?"

The vehicle's lights come on, blinding me for a moment. Then the car slips into gear and starts coming really fast up the street. I watch as the sedan goes by, trying to get a good look at the driver.

I do a double take.

It's an older woman, just like Mrs. Ryers said.

But that's not why I'm surprised.

I only caught a quick glance of her, but the old woman looks *really* familiar. I know her from somewhere ...

Whoever she is, she's gone in a hurry, moving too quickly for me to get her license plate.

I feel Mrs. Ryers's eyes on me.

"I told you," the older woman says.

I take a deep breath. I'm a bit shaken up, to be honest. But what are the chances that I'd have *two* people stalking me around the same time? One a career criminal who suspects my husband is leading a double life. And the other an old woman whom I think I know from somewhere? Like I said, I can't imagine they're working together. Jim Smith would have found a connection.

"It could be anything," I say. "Maybe she knows somebody in the neighborhood."

"I asked around," Mrs. Ryers says ominously, shaking her head. "Nobody on this street knows that car."

22

Brent is really late getting home that night. I'm already in PJs and thinking about turning off the TV. I want to curl up in bed with a good book—I need something to take my mind off the strange blue Chevy in our street—and I'm just going to bed when he finally arrives.

"Great news, honey," he calls, not even fully in the door yet.

"What's going on?" I ask.

He's beaming. "Another investor. I contacted him last week, and he didn't seem interested. Then, today, he hit me up out of the blue."

"Really?" I'm excited. This guy has to be better than Dorian. I mean, that's a really low bar, but still. "What's his name? Who is he?"

We sit down at the dining room table together, and Brent fills me in. This man's name is Alexander. He's bankrolled four tech start-ups in the last ten years, all of which have gone on to make millions of dollars. Three of the four were bought out by private equity firms, and the fourth just had an IPO, going public. Brent goes on and on about how much nicer this guy Alexander is than Dorian. The man is also, apparently, heavily into philanthropy.

"Wow," I say. "This is really exciting."

Brent nods. "I'm *pumped*. We could really be onto something here. There's just one thing ..."

Uh-oh. I didn't want this to be too good to be true. But there is always a catch.

"What is it?"

Brent makes a face. "He wants very similar terms. He'll put up half the capital, but he wants us to come up with the rest."

"Oh."

I'm not going to hide my disappointment. This is a nonstarter for me. I wonder why Brent didn't lead with this information. Instead he went on and on about how wonderful this new investor is, all while keeping the most important piece of the discussion to himself.

"Well, that's too bad," I say.

"I know." Brent is giving me a sidelong look. "But maybe it's time we start considering the idea? I mean, if we're serious about the business, then we should get serious about the money too."

I look down. How many times, and how many different ways, do I have to tell him I am not comfortable risking all that money? And why does he keep asking? Brent has never been this pushy before. In fact, that's one of the reasons I fell in love with him. Unlike most of the other men I've known, he has never pushed me into anything. He lets me take my time, and if I say no, he accepts the answer. This retreat sure has changed him.

"Brent." I look him in the eye. "I'm just not comfortable doing that. Okay?"

He grimaces, then gathers himself. "I understand, honey."

As he rises, he tries to hide the disappointed look in his eye. But he can't. He *really* wants this to work out.

I wish I felt the same.

23

BRENT – DAY SIX – APRIL 16

Last night they came into my cell to change out my bucket.

At least, I think it was last night. I can't really tell.

I was asleep when they came in, so I couldn't attack. But even if I had been awake, I probably wouldn't have tried anything, because when I came to, I realized he was holding a gun.

"Don't move," was all he said.

I thought about moving. I thought about it a lot. I didn't *think* he would shoot me. But I couldn't be sure. While I looked down the barrel of that gun, trying to put odds on whether he'd shoot and what my chances of escape would be even if he didn't, they replaced the nearly overflowing bucket of waste with another.

This morning, if it *is* morning, my stomach is in knots. I'm so goddamned hungry. All I get for dinner is an apple. That's it. And last night's apple was kind of small.

They're starving me.

At least they've been better about water. They gave me a bigger bottle two days ago. I've still got a little water from yesterday. I should ration it out, because I don't know when they'll be in again today. They don't seem to maintain much of a schedule with me, showing up willy-nilly with food and water. But I can't ration it out. I'm too thirsty. I chug what little is left.

It's not enough to ease the headache. I feel feverish too, and my tongue is like cotton.

The next time they open my door and come in to swap out the bucket, I don't have a choice. I don't care if they've got a gun pointed at me, or even a rocket launcher. I have to make a move. At this rate, I'll be dead in a few days.

I force myself to stand and move around the tiny space. I'm really weak now. It's amazing how quickly the body breaks down without enough nourishment. Crossing my tiny space a dozen times is enough to tire me out. I lie back down on the bed. I don't know if it's better to rest or force myself to move around.

I drift in and out. Some time later, the slot in my door makes a loud noise as it's pulled open. I come to, immediately alert.

"You awake?"

I sit up in the cot. That doesn't help with my headache.

"I need more water. My head hurts, and I'm dizzy all the time."

He raises his voice. "Brent's awake! Come on down!"

"Please," I say, trying not to sound like I'm begging. I still have a little pride left. "I need more water."

"You'll get more water once you're ready to talk."

"You have to let me out."

The slot begins to slide closed again. I jump off the bed

and put my hand in the open space. He closes my wrist in the metal opening. It hurts a lot, but I don't pull my hand back.

"No, please! Don't! I'll talk! I'm ready to talk now!"

"You sure about that?"

"Yes. Please."

"Alright."

He pulls the slot all the way open. I peer through and get a good look at him.

My father is sitting on the chair they've left outside the door. For a moment we just stare at each other. What kind of man could do this to his own son? What kind of monster? My parents aren't good people. They were both distant and abusive when I was a child, and they've always been criminals. By the time I was a teenager, nothing they did, or didn't do, surprised me anymore. But this ... holding your own son prisoner ... this is evil beyond comprehension. My father's eyes are steely. "Brent, you gonna cooperate with us?"

"Yes," I say.

"Good." He smiles. "That's for the best."

I hear footsteps. My mother appears. She sits on an old wooden stool beside my father. I haven't seen either of them in years. Mom has let her hair go completely gray. When I first saw her, I almost didn't recognize her. They've both aged —badly.

"Please give me some more water. I'm going to die."

"Oh, quit being such a baby," Mom says. "You were always so soft. If it were your brother in there, he would have broken out by now and probably killed us. But not you. You're so passive. You let the world run you."

I look at her in utter despair. I want to know why she ever chose to become a mother. If her heart was that hard, why would she want children? Maybe Dad convinced her in a moment of weakness, or maybe he forced her, or maybe it was just an accident. I don't know. She acts like she's tough and wouldn't let anybody push her around, but Dad has always run their marriage. Whatever he wants, he gets.

Dad says, "You don't get any more water until you prove to us you're going to cooperate."

"What do you want?"

"Well, son, as you've probably guessed by now, your mother and I didn't go on any stupid retreat and find God, or become one with the universe or whatever."

I should never have believed him in the first place.

He goes on. "We want to know everything about you and your wife."

"Why?" I ask.

He wags a finger. "You don't get to ask questions."

I'm really confused. What does this have to do with Mary?

"What do you want to know?"

"*Everything.*"

I don't understand. Dad must read the confusion on my face, so he finally explains why. By the time he's finished, I'm absolutely stunned. They want Mary's money. That's what this is about. And they were willing to put me in a dungeon for thirty days to get it.

I'd rather die than help them get Mary's inheritance. No way. I could never live with myself.

"You both can go to hell," I say defiantly.

"See?" Mom says. "I told you. He lets that bitch run his life."

Dad gives her a nasty look, and Mom turns away. My father holds his gaze on her for a moment longer, reasserting his dominance, until she fidgets nervously on the stool. Then he turns to me.

"You're going to help us," he says. "You have no choice, Brent."

"You're out of your mind if you think I'm going to help you. I will let myself rot in here. I will starve to death if I have to. I love Mary. I would never hurt her."

My old man smiles wickedly. "That's exactly why you're going to help us."

I'm not following. I look from my father to my mother. There is no sympathy in their eyes. None.

Dad says, "If you don't help us, we'll kill her."

24

THURSDAY – MAY 25

I haven't seen the blue Chevy sedan in a few days, not since the other night when I was carrying the weed whacker across the front yard. But still, I look up and down the street. Nothing like being stalked by one criminal, and possibly an older woman, to make you paranoid.

Brent is late again. He texted a few minutes ago to say he was going to work late at the office. Aaron has him working on some special project. That's a good thing. Aaron usually only hands those things out to people he really likes and trusts, which means that Brent is, miraculously, back on his good side. I didn't foresee this happening, I'll admit, especially because Brent hasn't exactly been keeping regular hours at work. I'm frankly amazed that Aaron is putting up with it, especially after he was gone for so long.

But for whatever reason, it sounds like it's working out. I'm happy for Brent. He's hated his job for a few years now. He deserves a change in luck.

Rather than sit around the house by myself, I decide to go exercise. The group exercise classes on offer when I arrive aren't appealing, so I decide to ride the stationary bike. Maybe I can duplicate the spinning workout I tried last week.

The gym is busy, and I spot the shockingly attractive blonde woman Brent was talking to last week. She's in the free weight area, doing deadlifts right in the middle of the floor. I'm pretty sure she's positioned herself strategically. She wants everybody looking at her butt as she hinges at the waist and picks the, I have to admit, heavy-looking weight up.

I plug earbuds into my bike and turn on the TV. Whoever was using the bike last was watching the local news, because that's what comes up. I'm about to change the channel when an image flashes on the screen.

It's a picture of Joshua.

The image is a close-up of his face. One eye is badly bruised, completely swollen shut. His beard is a little shorter, and he's not wearing sunglasses or a hat, but I know it's him. I recognize the scar running along the side of his face, near the eye that isn't swollen shut.

"... need your help in identifying this man, whose body was found yesterday morning in Hyde Park. The police are not releasing any other information at this time."

My jaw hits the floor. Joshua is *dead*?

A policeman wearing a blue uniform appears on the screen next. A reporter, whose back is to the camera, holds a microphone up to his face. His name and rank appear on the bottom of the screen along with the name of the police department. It's in my county.

"We cannot disclose any other information at this time because this is an ongoing investigation," the policeman says. "But we are asking for anyone to come forward who might have knowledge of this individual. At this point, we are simply attempting to make a positive ID."

The reporter asks, "Can you comment on the manner of this man's death? Have you ruled out foul play?"

The policeman shakes his head. "I'm sorry. Like I said, I cannot provide any other details at this time because this is an ongoing investigation. That's all I can say for now."

The news cuts to a different story. A message pops up on the screen of the stationary bike. The computer system is asking me if I want to pause the workout. Apparently, I stopped pedaling altogether when I saw the image of Joshua appear.

I get off the bike, my heart racing. I close my eyes and take deep, calming breaths. Once I get myself together, I head for my car on jittery legs.

I sit in the parking lot for a few minutes, my head spinning. But then a thought occurs to me.

Why don't the police know who Joshua is?

Jim Smith was supposed to file his police report several days ago. The police should have this man's information on file, including photographs of him in his SUV near my home. Hmm. Maybe Joshua died without ID on him ... but they'd still get fingerprints, wouldn't they? And this guy has a criminal record, so his prints are in the database. They should know who he is—

Unless the police couldn't *get* fingerprints?

I shudder at the sickening thought.

Joshua was a criminal. From what I read in his arrest record, he was not a good person. I won't say he deserved to die, but honestly, the world might be a better place without him.

All the same, if the police found his body and cannot

identify him, that means he was probably *murdered*. That means there's a killer running around out there. I should call. I should call them right now.

But first I text Brent.

> Need to talk. Call me as soon as you get this.

I wait a few minutes, but there's no answer. Then I respond to the group chat between my husband, me, and Smith.

> We need to contact the police ASAP. I just saw Joshua's picture on the news. He's dead. Can one of you call me right now?

Five minutes pass. Then ten. I've called Brent twice, but he hasn't picked up. This cannot wait. Even though I just found out about this, I feel like I'm obstructing a police investigation into a man's death by not calling them immediately. I pull up the general number for the county's department on my phone. Right before I hit the hyperlinked number and thumb SEND on my phone, Brent calls me.

"Hey, honey," he says. "I just saw your text. Sorry."

"Brent," I say, "Joshua was on the news. They ran a story a few minutes ago. The police found his *body*—"

"Whoa, whoa, whoa," he says. "Slow down, honey. Take a breath. Everything is fine."

"Okay. Okay."

I take a few deep breaths.

"Okay. I was saying, Joshua's been killed. The police don't know who he is, though."

"I know."

It sounds like he *already* knew. "You know?"

"Where are you right now?" he asks.

I don't like the sound of his voice. Brent sounds *cold*.

"I was at the gym. But—"

"Good. I'll meet you at the coffee shop. Be there in ten."

He hangs up without further explanation.

What is happening?

A terrible thought comes to mind. Did Brent have this man killed?

Or kill Joshua himself?

No, no. That's ridiculous. Crazy. Conspiracy-level insanity. I might as well put on a tinfoil hat if I'm going to start thinking things like that. Brent is not a murderer. It'd be stupid of him to murder this man, given that Jim Smith knows Joshua was stalking us. The detective could just go to the police and tell them everything.

Unless Brent killed Joshua in a fit of rage ...

I wouldn't have thought it possible two months ago. Or two years ago. Or when I first met Brent. He is a kind, gentle man, not prone to violence. He doesn't even like to kill spiders around the house. Whenever he can, he scoops insects up and tosses them outside rather than squish them.

But he's changed since he returned from this retreat. He's a new man now. It's undeniable. There is an aggressiveness to him that was never there before. I saw him nearly get into a fight at the gym, and that was over something stupid, something meaningless.

A man stalking and threatening your wife is *not* meaningless.

Maybe Brent decided to confront Joshua himself. Maybe he drove to the motel and knocked on the criminal's door. Maybe all Brent wanted to do was scare him away, but then things escalated. Maybe Joshua drew a knife or a gun, and Brent had no choice but to defend himself.

I could play the what-if game all night long and not get anywhere. I know this is stupid, but I can't help it.

Maybe Brent killed the other man in a rage. Maybe he let his emotions get out of control. Fearful that he'd be linked to Joshua's death, maybe he ... Oh my God, is this really happening?

No, no. It can't be. It just can't be.

But as I drive to the coffee shop, I can't ignore the fact that Brent *already knew* this man was dead and did not tell me about it. Why would he keep such a thing from his wife?

I arrive at the coffee shop before Brent does. Terry is behind the counter and greets me with a big smile.

"Hey, Mary! What can I get you?"

The *last* thing I need right now is caffeine. I'm so amped up, I'll already have trouble falling asleep tonight. Coffee will not help in that regard.

"Oh, nothing for me. I'm just here to meet Brent. I hope that's okay."

"Sure," he says. "I'll whip up his favorite."

Terry gets to work on Brent's drink while I head into the rear of the coffee shop. I find a table in the back so we can have some privacy. While I'm waiting for Brent, I search "killing Hyde Park" on my phone. It brings up a bunch of news stories. After reading the third one, I'm pretty sure none are going to provide any more information than I already have, so I put the phone down, cross my legs at the knee and try my best to remain calm while I wait for Brent.

When Brent finally arrives, he greets Terry with a huge smile. He acts like he doesn't have a care in the world as he pays for his coffee and then scoops up his drink. I wave to get his attention, and he strides into the back.

"Hey, honey." He sits opposite me. "Are you alright?"

"No, Brent." I shake my head, dumbfounded by how he's acting. "I am *not* alright. The man stalking me just turned up dead."

"Shhh." He holds out a palm, then looks over his shoulder to check for eavesdroppers. The only other customers are two teenaged boys seated about four tables away. They're more interested in their phones than what us boring thirty-somethings are discussing. "Keep your voice down."

"You knew about this but kept it from me?" I ask. "What the hell is going on, Brent?"

My voice hasn't gotten any lower.

"Please, Mary, not so loud." He leans in. "You have to let me explain."

"You'd better."

Brent cradles his cup of coffee and takes a deep breath.

"Jim found out last night," he says. "He called me this morning."

"You *knew* this morning?" I ask, incredulous. "And you didn't tell me?"

None of this makes any sense.

"I'll explain, but let me start from the beginning, okay?"

I don't like this.

"How did Jim find out?"

"That's what I was going to tell you," Brent says. "He still has a lot of friends in the department. Apparently, when the police catch an unidentified body, very often they'll contact local detectives to see if they can help with an ID. Somebody looped Jim in."

"Why didn't he tell them who Joshua is, then?"

"Because he's a professional," Brent says. "He called me first."

"Why?"

"Think about it, Mary," Brent goes on. "The guy was stalking you. We hire a detective to find him. A few days later, he's dead. How does that look to a cop?"

He has a point there. It doesn't look good.

"Did you have anything to do—"

"No," Brent cuts me off. "Absolutely not. But I don't have an alibi for two nights ago. Remember, I was working late? I was the last person in the office. I was alone for almost three hours."

I hate myself for wondering if my husband is telling me the truth.

"That's a big gap, and apparently, that might be when Joshua was killed."

"So he *was* killed?"

"Jim doesn't know for sure, but that's his guess. So the man stalking you has been murdered, and I have no alibi. Think about it. When Jim asked what I wanted him to do with the report, I didn't even hesitate. I told him not to file it."

"Brent ..."

"What?" He holds his hands out, palms up. "Do you want the police in our business at all? Do you want them taking me down to the station? Come on, Mary, it was the smart play."

"But the man's dead. You didn't do it," I say. "Surely the truth will come out."

"Don't be naïve," I say. "Innocent people go to prison all the time, Mary."

I don't know about *all the time*, but he does have a point. If there's even a remote possibility Brent could be charged with this crime, then I can't say he made the wrong decision.

Still, though, it feels *wrong* to keep this from the police.

"What if they find out anyway?" I ask. "Won't you look even guiltier then?"

"We'll cross that bridge if we ever come to it," he says. "Jim has been through the man's motel room. He's taken all the evidence with him."

"He can *do* that?"

Brent nods. "He's not a cop, so he's not bound by the same rules."

"I don't know, Brent. I really think you should reconsider. I just ... I don't know."

"You're not seeing the whole picture," Brent says. "If I'm arrested, hell, if I'm just a person of interest, how is that going to look? Word will get out. How long do you think Aaron will keep me around when he discovers the police are investigating me? More importantly, how many investors will be interested in doing business?"

He's got a point there. Aaron would probably fire him straight away, no questions asked. As for the investors, they wouldn't want anything to do with Brent. This could ruin his life.

Our lives.

But still ... we're hiding something from the police. That seems wrong.

No. It *is* wrong. Especially since we have nothing to hide.

"If the police ever make a connection, we will tell them we had no idea that he died," Brent says. "Okay?"

"What do you think happened to him?"

"Who knows," Brent answers with a dismissive shrug.

"The man was a criminal. He could have been up to anything."

"If he was *murdered,* though ..."

"It could have been an accident, Mary. We really have no idea. A lot of drug dealers work in Hyde Park. Maybe he went there to score or whatever and got into trouble? Or maybe he just OD'd. We don't know. The guy might have just had a heart attack."

That's possible. The man smelled like weed. But still, just because somebody smokes marijuana doesn't mean they use the harder stuff ...

"I don't know, Brent."

"Look, Mary. This is going to sound harsh, but I really don't care. Honestly? I'm glad he's dead. The guy was a lowlife, and he threatened you."

I wouldn't put it like that. Not exactly. And I'm not exactly relieved he's dead either, especially since Brent wants us to keep the stalking a secret.

"I think I should call the police," I say.

"Don't," Brent says, his voice suddenly dark. "You'll ruin everything."

25

BRENT – DAY TWELVE – APRIL 22

The questions are endless.

They want to know everything about Mary and me. How we met, how long we dated, when I moved in with her, when and where we got married, the names of our friends, the names of her distant relatives, the names of our colleagues and coworkers and managers and companies, how long we've been at our jobs, the names of our neighbors. On and on and on. They're always asking me questions. When one of them goes to bed or takes a break, the other one starts in. Over and over and over.

They asked for my passwords to my home and work email accounts. I refused. I refused until they pulled two of my fingernails out, anyway. Once they made it clear they would kill Mary, they were a lot more carefree about opening my door, about even stepping into my cell. Yesterday, they didn't even flash their gun when they came in to change out my bucket. I'm chained to the wall, I'm exhausted, I'm malnourished, and they will kill Mary if I don't cooperate. They know I'm not going to try anything.

How could I?

So I gave them my passwords. Now they know *everything*. They're reading over every email I've ever read and sent. They've asked me about the gym, about which bars and restaurants I go to, about what I like to do, about what I cook and what Mary cooks. They know everything now. They know literally every little thing about my life and about Mary's life.

They ask me the same questions too. They force me to go over things I already told them yesterday, or the day before, or the day before that. I've lost track of time now. I know I haven't been here a month, and I don't think I've been here more than two weeks. But I'm not sure about the latter. The worst part? Nobody is looking for me. Not yet. I'm technically not missing. Mary thinks I'm on a wellness retreat.

I've lost weight. They're not feeding me enough. They're feeding me *just enough*. Yesterday was a bad day. I was having trouble thinking straight. I couldn't form a sentence. They were kind enough to stop the questioning for an hour so they could give me more food. More apples. A few slices of bread.

They started in again this morning. It's awful. I've been over how Mary and I met a dozen times, what bars we used to go to, which restaurants. And I told them about how I proposed. We were away on vacation at the lake house we used to rent. I told them all about it. Mom laughed at how emotional I got, telling them the story.

I don't know what they're going to do with all this information. How do they think it will help them steal Mary's money to know that, six years ago, we used to get ice cream at that dessert stand that closed? I don't know.

Maybe they're just doing it because they enjoy torturing

me. It wouldn't surprise me. I always thought my parents were sadists.

Sometimes I wish I would just die. I wish I'd fall asleep and not wake up. That way, there'd be no more suffering, and they wouldn't be able to hurt Mary. I do wish I could see her one more time. I wish I could tell her how sorry I am, and how stupid I was. I've really messed things up. It's what I'm best at.

The door opens. The light from the main cellar area hurts my eyes. I squint and hold a hand out in front of me. Very slowly, I sit up in bed. I'm light-headed all the time. They're still not giving me enough water.

"Hello, Brent."

It's my father. But I can't think of him like that. Not anymore. I didn't think he or Mom could treat me any more horribly than they did when I was a child.

I was wrong.

This is much, much worse.

"Your cot looks crooked," he says.

"Does it?" I ask.

One of the legs came loose the other night. But I don't want him knowing that. I screwed it back into place, but later, when he's gone, I'm going to remove it again and see if it can be used for a weapon.

"You've been a good boy," he says.

That's the first time I've ever heard him speak those words to me. Of course, when he says it now, there's a dark undertone lining the sentence. I haven't been *good*. All I've done is *obey* while under duress. There's a huge difference between those things.

"Would you let me go?" I say. "I promise I won't go to the

police. I swear. I just want to get back to Mary. She'll give you the money. She will. I swear."

I wasn't even planning on saying that. It just came out, unprompted. I start to cry. I realize they've totally broken me down. I'm begging.

"We *will* let you go," Dad says. "When we know we can trust you."

"You will?"

"Yes," he says. "You're going to go back home, and you're going to do everything we say. Is that understood, Brent?"

I don't answer.

"Do I need to repeat myself?" he asks.

"You're sending me home?" I ask, trying not to sob. The thought of seeing Mary again lifts my spirits. "You promise?"

"You didn't listen to me, Brent," Dad says. "We will send you home, but first we have to know we can trust you."

"You can trust me," I say.

"You'll have to prove that to us," he says. "And then, after you go back home, you're going to do everything we say …"

26

SUNDAY – MAY 28

All weekend, I'm on edge. I can't sit still. Every few minutes, I'm expecting the police to knock on our door, or that I'll spot the blue Chevy sedan on the street, or that some other awful, unexpected thing will happen. The butterfly rash is really noticeable on my face, and my joints are swollen and painful. I cannot handle this upset anymore. The last time I had a flareup, I missed three days of work.

"Hey, babe."

I nearly jump out of my skin. I didn't hear Brent come into the living room. He's standing right behind the couch, looking down at me. He's dressed in a T-shirt and jeans, and his hair is slicked back in an unusual fashion. He's never worn it that way before.

"You scared me."

"Sorry."

He begins to massage my neck and shoulders and the space between. Normally, I'm always ready for a massage, but today I'm having none of it. I get up off the couch.

"Sorry," I say. "I'm not really in the mood."

He makes a sad face. "For a massage?"

"No, Brent. I can't relax."

"Aww, babe. Come here."

I don't move. He holds his arms out and waits, but I don't give in. Shrugging, Brent comes around the couch.

"Alright, then I'll come to you."

I'm stiff as a board when he hugs me. It takes all my willpower just to pat his back and show him some affection. I don't know how he can act like everything is fine. Joshua is dead, and we're keeping his identity from the police.

"I just heard from Alexander," he says. "He wants to sit down to dinner next week."

I can't muster any enthusiasm. "Okay."

"Okay? That's all you have to say? Why can't you be more excited? This is a big deal, hon."

"Brent." I move away from him to stand on the other side of the coffee table. "I'm at my wit's end. The last two weeks have been ..."

"Some bad things have happened," he says. "But for the most part, it's been great. Don't you think?"

No. I don't think it's been great.

And I don't understand how he can believe that.

I'm glad he's home. But the last two weeks have been far from great. How can we be that far apart on our shared experience? There have been times when he's scared me, when I've actually been afraid of my own husband.

My brain keeps sending me a signal:

Run.

To get out of this house, jump in the car, and put some distance between myself and my husband. But I don't know why. Yes, he got angry with me, but Brent would never hurt me, would he? It makes no sense. Where is this thought coming from? I'm panicked and I'm anxious and I haven't slept. I'm not thinking clearly.

"I'm sorry," he says, finally taking my mood seriously. "You're right. Things have been crazy. I haven't slowed down a second since I got back, and so much has happened."

I study my husband.

For a second, for just a moment, there is a look of panic in *his* eyes. But it's gone so quickly that I wonder if I imagined it. But I know I didn't. He was worried about something.

What?

I'm going crazy. I'm losing my mind. I'm starting to wonder if Mrs. Ryers was right. Is this man really my husband? Or is he somebody just pretending?

That's it. I am out of my flipping mind. I need to see a doctor, I think. Maybe I need the same medication that Brent was on before ...

"I think I need to get out of the house for a bit," I say.

"Alright, honey," he says, breaking into a smile as the awkward moment passes. "How about I make dinner tonight?"

"Sure. Great."

I stop by the kitchen to get a glass of water before I leave, but that's not really why I passed this way. I open the cupboard and pick up Brent's pill bottles. It's not like I counted how many were left when he came back, but the amount inside doesn't look any different.

Has he not been taking his medications? That might explain the erratic behavior. I quickly close the cupboard when I hear him coming and snatch the glass of water off the counter. He smiles on his way by, giving my rear end an affectionate pat as he passes.

"Do you want to meet for coffee?" Paige asks, over the phone.

"No," I say. "I need something stronger."

"Oh, I like the sound of that."

We meet up at a Mexican restaurant we used to go to a lot. Paige is waiting for me at the bar when I arrive. An absurdly large margarita is on the bar in front of her.

"You've gotta try this," she says, all but forcing the wide-rimmed glass to my lips.

I'm not usually into mixed drinks, but I have to admit this margarita is delicious.

"Watermelon and pineapple," she says.

"Really?"

"Want one?"

The bartender swings by, and I ask for what she's having.

"Better make it two," Paige says, even though she isn't half-finished with her own drink. "These go down easy."

The bartender leaves to prepare our drinks.

"So," Paige says, sitting on her stool. "What is going on?"

"Everything."

"Talk to me, girl."

I catch her up on the Life and Times of Mary and Brent. I never thought our lives would be this turbulent. I don't tell her that Joshua is the same guy the police just found killed in Hyde Park, though. When I finish my story, Paige lets out a whistle.

"You've been busy."

"Am I crazy?" I ask. "I mean, honestly."

"Honestly?" Paige thinks it over. "I think you have to ask him about his meds."

That's what I was thinking. It's reassuring to hear her echo my sentiments.

"You know, if he just stopped all of a sudden, that could really mess with his head."

I nod. "Right."

"What are you going to do about the investors?" she asks.

"I can't risk all that money," I say. "I've thought about it, long and hard, and I just can't do it."

She nods. "I wouldn't either, to be honest. Most new businesses fail within a year. I see it happen all the time at the bank. People come in with all kinds of ideas. Some of them sound really good, too. Nine times out of ten, they default on a business loan, and it's over inside a year."

"What do you think I should tell him?"

"The truth," she says.

"But what if ..." She knows where I'm going with this. "Paige, you haven't seen him recently. He's got a temper, and he's gotten impetuous."

"Brent? Impetuous?"

"I feel like if I say no about the money, everything will come to a head."

"That might be for the best."

"Paige," I say, "I'm not prepared to throw away my marriage."

"Mary." Paige gives me a hard look. She is about to drop one of her famous truth-bombs on me, I just know it. "I love you. You're my best friend. And I love Brent. He's had a tough life and I feel for him. I was happy when you got married. You seemed like a really good fit. And I've been cheering for you ever since."

"I feel a but coming."

"Huge but," she says. "Like, Kardashian huge."

Despite the serious nature of our conversation, I can't help but laugh.

Paige continues, "But if Brent asks you to risk all that money for him, and he's unhappy with your answer, then he can go take a hike. It's not right to put you in such a difficult position, where you have to choose between financial security and your husband. If he's that angry, if he threatens to divorce you, then, honey, you're better off without him. In my not-so-humble opinion, of course."

I cannot believe my marriage has reached this point, where I'm not-so-idly wondering if Brent is going to ask for a divorce. Or, if he doesn't, but he continues to put so much pressure on me about the money, I might have to leave him.

Now it's true that, before he went away, our marriage wasn't in great shape. But that had more to do with external factors, namely Brent's job and medical condition. While I had begun to wonder if we would split up, it seemed more like a hypothetical, unfortunate in nature but certainly understandable. We would have been those two decent people who tried really hard to make it work but couldn't find a way.

This is something else entirely. If we decide to separate now, it will be because Brent tried to force me to hand over all my inheritance to him. That's not an *externality*. That's *him*, my husband, directly responsible for what happens next.

"Sorry." Paige takes my hand. "I might have spoken too bluntly. People have told me I have that problem."

I can't bring myself to laugh. "It's alright. That's kind of where my head is, so it's good to know I'm not crazy."

"Well, we might *both* be crazy," Paige says. "You can't rule that out."

We share a laugh, but I'm only going through the motions. I feel hollow inside. I feel like I'm headed toward something ugly, maybe disastrous. Sure, I thought Brent and I might separate. But I never thought it would happen like this, over something like money.

"Come on," Paige says, trying to cheer me up. "Let's act like we're not going to eat anything while we order some appetizers."

She really is the best.

27

BRENT – DAY TWENTY-ONE – MAY 1

The metal plate screwed into the wall is finally loose.

I've been picking away at the concrete surrounding the plate with the loose leg of my bed. The cot has gotten even more crooked, though, so as I've worked on digging out the concrete surrounding the plate, I've had to adjust the other legs of the cot so it's not obvious that I'm up to something. Mom nearly caught me messing around with the bed yesterday, or maybe it was the day before, when she threw open the door to swap out my bucket.

The bolt through which I'm chained to the wall is attached to this metal plate. Getting it loose has taken a lot of work. But here's the rub. The one thing I have in here is a lot of time. They don't question me as much now, probably because they've asked me everything they could think of, and we've been over it all multiple times.

Anyway, the plate is loose! I can't hack through my chain or unhook myself from the bolt. And even if I had a knife or a sharp tool, there's no way I'd lop my own hand off at the wrist just to get free. I know people do that in movies, but that's not real. I'd probably bleed out before I got upstairs.

I've made up my mind. I'm going to kill my parents. It's such an odd thing to think: *I'm going to kill my parents.* But it's the only sane response to the insane situation I'm in.

Once the metal plate is no longer attached to the wall, I'll still have a chain around my wrist, but at least I'll be able to move around. I can even use my bonds as a weapon. I've imagined, God help me, wrapping that chain around Dad's neck and squeezing the life out of him. But that's a last resort move. I don't know if I have the strength to hold him down and choke him out.

I'm really weak. And still light-headed, too. They've given me a little more water, but it's still not enough.

I'm not kidding myself. There's a good chance Mom and Dad will simply overpower me when I attack them, even though they're old and don't get around so well anymore. I'm dehydrated, malnourished, sleep-deprived. They're not. And there's two of them. But I know one thing for sure: I'm not letting them decide my fate. Dad promised I could go home provided I do everything they say and continue to follow their orders. But I'd be a fool to trust him.

They're after Mary's money, and they're not above killing their own son or their daughter-in-law to get it.

So I have to get out of here.

Or die trying.

I unscrew the leg of the cot and continue my work. The metal leg is scratched and now bent badly out of shape. I have to be careful. I can't break it. Because then the cot won't be level, and it'll be obvious to them when they look in my room. If they catch me, the game is over. They'll probably take the bed out of here, and then I won't have anything but my fingers to try to dig the metal plate out of old concrete.

28

WEDNESDAY – MAY 31

Yesterday was a little better. Brent stayed home all day and didn't bring up the issue of money once. As a matter of fact, we didn't discuss work or his side business or Joshua at all. We mostly puttered around the house, taking care of chores. I was able to concentrate long enough to finish reading a novel. Amazing, I know. I even caught a nap. Brent woke me up by trying to put the moves on me, but I pretended like I had a headache and said I wasn't in the mood.

He was out the door early today, though not for work. He's getting a workout in at the gym before he heads to the office. I'm still waiting for the other shoe to drop with Aaron. Brent is kind of making up his hours as he goes now, sometimes working early, sometimes late. There's no rhyme or reason to it. I guess it just depends on how he's feeling that day.

He's been home three weeks today. It feels a lot longer, though. That day when he pulled into the driveway, full of confidence and charm and energy and positivity, seems like it happened a lifetime ago. A lot has happened since.

Around lunchtime, Brent messages me. This new investor wants to meet for dinner tonight. I don't really feel like going out, but it's important, and I should meet the man my husband is potentially going into business with before they agree to terms. Brent suggests another swanky restaurant in the city, but I put my foot down this time.

> Too tired for all that. Can we try Rindella's instead?

Brent puts up a bit of a fight about it, but eventually relents. I block out my calendar in the middle of the afternoon for a half-hour power nap. Tonight will be another late dinner, probably, so I need to recharge my battery. I send a few emails and then slip into the bedroom. I crawl under the covers, sort of dreading going out to dinner with another investor tonight, because I know it will only raise the issue of money again. I don't feel like talking about it anymore. I've made up my mind and made my position clear, but Brent isn't taking no for an answer.

Just as I'm dozing off, I hear the front door to the house open downstairs.

I'm instantly spooked. I pop out of bed and run to my dresser. I hid a knife in the back of my underwear drawer for self-defense. I know that a knife isn't the best weapon, but guns terrify me. It's better than nothing.

Holding the knife in front of me, I poke my head out the bedroom door.

"Hello?" I call out.

"Hey, hon. It's me."

I let out a huge sigh of relief, putting the knife back in my dresser. I hide it behind my underwear.

My relief is only temporary, however. Considering that he exercised this morning, Brent was late getting into the office. And right now, it's only two thirty. He's home very early. I immediately suspect something happened.

I come downstairs and find him standing in the kitchen. He's already cracked a beer and looms behind the island counter. Brent practically chugs the whole thing, then sets the bottle down a little too hard on the counter.

"Honey," I say, "is something wrong?"

Brent is staring off into space. But he shakes his head no and is smiling a moment later.

"No. Actually, everything is great."

His tone is off. I can tell something happened at work.

"But you're home kind of early."

"I quit."

I stop in my tracks, filling the threshold between the foyer and the kitchen.

"You quit?"

He nods, chugs the rest of his beer. "That's right. I told that asshole, Aaron, to shove the job up his ass."

I'm speechless. All I can do is stare incredulously at my husband.

Brent gets another beer out of the fridge. "Do you want a drink?"

"No, I don't want a drink, Brent. I want to understand what happened."

He comes out from behind the refrigerator door, second beer in hand. "There's not much to say, actually. Aaron was being his usual self. I called him out on his poor management and appalling leadership in a meeting. He was embarrassing Molly, one of my coworkers, and I'd had enough of it. So I told him to shut the hell up."

"Brent ..."

The room is spinning. How can Brent be so calm? The man just quit his job.

"What?" he asks, popping the cap of his second beer and taking a swig. "I wasn't going to stand there and say nothing while he talked down to a lady like that. Once the brass get the whole story, once they hear what really happened, they'll probably fire Aaron and beg me to come back to work. It's a win-win."

This is insane.

"You quit, just like that?"

"Hell yes. That place sucks anyway. I've been wasting my life there. To be honest, even if they *beg* me to come back, I might tell them no. It was time for me to go, honey. It was time to move on. There are bigger and better things on the horizon."

Brent watches me, as if waiting for a big reaction. I certainly owe him one. But I'm not going to give him the satisfaction.

I'm also not going to ask him about money. While that's obviously an important issue, especially since he's suddenly out of work, I don't want to go anywhere near that subject right now. If I suggest it's a problem, he'll just point to my retirement savings.

The worst part is my father saw this coming. I don't know how, but somehow he looked into the future and knew Brent would put me in this horrible position. How did he know? I wish I could ask him. I wish I *had* asked him. But that conversation with Dad was already challenging enough at the time.

"But, Brent," I say, choosing my words carefully, "you don't have another job lined up."

"Sure I do," he says with an irritating smirk. "I have my own business to start."

I am thinking a terrible thought. Brent purposely quit his job so I'd feel pressured to finance his new business. This is all a ploy.

"I ..."

"Babe," he says after another swig of beer, "what's the big deal? It's not like we don't have savings. We can manage while I get my business off the ground."

No, no, no.

"Brent ..." I'm not ready to go there yet. "I can't believe you just up and quit without talking to me first."

He narrows his eyes. "Mary, we don't live our lives in a laboratory under perfect experimental conditions. Things happen in real time. Aaron disrespected Molly. You should have seen her, she was practically in tears. I reacted to a situation that wasn't going to wait for me to call and check in with you. Once Aaron and I got into it, it was game on. He didn't pull his punches, so I wasn't going to either."

"In other words, you didn't think about me at all?"

"How can you make this about you?" he shouts. "I was stuck in that crappy job, not you. I took Aaron's abuse for years, not you. And I finally had enough, Mary. I'm sorry my well-being was inconvenient to you. God, Mary, you can be so *unsupportive.*"

I stare at him for a moment, then storm out of the kitchen. What happened at the office sounds awful, but that doesn't make Brent's abrupt departure right. I don't understand how he can't see that. I grab my purse and keys and head for the door.

"Where are you going?" Brent calls out. "We have to do this dinner tonight."

I'm out the door. I don't look back. Mrs. Ryers is sitting on her porch when I get outside. She watches me fly out of the house, nearly falling down the porch steps. I don't look up at her. I don't want to see the I-told-you-so look in her eyes. I can't deal with *that* right now too.

I hear the front door open behind me, but I don't look back.

"Mary, wait."

I get in the car. Brent is standing in the doorway. He's not coming out. I back out of the driveway, nearly hit an oncoming truck, whose driver horns me for a good three seconds as he proceeds down the street.

Brent is on the porch now, coming down the stairs. I have to get away from this man. He's no longer the Brent I married.

I manage to pull out onto the street without getting into an accident. Brent reaches the lawn. I drive away before he can get close to the car. When I reach the stop sign at the corner, I check my rearview. He's standing on the sidewalk, looking down the street at me. Before he can jump into his car and follow me, I make a quick left and drive way too fast through a residential area. I have to get away.

29

I meet Paige at a diner. We used to come here in high school, because it was always open late. We even sit in the same booth we occupied after prom.

"God, girl," she says. "Are you alright?"

"No," I blurt out.

The server stops at our table to take our orders. Paige asks for a salad. I can't even think about *eating* right now, so I just double-up her order. Once the server is gone, I let it all out. It's hard not to cry, but I manage.

"So, yeah," I say. "Brent quit. Just like that. Then yelled at me and accused me of not being supportive. I've had worse days, but I can't remember any of them right now."

Paige has been unusually quiet this whole time, not once interjecting with her quirky humor. When I finish telling her about my afternoon, she remains uncharacteristically silent. Squirming in the booth, she looks around the restaurant.

"Is something wrong?" I ask.

She puts on a fake smile and lowers her eyes.

"Mary," she says, looking into her iced tea for a moment,

"I don't know if what I heard is accurate or not, but I think you deserve to know."

"Deserve to know what?"

Paige chews on her lower lip. Sharing uncomfortable information is not usually difficult for Paige. It's one of the things I admire most about her. I'm the opposite. I have a hard time telling somebody they've been rude, even when they're outrageously so.

But right now, Paige looks as pained as I get when I have to politely ask someone to move their shopping cart so I can proceed down the aisle.

"What is it, Paige?"

My best friend closes her eyes and takes a deep breath.

"Molly and her friend from work came into the bank today ..."

Oh no. That means Paige heard about my husband's grand exit from somebody else already. And I'm getting the feeling their version of the story is not as flattering to Brent.

"Neither one of them said anything about Aaron being abusive toward Molly," Paige goes on. "I overheard them saying that Brent just flipped out over nothing."

"What?"

"Take this with a grain of salt." Paige takes another breath before continuing. This is the first time I remember her ever appearing stricken before. "You never know who to believe in these situa—"

"What did they say?" I ask, cutting right to the chase.

The server appears sporting two salad bowls. He places them in front of us and, sensing our strained conversation, makes himself scarce. Neither Paige nor I reach for our forks or the balsamic vinaigrette the server left on our table.

"I'm sorry," Paige says. "But from what I overheard, Brent didn't *quit*. He was *fired*."

"What?"

This doesn't make any sense.

But Paige is nodding. "They said since he came back, Brent hasn't been the same. The other girl, the one whose name I don't know, she said that it was like he'd completely forgotten how to do the work. Apparently, all Aaron asked him to do was a simple change in the coding. They acted like it was a quick fix and should have only taken a minute, but Brent *freaked out* and said it would take him all day."

I shake my head. I don't believe this.

No, that's not accurate.

I don't *want* to believe this. There's a difference. But I do believe it. I actually trust the word of two women I've never met before over my own husband's.

"Mary—" Paige says.

"What else did they say?"

"Aaron fired him on the spot, right out in the middle of the floor. Everybody saw ..."

I stand up. My legs are weak. I stumble on my way out of the diner.

"Mary, wait," Paige says.

"I have to be alone right now," I say.

"No, you need to be around people who love you," Paige says.

But I don't stop. I don't listen to her. I leave the diner. Paige has to run back inside to cover the tab. I use that as an excuse to get in my Prius and head off before she can stop me.

THE HOUSE IS dark when I get home. Brent's car is not in the driveway. He must be meeting with this new investor, Alexander, for dinner. Or maybe not? I don't know anymore what's real and what's made up. He just lied to me today about being fired.

I back in and park very low in the driveway. I don't want to think about why I'm doing that. I don't want to acknowledge the fact that I'm parking this way so that Brent cannot box me in with his car and I can leave much more quickly, facing the street, if I have to.

I sit in the driveway for a moment while darkness falls. Going into my own house is not that appealing right now. But where else can I go? I don't want to rent a room at some motel. And, besides, why should I have to? This is *my* home. I grew up in this house, and it belonged to me before Brent and I got together.

Before I even reach the porch, Mrs. Ryers calls out to me.

"Mary, are you alright, dear?"

I pretend I don't hear her. I climb onto the porch and unlock the front door.

"Mary!" she calls out.

I ignore her and go inside. I can't deal with one more thing, or person, right now. But I also don't know what to do with myself. I didn't eat at the diner, but I have no appetite. I could use a glass of wine, but I need to have a clear head.

What else has Brent been lying about?

I force myself to sit down and think this through.

It's possible he hasn't lied about anything else. Getting fired is one of the most embarrassing things that can happen to a person. Not many people go around advertising the fact they've gotten axed. Is it so unreasonable to think he'd make up a story about quitting because he's ashamed? People do that all the time.

Sure, they tell perfect strangers they quit. They tell acquaintances and friends they quit. *Maybe* they even lie about it to their close friends. But they don't make up a story about quitting for their wives. That's not right.

The truth is, I don't trust him anymore. If he's lied to me about this, then he's lied to me about other things too. Now I've figured out how to expend all this nervous energy: see if Brent has told me other lies. He's out to dinner right now. (I think.) That gives me a couple of hours to mull everything over and, if necessary, do some digging. I start from the beginning, when Brent came home nearly five hours late and offered some very vague excuses why. Come to think of it, he still hasn't named one other person from his retreat other than the owners, even though he went on and on about all the great friends he made there.

In my head, I replay every conversation we've had since he returned. Not once has he gone into more detail about his retreat other than the fact they meditated, exercised, worked the farm, and were out in nature frequently. He's repeated a couple of clichéd mantras, but other than that, he's told me nothing about his trip. Was he actually away? Or did he go somewhere else?

I look up how to ping someone's cell. Apparently, our carrier provides an app that reports the location of a phone. You're supposed to use it for finding a lost cell. I didn't even know this service existed. Unfortunately, the app doesn't provide historical information. It only tells you where the phone currently is. So I can't track his movements while he was gone, but I can see where he is right now. I ping the phone and wait.

The app takes a moment to run. But when it comes back with a location, I'm shocked.

Brent is at a shopping center on the other side of town, nowhere near Rindella's, where he's supposed to be meeting this Alexander guy.

I get a horrible feeling in the pit of my stomach. Five minutes in, and I've already caught him in another lie.

Now I'm really panicked. What else am I going to find?

As scared as I am, I force myself to keep digging. I need to know the truth now. I don't care if we're headed for a divorce. I deserve answers. I need to know what my husband has really been up to. I'm starting to think that all those hours he allegedly spent working on his side business were a lie too. I keep thinking about everything he's said since he came home. Pacing the house, I recall the things he's told me. The problem is, there's not much substance there. Most of our conversations have been about his side business, and I can't verify any of that information. Brent has done all his supposed work on his laptop, which he has with him right now.

While I'm pacing the dining room, I continue to think over every moment of the last two weeks. It's hard not to question literally everything he's told me. I even wonder if Joshua was telling the truth—if Brent is a criminal pretending to be a regular guy. Though, that still seems far-fetched. I've known Brent for ten years and, to be fair, his unusual behavior is a very recent phenomenon. Excluding the last two weeks, there is nothing in the last decade that would make me think Brent is some kind of criminal.

I'm not getting anywhere. I sit back down at the dining room table and think everything over. He'll be home soon. I don't know whether I'll confront him yet. Lying to me about getting fired is a big deal, but I wonder if I should wait till I have more information so I can point out more inconsistencies.

I log into our bank's website and review our savings and checking accounts. I don't see any strange charges. Then I check our credit card statement. Again, I don't see any unusual charges here, other than what we agreed upon: the expensive dinner at the Blue Star, my new dress, Brent's new suit—

I gasp.

His new suit.

I hear a car pull up outside. He's home already. I check the time. He's been gone for nearly two hours. I lost track of time when I fell down the rabbit hole of trying to catch my husband in as many lies as I could. Quickly, I close my laptop and slide it into the big purse. I also make sure I have my keys and phone on hand, in case I want to leave in a hurry.

I wait in the foyer. Brent had to park on the street because of where I left my car in the driveway. I'm sure he's not too happy about that, but I don't really care right now. Before he reaches the porch, I open the door. Brent stops to look at me with one foot on the step in front of him. He knows.

He knows I know.

"Hey, honey," he says.

The words are so forced, it's pathetic. I open the door wide so he can come in, then close it behind him. We've been together a long time. I'm already tearing up over the thought that this might be it for us. I'm not one of those hopeless romantics who thinks everybody gets a happily-ever-after, but I'm also not happy about a divorce. Even though I feel like I didn't do anything wrong here, I still can't help but feel like I failed somehow. Did I put too much pressure on Brent? Did I make him feel like he *had* to lie to me? Did he come back from his retreat thinking he *had* to really impress me so much that he spun this increasingly complicated web of lies?

I don't know.

"Hey," he says sheepishly.

When he moves in for a kiss, I take a step back.

"Brent, we need to talk."

"I know. We really do." Brent slides his backpack off one shoulder and puts it on the floor by his feet. "But there's something I have to tell you first."

I fold my arms.

"Alexander wants to invest," he says. "He's offering better terms than Dorian."

"Brent—"

He keeps going. "No, please listen. I think this is it, Mary. I think this could be the deal! I know I screwed up today. I should never have quit without talking to you first. I'm really sorry about that. There's no excuse for my behavior. But, like they say, onward and upward, right? I mean, this could turn out to be a good thing. Now I can focus all my time on the new business."

"Brent."

He won't stop talking.

"Alexander is ready to move forward. He was ready, like, yesterday. The only thing is, he wants us to put up our own money too. Apparently, that's normal when you're dealing with angel investors. They want to make sure that—"

"Brent, I know you didn't quit!"

He stops talking.

I close my eyes for a moment to slow my racing thoughts.

"I know that Aaron fired you," I say. "I hear—"

"No," he says, shaking his head. "That's not true. I mean, he's going to *say* that's what happened, obviously. He's that kind of guy. I don't know who you talked to, but Aaron is just protecting himself now. I mean, I told him I quit, and then he shouted at me to leave, so I guess he can sort of say he fired me. But the truth is, I'd already quit. You know that old line, you can't fire me because I quit? Well, I actually *did* quit; then he told me to go."

My head is spinning. I can't keep up with the implausible twists and unbelievable turns of Brent's life anymore. I'm angry, hurt, and disappointed in equal measure.

"Anyway," he goes on, "Alexander and I had this great meeting over dinner. Mary, when I tell you—"

"Stop lying, Brent. I also know you weren't at Rindella's."

Brent freezes. "What are you talking about? I was there twenty minutes ago."

I can't stop the tears. "Brent, I can't do this anymore with you."

"Do what?" he asks.

I don't answer.

In a small voice, he adds, "Be my wife?"

I open my mouth to speak, but no words come out.

"No." He's shaking his head. "No. I'm going to *prove* to you I just met with Alexander."

"Brent, I don't think—"

"No, wait."

Brent kneels and unzips his backpack.

"There's something I want to show you."

"Brent," I say, "I checked the credit card. You bought your

new suit last Wednesday, not Thursday like you said you did. You lied about that too."

He's not listening to me. Both of Brent's hands are rummaging through the bag.

I have no idea what he wants to show me, but at this point, I don't think there's *anything* that would change my mind. My husband has lied about too many things. He's not the same man I married. He's really not. As crazy as it sounds, I'm starting to believe that Mrs. Ryers was right. This man is an impostor. This is not the Brent I ever knew, and Brent was certainly never capable of becoming this person.

"Do you remember that time we wanted to go skiing? Neither of us had ever been. We took a twenty-minute lesson, then tried the bunny slope. We never made it once down the hill without falling. Do you remember?"

Brent stops riffling in his bag. He looks over at me, studies my face.

"I remember that."

I freeze.

Brent's eyes go wide. All the color leaves his face when he catches my reaction.

This man is not my husband.

We never went skiing.

Very slowly, I begin to edge my way around him. Brent goes back to picking through his backpack.

"Here it is," Brent says.

I'm almost to the door. Keeping one eye on this stranger, I reach behind me for the knob. As soon as I get this door open, I'm going to bolt. Forget the car. I'll never get in, start the engine, and pull out before Brent ... oh my God, what is he going to do to me?

Brent shoots to his feet, and the next thing I know, he

covers my mouth with a white rag. A horrible smell fills my nose.

"I didn't want it to come to this, Mary."

I can't believe what's happening. On some level, I'm aware that my husband is forcing me to breathe in some chemical, but I can't wrap my head around it. Instinctively, I begin to struggle, but he's too powerful, and it's too late.

"You actually weren't horrible in bed," he mutters.

It's the last thing I hear before I pass out.

30

BRENT – DAY TWENTY-NINE – MAY 9

D ad opens the door.

I'm really lucky. Only a few minutes ago I stopped trying to dig the metal plate out of the concrete wall. If he had come just a bit sooner, Dad would have caught me. I squirm on my bed like I'm nervous, but I'm only moving so as to block his view of the wall where my chain is linked. There's one stubborn screw holding the thing in place now. With a little more work, I think I can get myself free later today.

"Son," he says, "we're letting you out tomorrow."

Yeah, right.

He smiles. I wish I could clobber him and wipe that expression right off his face. But I remind myself to be patient. I'll get the chance very soon. Maybe the next time he opens this door, I'll hit him as hard as I can.

It had better be the best punch of my life, because I'm severely malnourished and weak. My forearms look skeletal. They've whittled me down to skin and bones. I'd better connect with his jaw for a knockout shot. Dad is old and doesn't move around so well anymore, but I'm so weak, a stiff breeze would topple me. I'll only get one chance at this. One good shot. I have to make it count.

I was never a good fighter. You would think that, after being bullied in school and at home, I'd pick a few things up along the way. But I never improved at fighting. I was always little more than Christopher's punching bag. He took his anger out on me, and my brother had a lot of anger.

"Did you hear me, son?" Dad asks. "Tomorrow is the day."

I manage a weak smile. My voice is hoarse and strained. "Great."

"But you have to do one more thing for us."

There is always a catch.

"What?"

"We need Mary's password to her personal savings account."

I shake my head. "I don't know it."

It's the truth. I *used* to know the passwords for our joint accounts, but Mary balances the books these days. I haven't logged into our bank's site in years. And I've *never* logged into her personal savings, where she keeps all the money her parents left her.

"I don't believe you," Dad says.

I immediately curl both hands up into balls. The fingernails on two of my digits have only just started to grow back. My fingers are still incredibly pained from when they tortured me.

Dad looks me over. "I don't want to have to hurt you again, Brent."

Maybe a few days ago, I could have come up with some witty retort to that. But I'm having trouble thinking clearly now. I've lost all track of time, though if I'm to believe Dad, tomorrow I'll have been gone for thirty days.

Maybe he's telling the truth, actually. Because if they don't let me go, then Mary will worry. When I don't show up at the house tomorrow at noon, like I'm supposed to, she'll try to contact me. If she can't get a hold of me, she'll call the police.

"We're going to let you go, son," Dad repeats. "But only if you tell us the password to her personal account."

"I don't know it." I force myself to look him in the eye. "And you have to let me go tomorrow. You don't have a choice."

Dad grimaces. "Son, I didn't want it to come to this, but you're forcing my hand."

Right. This is all my fault.

It's my fault they conned me, kidnapped me, and tortured me.

"If you don't cooperate," Dad says, "we are going to kill Mary."

My heart stops beating.

Dad nods. "What choice do we have otherwise? She's the only person on this planet who cares about you. Nobody else is going to come looking. We have to kill her."

"No." I shake my head. "You don't have to do this. You don't have to do *any* of this."

Dad sighs, like this terrible decision is being forced upon him by somebody else.

"Give us the account information," he says. "Or we're going to kill Mary."

"Please ..."

Dad stands up. He strides into my room and towers over me. A profound feeling of déjà vu overwhelms me. I can remember sitting on my bed at home, and my father looming over me just like this, before he proceeded to deliver a beating of some kind.

"Tell me!" he shouts.

"I don't know it." I look up at him so he can see my eyes and know I'm telling the truth. "I don't know it!"

Dad backhands me across the jaw. I see stars. He doesn't give me a moment to get my bearings, however. Dad forces me to sit up again.

"Honey!" he shouts. "Get the pliers!"

"No!" I scream. "Please, no!"

Dad yanks my arm out from behind me. I try to keep my fist balled, but I have no strength. Dad's able to open my hand up. Mom appears a moment later with that small pair of pliers in her hands.

"Come on, honey," he says. "Get in here and do it!"

I can't take this. Maybe one big wrench will free the metal plate from the wall. Then I can at least try to attack them both. I will have the element of surprise working in my favor. Neither of them are expecting my chain to come loose from the wall.

But if it doesn't work ... then I'm in serious trouble. They'll see I've been trying to get the metal plate free, and then they'll secure me to this wall, or elsewhere, in a different fashion. Maybe next time I won't be so lucky. Maybe next time there won't be any way to escape from my bonds.

Dad has the middle finger of my left hand fully extended. Mom is in the room now too. She tries to get the pliers on my fingernail, but at the last second I jerk my hand away and kick her hard in the knee. Mom howls. Dad rages.

He puts his elbow into my teeth, and I feel something come loose in my mouth.

"How dare you hit your mother!" he roars.

That's it. I have to do something now. They're not letting me out of here, I don't care what Dad says. And they're not above killing Mary. I clinch Dad and struggle to my feet. I'm so weak, so utterly useless, but I manage to stand up. Dad resists with everything he's got. I grab my chain and am about to give it one big wrench when I hear another voice:

"He doesn't know the password."

Dad and I stop fighting for a moment. I recognize the voice but can't believe it. Mom picks herself up off the floor and limps backward out of the tiny room. Dad shoves me back onto the bed hard; then he too leaves.

A new person fills my doorway.

"Are you sure?" Dad asks.

"I've been through all his emails. Mary once asked him if he wanted the password, and can you believe this, he actually said no," the other man says. "I guess he wanted to prove to his wife how much he loved her and that it wasn't about her stupid inheritance. God, going through your emails was so damned boring. What a minor, insignificant, utterly meaningless life you lead, Brent. Didn't you say, before you left, that you were going to do something important with your life?"

I can't believe it. I can't.

"You died," I say.

My brother, Christopher, sits on the bed next to me.

"Thanks for not coming to my funeral," he says. "Guess I know the answer to that question now."

When it was just Mom and Dad, I had a chance to escape. I have more fight left in me than I realized. Tangling with Dad, I felt like I could have overpowered him. Mom is a tough woman, but I don't think she could have stopped me if Dad was incapacitated.

But now that I know I'm dealing with *Christopher* also? There's no chance.

He was always faster, stronger, and significantly tougher than me. I lost count of how many kids he beat up in the neighborhood or at school. And looking him over now, he appears to be in freakishly good shape. The man could be on the cover of one of those fitness magazines.

There's no way I'm getting past all three of them.

And with that realization, a terrible comfort washes over me. I know I'm not getting out of here. I know I'll probably be dead soon. I know that Mary is in danger. And I know I don't have much of a chance at all to do anything about it.

In other words, I have nothing to lose.

So I might as well try.

I don't want to get into a grappling match with anybody, especially Christopher. If I allow myself to get tied up, then I'm not escaping. Once one of them has a hold, the other two will swarm. That leaves me with one option: hit each of them as hard as I can, hoping for knockout shots.

Christopher is sitting right next to me, making it an awkward angle to throw a punch. So I quickly get to my feet. Bad idea. I'm light-headed in general, and rising too quickly only makes things worse. Christopher is practically laughing at my fumbling attempt to hit him. I swing as hard as I can, but he sees the punch coming a mile away. My brother ducks and pokes me right under the ribs. I gasp, but it's like trying to breathe through a crushed straw. He hit me in exactly the right spot to knock the wind out of me.

"Still pathetic," he says.

I stagger, lose my balance, end up on the floor. I'm sucking air when Christopher steps forward and kicks me in the head.

"You're not going anywhere," Christopher says. "You'll stay right here until we have Mary's money. Then we'll decide what to do with you."

I'm having trouble focusing on anything. Christopher kicked me really hard. One ear is ringing. I peer up at him. There is murder in my heart. I never thought it possible to hate anyone as much as I do my family. I raise an arm and discover, to my horror, that the chain isn't taut.

It should be. I've sat on the floor here before, and my chain is usually maxed out at this distance from the wall. Too late, I realize I've given my concern away. Christopher notices me looking over at the metal plate, which has almost come out of the wall.

"Oh, look at this," my brother says.

No, no, no ...

Christopher examines the metal plate. Then he turns to give my parents a withering look. Mom shrinks under his gaze. Dad can't hold Christopher's stare either. The power dynamics between them have changed, clearly. My brother runs the show now.

"My God, how did you both *not* notice this?" he asks, scolding them like *he's* their parent. "The idiot nearly got free."

Mom and Dad look guiltily at each other. Dad, of course, is the first to recover.

"Didn't I tell you, *woman*, to check his chain?"

"You never said—"

"I told you!" he snaps.

I try to get up, I try to fight, but my ear is ringing. And I can't seem to make the world level, no matter how I position my head. That kick probably concussed me.

Christopher kneels beside me. While Mom and Dad argue about whose fault it was that I nearly got free, my brother lowers his voice to mutter in my ear.

"Nice to see you again, Brent."

31

CHRISTOPHER – THURSDAY – JUNE 1

My brother's wife isn't much to look at. She's not *un*attractive, but she's never going to turn too many heads. Mary is a plain Jane. She's that girl you meet in second grade and are sort of friends with forever. Then one night, when you're adults, you meet for drinks and catch up. One thing leads to another, and you wind up at her apartment, and the next morning you don't exactly *regret* what happened, but you're not proud of yourself, and you're definitely not going to repeat it. You sneak out of there early before she wakes up. The next time she calls or the next time you run into her, you just act like nothing happened, and she gets the idea.

But I wasn't lying to her when I said the sex wasn't bad. Amazingly, it wasn't. Then again, nothing mind-blowing happened. Mary was, surprise-surprise, kind of inhibited, a little shy, preferred to make love with the lights off because she's uncomfortable with her body. But there were a few times that I saw the hint of a wild side in her. Usually it came out after we'd had a few drinks.

Mary's not my type, so I did have to playact a bit. I like dirty blondes—the dirtier, the better. I like fit women with large breasts and skinny waists. What can I say? I was born that way. I think it's safe to say I've never been with a woman like Mary before. She's somebody you'd find working in a library, quietly putting books away. Not my type at all.

But sex was always an important part of my strategy. It can bring people closer together, and I used it to keep Mary distracted. I never let up. It was every night, especially early on. With a steady flood of endorphins, she'd be feeling too blissful to harp on about little things, like my leaving the toilet seat up (apparently, Brent always put it down for her), or that I'd forgotten this one little thing from five or six years ago.

I never worried that she wouldn't be interested in sex. Brent and I are twins, so I knew Mary would be attracted to me. And let's be honest, I keep myself in fantastic shape. I saw the look in her eyes when I "came home" from the retreat. I was Brent alright, but I was Brent on steroids. Broader shoulders, trimmer waistline, more developed chest. She didn't stop to think about how it would have been impossible for him to build a body like this in thirty days. Nobody looks a gift horse in the mouth, after all. That's why confidence games almost always work. People think they've hit the jackpot. They're too goo-goo, ga-ga to think rationally.

Anyway, the sex got boring after a while. I kept coming onto her though, because I didn't want to let up. I needed those endorphins constantly flowing through her body to elevate her mood.

Mary groans in her sleep. She stirs for a moment in our bed—really, *her* bed—but doesn't come to. I knocked her out with chlorophyll and then injected a sedative to make her sleep. I carried her upstairs and tied her to the bed and gagged her. She should be out till morning now. I'll even catch a few hours of shuteye myself, which is all I need. By tomorrow, it will all be over.

We'll have her money.

And Brent will be dead.

I didn't want the con to end this way. I prefer a clean getaway, where the mark doesn't even realize they've been duped. Once we knew that Brent could not access Mary's retirement account, the plan all along was to con Mary into transferring her inheritance into our account, which was actually an offshore thing, very hard to trace. When that was done, I'd leave for work the next day and never come home. A few weeks later, Brent's body would turn up somewhere, bruised, battered, broken. The police would never suspect me, since I'm supposed to be dead, and when they began to investigate the retreat, they'd only end up with more questions than answers. We have Brent's passwords and access to his laptop and phone, so we were able to permanently erase every electronic exchange he had with our parents and with the phantom owners of the retreat (just a sock puppet account worked by Mom and Dad).

But, like the man said, your plan does not survive its first encounter with the enemy. Despite working my magic with Mary, turning up the heat in the bedroom and turning on the charm in other ways, she never warmed to the idea of Brent starting his own business. I have to give her credit: she's right not to trust my brother. He's a pathetic weakling who doesn't have the stones to run a business. That takes vision and self-confidence and, above all else, *balls*. Brent doesn't have any.

He never has.

I also overestimated how easy it would be to fake my way through Brent's daytime job for a couple of weeks. While we kept him in the cell, I spent thirty days learning the very basics of coding. God, talk about boring. All these rules, all these ones and zeroes, all these syntax errors and this and that. One rule always bumping up against another rule. I can see why Brent likes the work—he was always a rule-follower. He wanted life to be neat and tidy, everything fitting nicely within a box.

Me, I'm the opposite.

I hate rules. I despise order. Rules are for the weak-minded, the sheeple who need to be told what to do. People don't realize that life is a game, and they also don't realize that they're playing by rules set up by other people. They don't even *see* the rules. They just blindly adopt them, blindly follow them, and wonder why they're so miserable.

Not me.

I see through it all.

But anyway, I realized pretty quickly that trying to fake my way through Brent's job would be impossible for any lengthy period of time. I figured I had a week, maybe two, before the wolves were at the door. It didn't help that my screw-up brother was already skating on thin ice with his boss. So I did everything I could at the office to distract from my ineptitude. I made every meeting less about the work and more about the personality conflicts. I challenged Aaron and pushed back against Rich and turned the charm on with Molly and the other ladies around the office so I'd have some allies in the conference room. Any other grifter would have been out of there inside a week, but I lasted two.

Joshua was also a wrinkle we never expected. I hadn't seen that crook in a long time. We worked together on two jobs. He took the rap for the latter. That wasn't my fault, but criminals aren't the most fair-minded. He went away for a few years and made it known he was gunning for me. While he was inside, he also managed to get in the ear of some other very nasty people, telling them I was responsible for their incarceration too. He made me out to be a criminal informant. None of that was true, of course, but his methods worked.

A lot of people wanted me dead.

So I killed myself.

It wasn't as difficult as it seems. Mom and Dad helped. Word got around that I was gone, and the people looking for me lost interest. I thought Joshua would too. But you can't see everything coming.

I'd made the mistake once of telling Joshua that I sometimes assumed my brother's identity when grifting. Bad timing here, but it turns out he was released recently and had been following Brent and Mary around. Oh well, what can you do except improvise and adapt and overcome.

Dad pretended to be Jim Smith, the private detective. While Mom stayed busy with Brent at the farmhouse, Dad followed Mary from a distance. It didn't take him long to find Joshua. We killed him—we had no choice, obviously. We cut off his fingers and pulled his teeth and buried him in Hyde Park. Dad was never going to file a report with the police, which, by the way, I'm shocked Mary believed. *She* would have had to file the report. But here's the thing: most honest citizens have no idea how the law works, because they're never in trouble. Mary didn't even question the fact that Jim Smith would file a report.

Anyway, Joshua wasn't supposed to be found for a while. But some guy with a metal detector was going through there, looking for coins or whatever, and there just happened to be something near Joshua's body. What are the odds?

These things happen, though, all the time. Most criminals are brought down by accident. Nobody except the real idiots leave obvious evidence behind for some cop who barely got through high school to find. The police usually are incredibly lucky when they collar pros. Hence the term "catch a break."

Dorian, Katya, and Alexander were all seasoned grifters I've worked with before. I didn't want to bring anybody else in, but I knew immediately I wouldn't convince Mary without the razzle-dazzle. We tried high-pressure sales tactics with Dorian, and that obviously didn't work. Alexander was going to be a kinder, gentler investor, more of a Silicon Valley hippie type who spoke in vague generalities, the type of guy who tells you he wants to change the world, by creating a new restaurant app. You know, one of *those* assholes.

But that wasn't to be. As soon as I caught a whiff of Mary wanting to leave me, I knew the jig was up. Even more so when she caught me in several obvious lies, and then, sneaky bitch, tripped me up about that ski trip that Brent and she apparently never took. I don't know where she got the idea I wasn't her husband, but I'm betting it came from Mrs. Ryers. Every neighborhood has that nosy old bat who can't go more than two minutes without getting involved in somebody else's business. I knew Mrs. Ryers would be a problem from the jump, after my brother shared all those cringey stories about how he helped her with her lawn work or carrying her groceries inside. I knew right away I had to nip that relationship in the bud.

Regardless, here we are. Most cons would freak out if

they were in my position, but it is what it is. I've been playing the game long enough to know I'm not beaten. Matter of fact, I'm pretty close to winning. When Mary wakes up, we are going to have a little discussion, and she will see things my way. She's going to have to die too, but she doesn't need to know.

That would be cruel.

32

They're going to kill me.

Dad keeps promising to let me go once Christopher has gotten the money from Mary, but I know it's a lie. They're only keeping me around for insurance right now. I'm not a criminal, but I know how my parents and brother think. If they can't trick Mary into handing her inheritance over, then they'll give up the con and resort to intimidation. They'll threaten her life or mine to force her to do what they want. The only reason I'm still alive is because that hasn't happened yet.

But I know I don't have long.

When they get their hands on that money, they'll definitely kill me. Like I said, I know how my brother's warped mind works. He's pretending to be me right now. When he has what he wants, he'll disappear. In a few weeks, a body will turn up—mine. Mary will identify me. There will be no trace of the money anywhere. No one will suspect my brother was involved because he's supposedly been dead for years.

If things don't go that smoothly for Christopher, he'll probably have to kill Mary too. Every minute I spend in here, the greater danger she's in.

Today I'm going to force my way out.

Once Christopher discovered the metal plate was loose, they had to decide what to do with me. Apparently, there was nowhere else on the farmhouse to stash me securely, though, so Mom and Dad went about trying to reattach the plate to the wall. While Christopher aimed a gun at my chest, Dad did his best, but it was pretty obvious they couldn't just patch it up and hope it would stay. The three of them, fortunately, could not figure out how I'd done it. They thought I'd clawed and scraped with my fingers and picked away. The wall was pretty shoddy, and my fingers were pretty chewed up from all my work, so they didn't think to check the detachable metal legs of the cot.

In the end, they decided to let me be. I'm still in the room, with a chain around my wrist, only now that chain isn't attached to the wall.

They just don't open my door anymore.

They still bring me food. An apple. Twice a day if I'm lucky. Once a day if I'm not. And a single bottle of water. That's it. That slot slides open, and they push it through. They don't talk to me, not like they did the first month. They have all the information they think they need. I tried my best to sprinkle some lies in with all the true things I shared. Being grifters themselves, Mom and Dad know how to spot a lie, so I had to be very careful. When they asked me about Mary's closest friends, I told them about Paige and Gwen, leaving out the fact that Mary and Gwen had had a bitter falling-out recently. There were other things I lied about, little things, but noticeable ones that hopefully Mary picks up on. Like Mary having rheumatoid arthritis instead of her actual diagnosis: lupus. That's not a thing I would ever forget. And like my starting a business. Sure, Mary and I talked about it, but I never planned to do freelance coding, as I led Christopher to believe.

And most importantly, this lie: I told my brother we did not keep any weapons in the house. He has no idea about the knife in her dresser.

I hope she doesn't need to use it on him.

But I can't think about that right now. My problem is the door. It's great I've broken the metal plate off the wall, but it hardly matters if I can't get the door open.

They don't swap the bucket out anymore. Now I pee in the corner farthest from my bed. It's an unfinished basement with a French drain, so at least my urine seeps through to the underground and doesn't collect in the room. The bucket is, however, overflowing. Dad promises he'll bring me a new one when he feels like he can trust me again. But I know that's a lie.

I've dug the plate out of the concrete using the detachable legs of the cot. Since Mom and Dad don't come into my room anymore, I don't worry about their inspecting my bed. Now the bedspring is on the floor. Three of the four legs are whittled down to tiny flimsy shards. Only the fourth is in reasonable shape. It's my only hope.

I sharpened it against the wall.

I'm waiting for them to come today. When they pass me food, I'll grab a wrist and jam the sharpened metal into flesh and hold on to that arm, whomever it belongs to, and demand to be let out. I'm so weak and emaciated now, though, there's little chance it'll work. But I'm out of what few options I ever had.

While I wait for the inevitable violent confrontation, I go to that place in my mind. I think about my honeymoon with Mary. I recall the sand on our toes, the smell of the warm salt water, the long, late nights at the resort where we made love. The future seemed so bright then. Sure, I wasn't crazy about my job, and I still had issues to work through, but it seemed like things could get better. A lot of the details are vague, fuzzy now, because of the state I'm in, but a few memories remain sharp and well-defined. I can still picture her in her wedding dress, looking absolutely beautiful as she came down the aisle, and I can still imagine waking up next to her, the way she'd get goose-bumps if I kissed the side of her neck. I can still smell her too.

Everybody has their own smell.

There's a knock at the door.

At first, I think I'm imagining things. They never knock. Then, for the briefest of moments, my hopes soar. Maybe it's a neighbor or the police, somebody who got suspicious and is now checking the property. But then my hopes are deflated.

"Son, you awake?" Dad asks.

I don't answer. I want him to go away. I don't want to interact with either of them again until they open that slot in my door ...

"Son!" Dad shouts. "Wake up!"

He pounds the door. The noise is enough to ignite another of my frequent headaches. I cover my ears, but it's not enough.

"Stop!" I call out.

"What the hell's the matter with you, boy?" Dad asks. "I've been calling out to you."

Gee, let me think. I've been malnourished, beaten, kept in a cellar for over a month. I wonder what's wrong.

"What do you want?" I ask.

"I need to open the door," he says.

I scramble to my feet.

"Move against the back wall," he says.

He pulls the slot open.

I forgot to grab the sharp piece of metal!

"Go on, move," he says. "And keep that wrist with the chain out in front of you, where I can see it."

I pretend to be light-headed, which isn't difficult. I wobble and keel over, break my fall with a hand on the cot.

"What the hell's the matter with you?" he barks.

"Dizzy," I say, snatching the metal with my non-cuffed hand and quickly putting it behind me. I shuffle back to the wall and slide the piece of metal between my belt and pants at the small of my back.

"Okay," Dad says. "Now I've got a shotgun, boy, so don't try anything."

I hold my cuffed wrist out to show I'm not a threat. But I angle my body so I can keep my other hand almost behind me, close to my makeshift weapon.

"What's happening?" I ask. "What are you doing?"

"Just be quiet."

The door groans open. The light blinds me for a moment. Then my eyes adjust. Dad stands in the doorway with a shotgun pointed at my chest. Mom appears, crouching so she's under the barrel.

"God, it stinks in here!" she says with a look of disgust.

What did she expect?

Pinching her nose with one hand, Mom grabs my bucket with the other and shimmies her way out of the room. The shotgun has never wavered. Dad has it aimed at me, center mass.

"Come more into the light," Dad says. "Not too far, though."

"Why?"

He shakes the shotgun. "You want me to blow your damned head off? Do what I say!"

I come forward a little bit. The end of the barrel isn't quite in my doorway. It's a little more than one big stride away from me.

"What do you want?" I ask.

When Mom reappears, I'm expecting her to slide a new bucket into my room. But instead, she ducks under the barrel again and points a cell phone at me.

"Stand still," Dad orders.

"What are you doing?"

"Shut up!" Mom yells.

She taps a few buttons on her phone and then steadies it while facing me. Then I realize she's taking a picture of me.

"Why are you doing that?" I ask.

Neither of them answer.

My mind is racing now. The last thing they'd want is photographic evidence of their son looking like this, being kept in a dungeon, basically. Unless they need an image of me to intimidate Mary.

Oh God ...

I begin to reel, like I'm light-headed.

"Stand still!" Dad snaps.

I groan and clutch my stomach.

"I can't ..."

I totter to one side, plant one knee on the cot, make sure to lower my head so they can't get a good picture of my face.

"Did you get the picture?" Dad asks.

"No!" Mom snaps. "He was moving around too much."

"Oh, hell," Dad says. "Just get one of his face, then. Brent, look up at your mother."

I groan. It's really not difficult to act like you're dying when you've got a migraine and you've lost probably forty pounds in a little over a month.

"It's an act," Mom says.

Dad laughs. "It's no act. Look at him. The boy can barely stand. He looks like those people starving in the third world. Just grab his hair and lift his face and get your picture. Go on. I've got the gun. He won't try anything. I mean, just look at him. Do you think he even has it in him to try anything at this point?"

I edge forward so I'm a little closer to the door, making sure to keep my head down. As soon as Mom gets close, I'm going to make my move. A shotgun is a terrifying weapon, but it's not ideal for this situation. All I have to do is grab Mom and use her as a shield. Dad can't shoot me then.

"Alright, Brent," Mom says, snarling. "Don't you dare try anything! Forget the shotgun, I'll scratch your eyes out, you miserable child! All you ever did was look for ways to ruin this family, and now you're finally going to pay us back!"

This is it.

This is it.

I love you, Mary.

33

MARY – JUNE 1

When I wake up, I feel really groggy. My tongue is thick and cottony, like I had way too much to drink last night and a hangover headache is about to hit me with everything it has got.

Sunlight is coming through my bedroom door, as opposed to my window, so that means it's early morning. I don't remember anything about last night. Did Brent and I go out? Did we drink too much?

Then it all comes back to me.

I open my mouth to scream, but I realize I'm gagged. I can only manage what sounds like a frustrated grunt. My head immediately starts to pound. I try to pull the gag out of my mouth, but I can barely move my arms.

I'm tied to the bed.

What the hell is happening?

Think, think, think ... Brent and I were arguing. I caught him in several lies. Then ...

Oh God.

He put a white rag to my mouth, and I blacked out. He

knocked me out with something, just like the way they do in movies. Then he carried me up here and tied me to the bed.

"You're awake."

Brent stands in the doorway. He's wearing that new, expensive business suit he bought last week.

But he's not Brent, I know that now. So who is this man?

He holds a finger up to his lips.

"Shhhh. Don't make a sound." He reaches into his pocket. I squirm, thinking it's a weapon, but he only pulls out his phone. "I'm going to show you a picture. It will shock you. But do not make a sound. Do you understand?"

I reluctantly nod.

The man approaches the bed. I try to shift away from him, but he's tied me up pretty tightly. I can't move much. He sits on the bed, his hip brushing up against mine. My skin crawls.

"I know." His smile is cartoonish, grotesque. "I know this is a lot."

He holds the phone toward me so I can see the screen.

It's a picture of ...

Brent.

Oh my God, he looks *horrible*. He's all skin and bones, and he's bruised, and his hair looks like it's started to fall out and—

"Quiet," the man says.

He puts the phone away. I stare up at him, wild-eyed. I'm gagged and tied to a bed. He could do anything he wants to me. I shudder at the realization—he already *has* done whatever he wants to me.

"Yeah," he says nonchalantly. "I'm not Brent. But you probably figured that out by now."

No, no, no, no ...

"We do resemble each other," the man says, rubbing his face. His hand passes over the tiny cut along his jaw. "But I was always the better-looking twin."

My whole body is trembling.

"Aww, you're cute when you're scared," he says.

I close my eyes. But I can't keep the tears from escaping.

"I'm Christopher," he says. "Nice to meet you, finally. It's a shame we're only just now meeting, under these circumstances."

No, Christopher is *dead.* He can't be sitting on the bed with me right now. That's impossible.

"Did Brent never tell you?" the man asks. "We're identical."

This cannot be happening.

Brent does not like to talk about his childhood or his family. But most of all he does not like to talk about his brother, Christopher. On the rare occasions I brought him up, Brent either shut down or changed the subject. Aside from the handful of horror stories Brent shared with me about his brother, I only knew two things about Christopher—

He was a sadist.

And he resembled Brent.

I never knew they were *identical* twins. I'm guessing Brent keeps that from people because he doesn't want them wondering if he's exactly like his brother, beyond mere appearance.

He touches my neck. I scream, but it comes out muffled against the gag. I twist away, my eyes flying open.

"Shhhh," he says. "If you make any noise, Brent will die."

I manage not to. But I can't stop shaking violently.

"I didn't want it to end this way," he says. "I was going to disappear. You wouldn't have been any the wiser. You were supposed to think Brent vanished, finally lost his mind and flaked out or whatever. That's all. No harm done. In fact, I'd sort of be doing you a favor. Brent's a loser, isn't he? We both know it. You were ready to leave him before he went away. You were only keeping him around because you felt bad, weren't you?"

I shake my head.

"Don't bullshit a bullshitter," he says. "My brother is a complete screw-up. You would have breathed a sigh of relief if he disappeared. Then you wouldn't have had to officially end the relationship, or pay him alimony, or do any of that."

"No," I manage to say through the gag.

No matter how bad things had gotten, no matter how bad things could get, I would have died if Brent had just disappeared without a trace. Even if we were separated when it happened, it wouldn't change how I feel. I love him, no matter what. This man—*Christopher*—is a sociopath, however. He wouldn't understand that two people could share a deep connection like that.

"But here we are," Christopher says. "There's only one thing left to do. When the bank opens this morning, we'll be first in line. You are going to transfer your inheritance to my offshore business account. This is the type of transaction that can only be done in person, so as not to arouse too much suspicion. So we are walking into that bank together, and you are transferring the funds. I'll have a line open to my partners the whole time. If you try anything, Brent dies immediately."

It all makes sense to me now. Christopher was after my money, nothing more. The side business, the investors, it was all a ruse. Brent told me how gifted a con man his brother was—and apparently still is.

"Once that's done, you and I are going on a nice, long drive."

"No."

He smiles. "Don't worry. I'm not going to kill you. So long as you play along, both you and Brent will get to live out your lives. I promise."

I don't believe him.

34

BRENT – JUNE 1

The drive home takes me two hours. I pushed it on the turnpike, doing almost eighty. It's surreal when I pull into our neighborhood at this ungodly, early hour. The false dawn brightens the horizon as I come to a stop along the curb, about a block away from our home.

After the confrontation with Mom and Dad (I can't think about what happened), I took a picture of myself with Mom's phone and sent it to Christopher. That's what they were after, proof of life. That way they could threaten Mary with my death if she didn't cooperate. She must have figured out Christopher wasn't me.

I found bread and cold cuts in the old fridge upstairs and grabbed several bottles of water. I wolfed the food down during the car ride, but I barely ate half the sandwich before I felt full. My stomach isn't used to handling that much food right now. I was careful about the water, making sure not to chug it. I read somewhere that you can't gulp a ton of water down after you've been dehydrated for a long period of time

... or maybe I saw it in a movie. Who knows. Either way, I was careful.

I haven't had this full a belly in a long time. It made me feel sluggish and almost sleepy. But there was no way I was going to doze off. I've got to get home.

I pad along the sidewalk quietly. A jogger breezes past me. It's a woman from a couple of blocks away. I recognize her because she likes to run up our street. She says hello, then does a double take when she gets a better look at me. I must be a sight. I'm emaciated, and my face is badly bruised with both old and fresh wounds. I'm also wearing Dad's clothes. Mine were torn to shreds and partly soiled. I'm swimming in Dad's pants and shirt—he was always a bulky man. I must look homeless to this woman.

She quickens her pace and hurries along. I hope she doesn't call the police. I'm not ready for them to arrive yet.

I try to run, but I'm so weak. After a few steps I'm out of breath, and my knees ache terribly. I hurry as best I can around the corner and up the sidewalk, pulling my baseball cap low. If anybody happens to notice me, I want them thinking I'm just a guy out for a walk.

I make my way to Mrs. Ryers's house. She's always up early. The old woman barely sleeps anymore. All the same, she's still surprised to see me standing on her porch at this strange hour.

"Brent ...?"

"It's me." I nod. "I need to get into my house. Do you still have the spare key?"

"My God, what's happened to you?"

"I don't have time to explain," I say. "There's a man in there with Mary. He's pretending to be me. She's in terrible danger. I need the key so I can sneak in without him realizing."

She looks at me warily. "How do I know it's really you?"

I don't have time for this. I think back over our many conversations, trying to conjure up some memorable exchange.

"What did you think of my orchids?" she asks. "Remember, I showed you last summer?"

I smile. "You *hate* orchids. You've never had any in your garden."

Mrs. Ryers nods. That's enough for her.

"Come inside."

―――――――――

THE SUN IS ALMOST up when I slip out the back door of Mrs. Ryers's house.

"Brent," she says, "are you sure?"

I'm making this up as I go, but I can't think of any better way to make sure Mary is safe.

"Yes," I say. "Give me ten minutes, okay? Then call."

She regards me skeptically, then nods. "Alright."

I take the spare key to my house from her and thank her once more. The neighborhood is beginning to wake up. I don't have much time. The lights in the house next to ours are all on. I wait for a car to pass before I cross the street.

The house looks strange to me, almost alien. Like it's somehow changed. It looks bigger, the dimensions different. But I know it hasn't changed. I have.

I hurry around to the back, carefully look through the windows. I don't see Mary or Christopher downstairs. Maybe they're still asleep. That would be best.

I insert the key and turn it very slowly. In an otherwise quiet house, a lock turning can sound like a bomb going off. But there's no commotion when I flip the lock or gently open the back door. I slip inside, make my way into the kitchen to grab one of the knives out of the block. Even though guns scare me to death, I wish I had one on me. Back at the farmhouse, the shotgun went off and ... I don't want to think about it. I couldn't find any other shells for it, and I was in a hurry to leave, so I didn't bring the bulky weapon with me.

Holding the knife out in front of me, I tiptoe into the foyer and stop before I reach the foot of the stairs. I hear someone talking. A murmur. It's Christopher. He's already awake.

My heart races.

My brother has always gotten the best of me. Both mentally and physically. I've never been a match for him. For years I suffered his torments in silence because I was too scared to stand up to him. When at last I found the courage to tell my parents just how sick and twisted he was, they were dismissive and unsympathetic. Boys will be boys; you have to stand up for yourself, yadda, yadda, yadda. The abuse continued until finally I stood up to him.

Bad idea.

Christopher is a dangerous man. He is a sociopath with a vicious and violent streak running through him. I don't have that in me. When I finally hit him with a good punch, I thought that was it, I'd made my point, there was nothing further to discuss.

But then he hit me, even harder.

He knocked me to the ground. I pled for him to stop. Told him I gave up. But that didn't stop his assault. He kept hitting me and hitting me and hitting me, long after he needed to, long after it was obvious I had given up trying to fight back. He was a sadist, and apparently he's only gotten worse.

When I go up these stairs, I have to confront him in what I know will be a life-or-death fight. I have a knife on me. I know what I have to do with it. He'll probably be armed too. Maybe he'll have a gun on him. I don't know. But it doesn't matter. I have to be the aggressor here. I have to kill my brother, even if it means trading my own life, to ensure that Mary is safe. Because right now, she's all that matters.

I steel myself for what's about to come. Then I walk to the stairs.

35

"I'm going to untie you now," Christopher says. "We have to get you cleaned up and looking pretty. I can't have you walking into the bank looking a mess and asking to transfer hundreds of thousands of dollars. It would be suspicious."

I shudder as he touches my ankle. He sees my reaction, takes a perverse joy in it. Before unknotting my ankle, he runs a hand up my thigh. Thank God he didn't undress me last night. The thought of his hand on the skin of my inner thigh is disgusting.

"You really aren't my type," he says. "But maybe, after everything we've been through, we should have one more roll in the hay. What do you think?"

I can't even answer that question.

He laughs. "I'm joking. You were kind of a bore. I don't know how Brent deals with it. He must be a bore too. You hit the jackpot when I showed up, lady. I know how to please a woman."

I look away from this disgusting man. He stops rubbing

my thigh and finally unknots my ankle, then the other. My
feet are asleep. Being stretched out like this overnight, with
the bonds really tight, my circulation got cut off. My toes
hurt, they're tingling so badly.

"I'm going to untie your wrists now," he says. "Don't try
anything."

He reaches into his pocket and takes out a revolver. I am
terrified of guns. I let out a smothered shriek when the cold
metal of the barrel pokes my side.

"I mean it, do not try anything."

I nod vigorously. He puts the gun back into his pocket
and unties one wrist. Just like my feet, my hand is numb.

"I'm going to leave the gag in for now," he explains. "I
don't think we're ready to take that off. After you get fresh-
ened up and dressed, we'll see."

He moves so he's standing by the foot of the bed. I'm
waiting for him to unknot my other wrist. But Christopher
doesn't. Instead he reaches into his pocket and takes out the
gun again. He motions at my tied wrist.

"You have a free hand," he says. "Unknot it yourself."

Keeping the gun pointed at me, he watches me struggle
terribly. My free hand is numb, and I can't quite use my tied
hand to help with the knot. It's a slow, painful process. When
I look over at him, begging with my eyes for his help, he just
cracks a smile and laughs.

"Get it yourself, bitch."

I sit up and put my feet on the floor. The pins and
needles sensation in my feet is really painful. I wonder if I've
suffered nerve damage, that's how bad it is. But I ignore that
and keep working on the knot. Sensation has returned to my
free hand. After what feels like ten minutes, I manage to
undo the knot, and now my other hand is loose.

"Stand up," he says.

I follow his instructions. My feet and ankles are still a little numb, so standing is difficult. He laughs at my awkward attempt to get upright.

"Take your clothes off," he orders.

I hesitate. I don't want this man to see me naked ... I mean, he already has, and I can't think about that, but I—

"You're going to be shy now?" he says, shaking his head. "I've seen the goods, Mary, and they're nothing special. Now hurry the hell up!"

I whimper at the sound of his scream. I'm going to do what he wants. I'll transfer all the money into his account. For a moment I toyed with the notion of attacking him. I've got that knife in my dresser, tucked away behind my underwear. But once he pulled the gun, I knew I had no chance. All he has to do is pull that trigger, and it's over. Not only will I be dead, but then he'll have to kill Brent too.

The best time to try anything is at the bank. Maybe I can slip a note to Paige or write something on the form I have to fill out. She can act like she's transferred the money—she told me they have training for these situations. She has a way of alerting the security guard discreetly. Maybe we can tie Christopher up in the bank and keep him from alerting his friends. I know I'll be putting Brent's life in jeopardy, but I don't really have a choice. I don't believe Christopher when he says he'll let Brent and me go. The only chance one or both of us have to live is by me doing something at the bank.

"Hurry up." Christopher moves away from the bed, maintaining about ten feet between us. "Get some clothes on."

I pull off my shirt and pants, but leave my underwear and bra on. As I walk to the dresser, I see a flash of movement in the hallway outside the bedroom. There's somebody else in this house. Maybe it's a cop? Perhaps the police are here.

"Come on," Christopher says, oblivious.

I open the bottom drawer first and fish out a pair of jeans. Then I grab a long-sleeved top from my middle drawer. I look toward the hallway again, allowing my eyes to linger for a moment. I want him to think I'm considering running.

"Oh no you don't."

Christopher positions himself between me and the door to cut off my escape. But he's facing me, which means his back is to the hallway outside the bedroom. Whoever is out there, now they have a chance.

"What are you doing?" he asks. "Put your shirt on. Let's g—"

A strange man appears in the doorway. He's bearded, bruised, and looks skeletal. He's also carrying a knife.

It's my husband.

It's Brent.

He's alive!

36

Brent lunges at Christopher with the knife.

But Christopher senses the attack coming. Spinning around, he slaps the knife hand out of the way. Brent screams and continues to charge, plowing into his brother. The gun goes off. For a moment I freeze, fearful somebody has been shot.

But I'm not hit, and I don't see a spray of blood anywhere.

Brent and Christopher get tangled up. The gun goes flying out of Christopher's hand and ends up near the doorway. Brent pushes his brother back toward the bed. I should do something, but I'm scared out of my mind, and Brent still has a hold of the knife somehow.

They struggle against one another until Christopher pivots and turns and throws Brent over the bed, onto the other side of the floor. My husband lands badly on his shoulder and lets out a yelp. Christopher spins around, his eyes savage, a vein throbbing in his neck, to glare at me. I hold my hands out to show I'm no threat. He forgets about me and looks around for the gun he dropped. Spotting it, Christopher rushes back to the doorway.

I have no choice.

I have to kill him.

Pulling open the drawer, I snatch the knife hidden in the back. Christopher is almost to the gun. I sprint toward him. He's got his hand on the weapon. He stands and turns around, ready to fire.

But I'm already there.

I plunge the knife as hard as I can into him.

37

They have to take Brent to the hospital. He's severely malnourished, and his organs are probably close to failure. They're afraid that his brief fight with Christopher might have caused some internal bleeding too, which they will be hard-pressed to stop. He's in really bad shape. It's amazing he was able to drive himself home.

At first, the EMTs don't want me joining them in the ambulance, but I demand to sit in the back with my husband. The driver activates the siren, and we're off. The police follow the ambulance. They've obviously got a lot of questions for both of us, but I insisted I accompany my husband to the hospital when the EMTs told me Brent's body might shut down without immediate medical care.

They've got Brent on a stretcher. One of the medics runs an IV. I hold Brent's hand.

He looks terrible. Whoever was keeping him barely fed him. And he bears the marks of several beatings. I can't even look at the fingernails—or lack thereof—on his one hand.

"What happened to you?" I ask.

He shakes his head. "It was my own fault."

I frown. "What do you mean?"

"I'll explain everything, I promise."

I take his good hand and squeeze. "Okay, honey."

They take us to the nearest hospital, where Brent is admitted to the ER. I never leave his side. When they ask him to change into a hospital gown, I'm utterly shocked by how skeletal he looks. I can see practically every bone in his body. And the bruises, scars and other terrible marks running up and down his body are nightmarish.

"Brent ..."

He gives me a sad look as he slips on the hospital gown. "It's alright. It's over."

The ER doctor checks him out. They run a bunch of tests and do bloodwork. All of it takes a long time. There's nothing quick about a hospital visit. I don't let go of him.

"How did you get away?" I ask.

Brent looks away from me. "I don't want to talk about it right now."

I can tell by the haunted look in his eyes that he had to do something awful to escape from wherever he was.

"Why didn't you call the police?" I ask.

"Maybe I should have." He manages a weak smile. "But I was scared. I didn't know if the cops would believe my story, that I was me and he was him. And also, if they *did* believe me, I didn't want the police surrounding the house. Christopher would have taken you hostage or something. He would have done anything to protect himself. *Anything.* I thought our best chance was if I got the spare key from Mrs. Ryers and snuck in. That way he wouldn't see anything coming. She was supposed to wait ten minutes and call the cops, in case I didn't ... in case I screwed something up."

"You didn't screw anything up, Brent," I say.

We hold hands while we wait for all the medicine and doctors and nurses to take their course.

"It was all my fault," Brent says.

"No, honey," I answer. "Don't—"

"Mary, *listen.*" He sits up in his bed. He's *painfully* thin. It hurts to look at him. "My parents tricked me. They set this whole thing up. They told me about the retreat, but it wasn't real. I believed them. It's *my* fault. I'm so sorry."

The whole world stops. It takes me a moment to process what Brent has just said.

His *parents* were involved too?

I have so many questions that I don't even know where to begin. When did he start talking to them again? Brent never said a word about that. After everything that's happened between them, why would Brent ever think they had his best interests at heart?

I let go of his hand, really angry with my husband. How could he keep this from me? If only we had discussed this, if only I'd *known*, then all of this could have been avoided. I would never have let Christopher into my home and ...

I can't think about it.

"I didn't want to ..." Brent closes his eyes. "I had no choice. To get back to you, I had to ..."

Then it hits me. I understand immediately why Brent didn't want to talk about his escape a moment ago. It was his parents keeping him prisoner.

Did he kill them?

I'm still terribly upset with him, but this bit of information cuts right through my anger. Brent cries while he repeats over and over how sorry he is. Though they were horrible people, Brent has literally lost every member of his family today. Two by his own hand, one by mine. The fact that I ... it has not sunk in yet.

"Don't worry about that right now," I say as calmly as I can manage. "Let's make sure you're going to be okay first."

I haven't told him how angry I am, but Brent knows me too well. I tell him I need to be alone for a few minutes. He nods, giving me a sad look. We've both just been through hell.

EPILOGUE

SIX MONTHS LATER

I t's taken some time, but I've forgiven Brent.

He moved out of the house for a bit. I needed him to. He respected my wishes and did not argue.

But as one month turned into two, I found myself really missing him. When he came home, I was so happy, I cried. I'm not a woman who sheds a lot of tears. But when Brent pulled into the driveway, I raced out to meet him on the lawn. We must have stood out there and hugged for fifteen minutes straight. Mrs. Ryers, naturally, watched us the whole time from her porch. I'm sure the whole neighborhood knew what was going on about five minutes later.

Once we got through the seemingly endless questions from the police, once we proved to them several times over that our lives were threatened and we did everything in self-defense, they finally closed the books on this case. It was incredibly difficult, having to go over all these awful things again and again, with the feeling that the police did not believe us and, at times, suspected us of murder. I had to see a therapist for a while to process everything and get on with my life.

We had to move. It was easier to sell the house I grew up in than I anticipated because of everything that had happened. The story made the rounds, and it was awkward to interact with the neighbors when I knew, in the back of their minds, what they were thinking. They were all wondering how Brent's brother could have deceived me for so long. Nobody came out and said that, but I could tell. So we sold the house and moved to a different state.

Brent continues to take all the blame for what happened, but this isn't entirely his fault. It's not even *mostly* his fault. Sure, he could have told me about speaking to his parents again, but even if he had, I can't say with any certainty I would have suspected them of setting up this elaborate con. The truth is, I wouldn't have known either.

I only interacted with his parents on two occasions, so I would probably have deferred to Brent's judgment. If he told me he trusted them, I would have too. Besides, who could have ever guessed that the retreat was all made up, and that they planned to keep Brent locked away in a farmhouse cellar for over a month while their supposedly dead son tried to steal my inheritance?

Nobody.

So, no, I can't blame Brent for this. Bad people do bad things. It's not Brent's fault his parents took advantage of him while he was in an emotionally vulnerable state.

I check myself in the bathroom mirror again. I've managed to get a tan for the first time in a decade, and I've also lost a few pounds. I can't wait to see the look on Brent's face when he sees what I'm wearing. I fuss over my hair some more, knowing full well I'm not going to make it any

better at this point. I am who I am, and Brent loves me
for it.

I take a deep breath and exit the bathroom.

The sliding glass doors are open. An ocean breeze wafts
into the room, carrying the smell of the sea. On the beach
outside, I see my husband standing with his back to me in
his nice new suit. Over the last six months, he's done a lot of
work on himself. He's in therapy again, and he's trying a
different mixture of medication. He's exercising a lot,
spending more time outdoors, and working on mindfulness.
Brent got a new job at the mall. It doesn't pay well, but that's
alright. We're okay on money, and we—knock on wood—
always have my inheritance in the event of an emergency.
Brent is hardly spending any of his money now, instead
saving up what he can to go back to school. He wants to
become a therapist. He thinks he can help other people.

I step through the big sliding doors onto the patio. It's a
calm day on the sea as the sun sets, turning the horizon
purple and gold and orange. Brent promised not to look
until I came up beside him. Only the minister can see me.

I walk, barefoot, across the sand to meet them on the
beach. As I draw up beside my husband, I take his hand in
mine. He looks over—gosh, he's so handsome—and his
breath catches in his throat.

"Mary," he says, "you look beautiful."

I smile. "You don't look so bad yourself."

That is an understatement. Brent is one of those men
who don't realize how good-looking they are.

He shakes his head. "I loved that dress on you the first
time. But it looks even better now."

I'm wearing my wedding dress. I never thought I'd be
able to fit back into it, but here I am. I have to admit, I look

pretty good. I feel healthy and irrepressibly happy. Six months ago, things looked pretty bleak. But now they don't. Now the future is filled with possibilities. And that new future starts here, with us renewing our vows.

The minister smiles at us. "Shall we begin?"

"Yes," I say. "We'd like to begin again."

THANK YOU FOR READING

Did you enjoy reading *The New Husband*? Please consider leaving a review on Amazon. Your review will help other readers to discover the novel.

ABOUT THE AUTHOR

Brian R. O'Rourke has been writing stories since he was eight years old. A lifelong, avid reader, Brian believes that fiction has the power to change the world. He enjoys spending time with his family, exercising, playing the violin, and golfing.

He also writes mysteries and thrillers under the pen name Evan Ronan.

Made in the USA
Middletown, DE
05 December 2023

44724630R00196